COMBUSTION

MARTIN J. SMITH

DIVERSIONBOOKS

Also by Martin J. Smith

The Memory Series
Time Release
Shadow Image
Straw Men
The Disappeared Girl

Diversion Books
A Division of Diversion Publishing Corp.
443 Park Avenue South, Suite 1008
New York, New York 10016
www.DiversionBooks.com

For more information, email info@diversionbooks.com

First Diversion Books edition September 2016.
Print ISBN: 978-1-62681-920-7
eBook ISBN: 978-1-62681-919-1

For Molly Boulware

1

The closing credits were still scrolling up the screen of Starke's iPad when his cell phone jolted him straight up in bed. What time had he finally fallen asleep? He scanned the darkness for some sign of the time.

His phone *chirruped* again, like a cricket trapped somewhere in his one-bedroom cave. Where'd he left it? He moved the tablet to the side, slid his feet off the twin mattress and onto the worn carpet, and stood with a riotous popping of cartilage. He was naked. The compressor of his window air-conditioner had been busted for months. Since the apartment was above the Suds-Your-Duds laundromat on the ground floor, the dryer vents leaked warm, moist air through the ductwork. It was like living in somebody's armpit, but he just hadn't had the energy to move, or do anything besides work, since Rosaleen.

Chirrup.

The pocket of his jeans? He found them draped over the single folding chair in his kitchen, but no phone. He glanced at the microwave clock. Nothing good could come of a phone call at 4:43 in the morning.

The third ring drew him to the counter, where the phone glowed beside his Toast-R-Oven. He unplugged it from its charger and carried it to the refrigerator, opening the fridge door to enjoy the cool air. Good thing he wasn't hungry. Not much you can do with condiments and half a sixer of Newcastle.

He cleared his throat and answered. "Ron Starke."

Donna Kerrigan's voice brought him fully awake, like a nearby screech of brakes or a late-night smoke alarm.

"He's dead," she said.

Starke reached for a Newcastle and pried off its cap. Man, it was hot. "A cheerful good morning to you as well, Chief Kerrigan."

"I know it's early, but I need you at the morgue."

"You're sure it's him?"

"Ninety percent. I want a fast start on this."

Starke had a flickering thought: TV news would be all over the story, and Paul Dwyer's family shouldn't find out that way. While he was no fan of Shelby Dwyer, the new widow deserved better. He took a long pull, certain the delay was spiking the blood pressure of a woman whose smile he had yet to see during her first few months as his boss. She was a puzzle.

Finally: "OK, what do we know so far?"

"Body dump. In one of the ponds where they're building that residential tract, the big one—Villa Cordero, I think it's called."

One of Dwyer's own developments, Starke thought. *Interesting.*

"Some high school kids partying up there last night

found him," Kerrigan said. "Condition puts DOD at weeks, not days, meaning he's been dead since right after he disappeared. That's all we know at the moment. But you need to roll now. They're waiting for you to start the exam."

"The notification?" Starke said. "They have a daughter, a teenager. Somebody needs to tell Mrs. Dwyer soon."

"Agreed."

He remembered the unexpected note Shelby had written him two years before. It hadn't helped. But given their complicated history, he'd appreciated the gesture.

"I'll swing by their house on my way to the morgue," he said.

"No."

He waited a long moment for Kerrigan to elaborate. She didn't. "What's the media situation?" he said at last.

"I'm sure they heard the radio traffic."

"Then I really think someone needs to—"

"I'll go," Kerrigan said. "You need to be there for the exam. I can handle the notification. Widow's name again?"

"Shelby."

Starke pressed the cold bottle to his forehead, then dumped the rest of the brown ale into the sink. He set the empty bottle on the counter. Kerrigan was probably right. He needed to be there for the initial examination of Paul Dwyer's body. For a lot of reasons, he also wanted to handle the notification, to look into Shelby Dwyer's eyes at the moment she heard the news for any sort of tell. Both things needed to be done now, and he couldn't be in two places at once.

"Just—don't wait, OK?" he said. "Get there before the satellite trucks."

"Walking to my unit now," Kerrigan said.

Starke hoped what he was about to say wouldn't sound patronizing, but he didn't want to leave it unsaid. "This one's wide open, you know."

"Meaning?"

"Watch her carefully."

This time, Kerrigan took her time responding. "You think the wife knows more than she's saying?"

He hoped Shelby didn't. He hoped her husband's murder was a business deal gone bad, or a carjacking, or a life insurance hustle, or a jilted lover's revenge. He hoped Paul Dwyer had some sort of secret life that would explain it all and provide a logic for his death.

Because, more than most, he knew death without logic was the worst death of all.

"It's just—" Starke swallowed hard. "It's wide open."

"Never met a woman without secrets. On my way," Kerrigan said, and ended the call as abruptly as she'd started it.

Starke closed the refrigerator door slowly, erasing its wedge of light until he was alone again, sweating naked in the dark.

2

What drew her to the front door that Saturday morning, Shelby couldn't say. It started with an improbably hot breeze, as light as a lover's touch, that stirred the curtain beside her bedroom's open French doors. It seduced her from the bed where she'd been crying, into her satin robe, into a crackling alert mode. That's when she noticed the low thrum of a motor as it eased up her long driveway, followed by the thump of a heavy car door. By then she already was at the mirror in the marbled front hall of the silent house, checking the redness of her eyes.

She opened the door as her visitor reached for the bell, catching the woman by surprise.

"Oh," the woman said, finger poised. "Shelby Dwyer?"

"Morning."

"The driveway gate was open." She stuck out her hand. "Chief Kerrigan, Los Colmas PD."

Shelby looked past her. Had Chloe left the gate open

again? She took the woman's offered hand and looked her directly in the eye. "Nice to meet you."

There had been other cops in the past twenty-one days, maybe a half dozen. The first two had been women. They'd taken the empathetic approach, sister to sister, trying to coax information from her. When the women came up with nothing useful, they'd sent men, good-cop-bad-cop players she'd found laughably transparent. Now what? This lady cop was less manly than the first two—pretty, in fact, with her auburn hair pulled back and tied with a navy-blue silk ribbon that matched her business suit, which was nicely tailored to the small hips of an athlete without children. The whole executive top-cop package was softened by almond eyes that dipped at the corners, giving her the face of someone who Cared Deeply.

The lady cop reached for her ID, actually held out the badge and ID long enough that it was easy to read the full text: Donna Kerrigan, Chief of Police, City of Los Colmas, San Bernardino County, California.

"Where's Ron?" Shelby said.

"Ron?"

"Detective Starke."

Kerrigan raised one perfect eyebrow. "So you have a personal relationship with Detective Starke?"

Shelby just smiled. "Small town. But you're new here, right?"

After a long moment, Kerrigan continued. "He had another appointment this morning. But yes, it's his case. Mrs. Dwyer, I'm—"

Shelby snapped her fingers. "The Dwyer Foundation. Fall fundraiser, two years ago. You and your husband drove all the way from LA to deliver that wonderful donation. You were talking to Paul."

Kerrigan flushed pink, then opened her mouth to answer. Nothing came out. She tried again, managed: "I go to a lot of events."

"I've got a memory like an elephant," Shelby said. "Your husband's gift made a huge difference that year."

Kerrigan smiled, but it seemed forced. "Ex."

Shelby cleared her throat and waited. Finally: "I'm sorry."

"But that's—I have some news for you and your daughter, Mrs. Dwyer."

Something in the way she shifted told Shelby this was different. Donna Kerrigan was working, watching her for a reaction. Shelby caught herself before she could look away, fixed her eyes on the stranger's with the anxious stare of someone who desperately wanted to know whatever news she'd brought. She bit her tongue and waited. She'd never given anything away, and wasn't going to start now.

"There's a pond up near the new Villa Cordera tract, Mrs. Dwyer. Know it?"

Shelby untied and retied the satin belt of her robe. "Known Jean and Harv Shepherdsen a long time. That was their ranch. But it's been years since I was up there. Can't imagine there's any ponds left in those foothills."

The police chief nodded. "It's building up so fast. One of your husband's residential projects, if I'm not mistaken."

Shelby nodded. "Can't build on water, he always says."

Paul Dwyer was one of the few locals not troubled by the sparkle-creep of million-dollar tract homes across the remaining swathes of wild Southern California. Development was what most people bitched about here, like rain in Seattle or snow in Buffalo. Los Angeles was caught in a human tidal wave that was pushing the strivers into the inland foothills, where her husband sold them master-planned four bed, three bath, 2,400-square-foot Mediterraneans for two-thirds the median price of homes in the city they'd just fled. "Win-win," Paul used to say, even though their salaries ended up in his pocket, and four of their Dwyer Development dream homes would have fit neatly inside the house where she and the police chief now stood. But watching the landscape of her rural childhood scraped clean by earthmovers was particularly rough on Shelby, who'd grown up to become the second wife of the man some of her hometown friends accused of destroying their paradise. She'd adapted.

"We found a body yesterday, Mrs. Dwyer," Kerrigan said at last. "Adult male. At the bottom of the pond. Looks like somebody sunk it there on purpose."

Shelby reached behind her, feeling for the edge of the doorframe. When her right hand found it, she eased herself backward and leaned her full weight against the solid wood. It wasn't a calculated reaction. She felt suddenly lightheaded. The bottom of a pond? Less than five minutes' drive from their house?

"No final ID yet; they're working on it now." Kerrigan paused. "You should know—Mrs. Dwyer, we're proceeding on the assumption that, if this is your husband, he was killed shortly after you reported him missing twenty-one days ago, maybe even before. Right now that's all we know."

Shelby knew this woman was watching her every gesture, waiting, analyzing, sifting for the precise wording she would use for this latest chapter in the investigation file the cops were keeping about Paul's disappearance. Spouse's immediate reaction to the news? Spouse's demeanor in the moments afterward? In the past, Shelby had performed for these official visitors. This time, her reaction was genuine. She guided herself down the door frame until she was sitting on the apron of travertine stone that spread in an elegant fan from her front door. She crossed her legs yoga style.

"You must think it's him," she said. "You wouldn't be here if you didn't."

"We'll know soon enough, Mrs. Dwyer. Are you OK?"

Shelby nodded. "Who found him?"

Kerrigan waited a beat before answering. "High school kids. I'm told the pond used to be about an acre, acre and a half."

Shelby had skinny-dipped there for the first time, or at least the first time with a boy.

"Of course, it's not that big anymore," Kerrigan said. "Golden Creek used to drain into it, but apparently your husband diverted the creek so he could build out Villa Cordera. So—" Kerrigan paused again. "With no rain for so long, and the creek diverted, the pond's drying up. Just a puddle now. Almost gone. So that's how the body was discovered."

Shelby looked away. "That's it, then? It's over?"

"What's over, ma'am?"

She waved her hand and found herself watching it flutter. "All this, then. If it's him, it's over."

The new chief hooked her badge over her belt and smoothed the sleeve of her midnight-blue jacket. "If it is him, that's one question answered, yes ma'am, if that's what you mean. Nearly a month since he went missing. Maybe now he's not."

Shelby's eyes fixed on a crease in the concrete. "But you all, it won't stop. You'll still have questions, won't you?"

"Depending what the coroner finds, yes, we will. We may have a lot more questions. Do you understand what I'm saying, Mrs. Dwyer?"

Shelby stared across her vast front lawn, where dozens of sprinkler heads were maintaining the illusion of a lush paradise despite the governor's drought-relief order. How would it all end? How could a life so carefully lived have led her to a juncture as improbable as this?

The chief of police eased forward. Shelby caught a whiff of good perfume, and for a moment Kerrigan looked like she actually might reach across the distance between them and pat Shelby's shoulder, or push the strand of fallen blond hair back off her forehead. But she didn't. Instead, she lifted one leg onto the porch step and set her tanned forearm on her own slender knee. She leaned in close and pitched her voice real low.

"Don't leave town, Mrs. Dwyer. We'll be in touch."

3

Ron Starke peered through the tiny, double-sealed window into the main examination room of the San Bernardino County Coroner. Except for the gruesome mass at its center, the exam area was impossibly bright and cheerful. Riotous spider plants hung in every upper corner to mitigate the airborne stew of alcohol, formaldehyde, and xylene. The only sound coming from in there was the constant trickle of water down the angled, stainless-steel autopsy tables.

"Today's your lucky day, detective," the deputy coroner said, clapping him on the back. "A big ol' floater."

Starke was already fighting one of the monster headaches he got when the Santa Anas were blowing. He closed his eyes and tried to imagine he was about to step into a cool and verdant glade. "How long in the pond?" he asked, eyes still closed.

Eckel, the deputy, grinned. "At least two weeks, maybe three. Nice'n ripe."

Starke sighed, smearing his upper lip with the VapoRub

Eckel offered. He snapped on a pair of gloves and they stepped into the exam room.

Starke looked away. Seeing the body and smelling it at the same time was too much at once, a sensory overload. He gagged as his eyes roamed the room, from spider plants to Stryker saw to washbasin. He steadied himself on the edge of a gurney parked just inside the door. When his eyes finally settled, they did so on Eckel and his satisfied grin.

"I've seen that shade of green before," Eckel said, "but never on someone's face."

"I'm fine," he said, and gagged again.

Eckel's grin got wider, and he flared his nostrils. "He sure smells like a developer."

"Stop. Just show me what you've got."

What they found on the table looked like a smallish Macy's parade float, the result of what happens when a submerged human body fills with the off-gasses of decay. The body's face was a tight mask of swollen tissue, puffed and unrecognizable. Bits of moss and mud clung to the hair like stubborn crabgrass. But that wasn't what most interested Starke. He stepped in for a closer look at what appeared to be a large portable TV, its busted screen a maw of jutting glass shards. Besides the bloated body, it was the biggest single item on the table. A length of plastic-coated steel cable had been looped through its carrying handle, looped again around the body's neck, then fastened with what looked like a combination lock.

Eckel nudged Oswaldo, his assistant, who'd done the prep work for the initial exam. "I could be wrong," he said, pointing to the unorthodox anchor, "but this may suggest foul play." He turned to Starke. "'Like a midget at a urinal, he was gonna have to stay on his toes.'"

Starke recognized the paraphrased quote right away. "Frank Drebin. *Naked Gun 33⅓: The Final Insult.* Nice pull, Eck."

He'd worked with the pair on other cases. They were jesters on the most macabre imaginable stage, but he appreciated their exuberance. In Oswaldo's case, it was especially incomprehensible, because he wasn't salaried, just a $15-an-hour lackey. But not even the rankest chores seemed to dampen his enthusiasm.

"Thanks," Eckel said. "I know you're a connoisseur of fine cinema."

Starke nodded to the TV. "So what am I looking at here?"

"Computer monitor, an old CRT, ancient, practically antique," Oswaldo said. "Still checking on the brand; never heard of it. But it weighed thirty-five pounds even before it filled up with water. The cable's just your basic bike lock. Four-foot, quarter-inch Master, costs about six bucks. Did the trick pretty well, though. Our boy'd still be underwater if there was still an underwater there. But there's not."

Starke crossed his arms over his chest and turned to face the young assistant. "In a language I can understand, Oswaldo. Help me out."

"One of those dried-up ponds. It was there; now it's not. Just a damp gully between the fucking McMansions. Some of the local juvenile delinquents found him floating like a buoy after the water level dropped."

Eckel smiled. "'Look what I found, Ma. Can I keep it?'"

"Guys, check this out." Oswaldo led them to the head

of the exam table. The assistant squatted and angled his penlight into the shadow just behind the right ear. Starke could see a jagged gap the size of a dime.

"Looks like his head has too many holes in it," Eckel said. "There's an exit wound on his neck on the other side. I'm guessing somebody shot him, then wrapped the steel cable around his neck, laced him up to the anchor, and hauled him out into the water figuring he'd stay down for a while. And he probably would've, except they picked the wrong pond. One of the local land rapers diverted the creek about a month ago, no permit probably. Then this heat."

Starke suspected they were looking at that very land raper in question, but said nothing.

"Might as well have dumped him on the I-10," Eckel said.

"Rookie mistake, if you ask me," Oswaldo added. "And, here, look at this." He led Starke and Eckel around the exam table to the body's left hand, which looked like an inflated surgical glove, blue sausage fingers. The ring finger had a curious crease just below the middle knuckle where the flesh had swelled around something. Starke could see a hint of gold.

"Wedding band." Oswaldo held up a pair of special, heavy-duty pinking shears. "May I do the honors?"

Eckel nodded his assent as Oswaldo snapped on some latex gloves, then turned toward Starke, catching him trying to filter a few deep breaths through the shirt fabric at the crook of his elbow. "This could make your ID job a lot easier, detective."

Starke suppressed another gag. "You ever get used to this?" he asked, his voice muffled.

"To what?" Eckel said.

Starke stepped back to the exam table just as Oswaldo was sliding the ring from the now-detached finger. He laid the finger back down beside the violated left hand before retreating to a nearby faucet. He came back with the cleaned ring in his palm. It had a delicate beaded scroll around each rim. The gold on the outside of the band was dull and scratched, but the metal inside still gleamed.

"Bingo," Oswaldo said, squinting into his palm. "There's an inscription."

Starke lifted the ring and angled it back and forth under the magnifier's high-intensity light. He could see tiny block letters engraved along the inside surface of the ring, but he still wished he'd brought his reading glasses.

"P.W.D.–S.L.D," Oswaldo said.

Eckel smiled. "You know, Oz, I'm gonna go out on a limb here. This may be a clue."

"Gotta be him," Oswaldo said. "Of course we'll do the science, just to be sure."

Eckel clapped Starke on the back again. "We'll disassemble him, amigo. We find anything else, we'll let you know."

Starke was more than happy to skip the autopsy. "You've got my cell, right?"

The deputy coroner saluted. "Hope you're not planning a vacation anytime soon."

4

The Shepherdsen spread, or what was left of the small subsected ranch, was one of the few large properties in Los Colmas still in private hands. It seemed much larger and more remote than it actually was. The remaining land was about three miles west of Los Colmas and shaped like a giant slice of pie, wide as a football field at the driveway and maybe a quarter-mile deep, but only twenty-five feet across at the back property line as it rose up a steep slope. A grove of California oaks stood in the late afternoon light at the rear, but it was a feeble partition between the property and the suburban blight that had sprung up on either side of the wedge's tip. Still, the trees obscured the dry brown patch at the crest of the hill that once was a creek-fed pond.

Starke led Kerrigan along the steep, overgrown path. Neither had said a word since they left the cars in Shepherdsen's driveway. He resented her big-footing his case, second-guessing everything he did. After fifteen years at Los Colmas PD, continuing a professional legacy begun by his father, he'd risen steadily through the ranks with an unblemished record of service. He'd been a top contender for the chief's job after Barry retired. Then? They bring in an outsider, a woman no less, who'd never set foot in the community before her job interviews nearly a year ago. Who despite her considerable professional accomplishments had the people skills of a rattlesnake. Who, despite his occasional rudeness and borderline insubordination since her arrival, had remained annoyingly professional.

Eckel had released a tentative ID on Paul Dwyer an hour ago based on the engraving inside his wedding ring. The dental charts and DNA samples were in hand and, barring surprises, would confirm what everyone already knew. How Dwyer died was still a mystery; the single bullet hole in his skull probably killed him, but Eckel still wanted to make sure he wasn't breathing when he hit the water. The crime-scene guys had sifted pond mud since yesterday, looking for the bullet. Just ahead, mounded piles of dirt surrounded the spot where his body was found, testifying to their diligence. But they'd come up empty.

Starke ducked under the fluttering yellow tape that secured the area between five of the oak trees, then lifted it so Kerrigan could follow—an unthinking habit drilled into him by his dad. They passed the massive granite boulder into which generations of Los Colmas teens had etched their initials. Somewhere on its backside were his own initials, right beside Shelby Dwyer's. Starke noticed that even a few gang tags had begun to appear as the city's demographics changed.

Kerrigan squatted beside him at the edge of a restricted area about the size of a two-car garage. The pond had been bigger once, back when Starke swam naked here as a younger man, but quickly shrank as Paul Dwyer's bulldozers redirected the water from Golden Creek; the sun evaporated what was left, and the pond gave up its secret.

"I used to swim up here," Starke said. "Partied here as a kid and in college. Harder to get away with that now, it's so built up."

He stood. Two faux Mediterranean villas flanked the site, each about a hundred yards away. They were so new that the manufacturer's stickers were still on some of the windows, and the sod had yet to be delivered for their instant lawns. They sat like twin wedding cakes in the middle of their scraped-brown half-acre lots. The house to their right already featured a Greekish statue of a nude Adonis pissing into a black-bottomed spa. To the left, a bright yellow Hummer sparkled in the semicircular driveway. A year ago, this spot might have looked the same as it did a century before, when old man Shepherdsen carved out his little piece of the California dream and started his groves of avocados, lemons, and walnuts. Today it looked like a lot of places in Southern California, a laughable montage of carefully chosen and carelessly financed image statements.

"How many ways to get up here?" Kerrigan asked.

Starke circled the restricted area and walked to the top of the downslope on the other side. The scene that spread beneath his feet could have been most anywhere in Southern California, a circuit board of residential streets and cul-de-sacs knitting together a nearly finished housing tract quickly filling with LA refugees. Paul Dwyer had called this development Villa Cordera—Villa Cordwooda to cynics who saw numbing uniformity in houses stacked so closely together. Amid all that newness, though, County Route 64 stood out. What Starke and other locals knew as Spadero Road ran along the ridge about a quarter mile below where he stood, bisecting East Villa Cordera from West Villa Cordera. From Spadero Road, especially at night, free movement up the once-wooded hill would have been possible. Not easy, but possible.

"Only two ways in, both on foot," Starke said when Kerrigan joined him at the crest of the hill. "The way we just came, along the steep path past the Shepherdsen place, or up this back slope."

The terrain was telling. When Starke had carried pony kegs and cases of beer up here as teenager, he preferred the path from then-isolated Spadero Road that followed the lazy switchbacks up through the little canyons. It was a lot easier than the steeper route past the Shepherdsen place. Besides, old man Shepherdsen was a light sleeper, and ornery. A winding, inlaid-stone driveway now covered the spot where the switchbacks used to be.

"I'd guess they came from this direction, up from Spadero," he said.

"You'd guess?" Kerrigan said.

"We know at least two people got here undetected," he said. "We can probably assume it was at night. Since no bullet was found here, it's possible that one of them may have been transporting the other's body."

Kerrigan looked skeptical. "Even in the dark, that would take some doing," she said. "They'd have had to park along the road. They'd have had to cut through these new properties, which all have security gates. They'd have to be pretty strong, or else have some other way of moving two hundred pounds of dead weight."

"And let's assume male, given the—"

"Let's not assume anything," Kerrigan interrupted. "Could have been two people. Three. A lynch mob. You're sure no one at the Shepherdsen place saw anything?"

Starke shook his head. "Talked to them myself."

Kerrigan turned around and swept her arm across the path they'd just climbed. "How thoroughly did the crime scene guys work this steeper path?"

Now he was really pissed. A full sweep of the area was a low-percentage shot for an understaffed department already reeling from budget cuts. The path they'd just walked was too steep. And even at his age, Harv Shepherdsen was a light sleeper. So Starke's scene team focused on the downslope beyond the rear of the property, an unpopulated wooded trail a year ago. It was now a crazy quilt of private, heavily mortgaged home sites, but there were only a few finished houses, and not all of them were occupied. He choked it all down before he answered.

"We can send them back if you want," he said. "They concentrated on the pond and the area around it, looking for the bullet, not on the possible access routes. It was an issue of resources."

"Who made that call?"

"I did."

In the long, uncomfortable pause that followed, Starke could hear birds in the oak trees behind them. In the distance, a lawn mower buzzed across someone's new sod. A semi roared along Spadero Road, upshifting as the road angled down.

"Mode of access is going to tell us a lot," Kerrigan said. "I want to know how the killer got up here. We're going to build this case on physical evidence, not guesswork and assumptions." She turned and fixed him with a stare. "Bust the budget if you have to, but get the crime scene crew back here first thing tomorrow."

Starke tucked his boss's second-guessing into that special place where he stored the things he would never forgive.

"And how well do you know Shelby Dwyer?" Kerrigan asked.

He forced a smile. "Small town."

"And you planned to mention that sometime, right?"

Starke clenched and unclenched his jaw before answering. "I'm not sure I like your implication."

The police chief just shook her head, then stepped around him, heading back down the path to her car.

5

Shelby had waited until the chief's black-and-white Ford was out of sight before she tried to stand, and even then she braced herself against the door frame. Her breath was coming now without effort, but her heart was racing. She could feel her temples throb, hear her pulse. Had Kerrigan heard it too?

She ran her fingertips across her forehead and they came away damp.

Through the open gate at the end of her driveway, she could see Craig DeMott standing on the opposite curb. He lived two houses away, but there he was again, ever vigilant. He and Paul were friendly—rather, Craig didn't know Paul well enough to see through Paul's bullshit—and he stood with his arms crossed over his chest, looking at her the same way he'd looked at her since the moment he'd heard that her husband had disappeared.

She waved. Craig didn't.

Shelby stepped across the threshold and back into the

dead-quiet house, cherishing the silence, and closed the door behind her. Chloe was still asleep, unconscious in the profound way only seventeen-year-old girls can be at ten on a Saturday morning. She thought about waking her, but opted instead for some extra time alone. Her daughter would be up by eleven, and then she'd tell her about the police chief's visit, about what they'd found.

In the kitchen, she rinsed last night's cup and filled it from the carafe. She sipped the coffee, not bothering to microwave it or even spoon in sugar from the bowl, and fished a cigarette from the spot behind her cookbooks where she hid them. It was her secret vice; never in public. She was less concerned with her image than the Dwyer Foundation's, which funded public-health initiatives throughout the Inland Empire. But right here, at the kitchen window overlooking the broad patio and the pool beyond, she did her best thinking with a cup in one hand and smoke curling up to the ceiling. There was a lot to think about, so she made a checklist in her head.

First, Chloe. Shelby had prepped her for the worst, but if they'd actually found her dad's body, there was no telling how she'd react. With him gone the past few weeks, she'd seemed to open up a bit, to breathe right for the first time since the summer before when it all went so bad, when Paul had both of them cowering and clutching each other on the kitchen floor, wondering if they'd survive the night. Still, Chloe and her dad did have a relationship, and even a relationship rooted in fear still means something to a kid. The first glimpse of death is always a shock.

Second, the police. They'd be around a lot more now, watching her, everything she did. Today was just the tip of the spear. It was about to get intense, and she'd have to be strong. And smart. For Chloe. It was just them now.

Finally, the rest of it—reporters, the Dwyer Development and the Dwyer Foundation people, the people at church. All the testing questions, the sidelong glances, the well-intentioned snoops who offered their help "if you and Chloe ever need anything," but who used their pretense at charity as a license to pry. He hasn't been in touch *at all* since he left? Not even on Chloe's birthday? He hasn't used his credit cards even *once*? No one had said it, but they knew all along that Paul was dead.

How much time passed, Shelby couldn't say. She was aware of nothing but the swirl of anxiety until a searing heat blistered the web of skin between her fingers. She flinched, and two inches of ash dropped from her cigarette into the sink, leaving a tan filter wedged between her knuckles. The burn and the cold tap water she used to ease the pain brought her back to the moment, and she suddenly felt more alone than she could ever remember.

She unplugged her cell phone from its charger on the counter, then pulled Ron Starke's card from her purse. When he picked up, she could tell by the hollow background noise that he was in his car.

"Ron? It's Shelby Dwyer."

She waited though a long, tense silence. Finally: "Shelby, I'm so sorry."

"Thank you."

"And I'm sorry I wasn't able to tell you personally. I needed to be somewhere else this morning, then up to the scene."

Shelby lit another cigarette and let Starke wait as she

took a deep draw. "There's nothing you could have done. God, this whole thing is just so unreal. I mean, why kill him? He was a good man, Ron. Maybe not the most popular man, but a damn good man who did a lot of good things around here. And somebody killed him and dumped him like garbage."

"What'd she tell you?"

Everything and nothing, Shelby thought. "In Shepherdsen's pond. They shot him and sank him in the water. And I'm trying to absorb all this and—let's just say your boss could use a little work on her bedside manner. She obviously thinks I was involved. She made that real clear. I mean, what the hell, Ron? Where's *that* coming from?"

"It's an active investigation, Shel. You know I can't—"

"We've got a lot of history between us, you and me. Ancient history, I guess. I hope. I'm counting on you to be straight with me. Where's this going?"

"My job is to look at every possibility."

"So why is this—" Shelby glanced at the business card the lady cop left behind. "Chief Donna Kerrigan. She's after me. Why is she even involved?"

"No one's after you," he said. "That's the truth. Let me do my job."

"Seems like *she's* doing your job."

Shelby regretted it as soon as she said it.

After a long pause, Starke said: "The coroner's call came this morning. I was needed elsewhere, and we didn't want to delay notification. Didn't want you to hear it on the news. But you have to understand the pressure here, Shel. Because of who Paul was, there's a lot of attention on this. And it's not just locals. His big project in LA, the coastal one out on the peninsula, has got the media there lathered up, too. The *Times* story last week was just one thing, and that was before we knew what happened. Now we're getting calls from everywhere, out-of-town papers, radio, network TV. This is Kerrigan's department, her reputation. Right now it's under the most intense scrutiny ever. She's pretty new, and she wants to get it right. We all do."

"She made me feel like a criminal."

"I'm sorry about that."

"I've been straight with you, Ron. You guys just be straight with me, OK?"

Shelby didn't like the way he waited before answering.

"Shel, remember when I asked you in that initial interview about things between you and Paul? And you told me things were good? 'Great, actually,' you said. I need to know if *you* were being straight with *me* then."

Shelby closed her eyes. Could he know? They had so many friends in common, having both grown up in Los Colmas. People gossip. Rumors spread. She'd told no one, but maybe the turtleneck and make-up hadn't covered her neck bruise last summer quite as well as she'd thought? Maybe Chloe was talking?

"We had problems just like everybody else," she tested.

"That's different from 'great,'" he said.

"Oh come on. Goddamn, Ron. Not you, too."

"Straight, Shel."

He could be bluffing.

"I talked to Chloe's school counselor," he prompted.

He wasn't bluffing. Shelby snuffed her cigarette against the side of her kitchen sink and washed the black ash down the drain.

"Shel?"

"Damn you. God*damn* you." She took a breath. "OK. OK. I'm going to be completely honest with you, but it has to stay just between us."

"I can't promise that."

Another breath. "Fine. I'll tell you anyway. And I'll tell you right now it has absolutely nothing to do with what happened to my husband."

"So noted."

Shelby tucked a loose ribbon of blond behind her ear. "Everybody knows Paul, right? Love him or hate him, everybody knows him. Knew him. He was the visionary, the man who built the Inland Empire. Or he was the son-of-a-bitch developer who knew the best prices for concrete and lumber, and who rode his contractors like a slavemaster. Or he was the guy whose foundation gave away all that money to the colleges and hospitals around here. Or he was the guy whose wife sat on every charity board in the county. Everybody knew Paul Dwyer, or at least some version of him. But Chloe and me, yeah, we knew another Paul, the one nobody else knew."

Starke said nothing.

"There was a part of him... a private part, an ugly part. Mean. Know what I'm saying? When he drank, he could be just... mean."

"I hear he drank a lot," Starke said.

"'Just part of the business,'" she replied. "That's what he always said. It was bad, but not intolerable."

"But sometimes he brought business home with him?"

"Sometimes."

"A lot?"

"He'd get angry about some stupid thing, or something that happened that day…. Things happened. Look, you know me well enough to know I'm not one of those women who lay down and take it. I give as good as I get. But you can't actually believe I'd—"

"Did he ever hit you?"

Ten seconds passed. "Sometimes, yes."

"Chloe?"

Shelby hesitated. "I was always there for her. She knows that. It was just her and me sometimes when he'd go off, so we're tight. That's all." She felt Starke's silence pushing her toward a terrifying edge. "What was I supposed to do? File a complaint every time something happened?"

"The law was always there for you, Shel," he said. "You know that."

"Oh Christ. Pull your head out of your ass, Ron. Put all this on public record? Do you have any idea what that would have done. To his business? To the foundation and all its good work? To him? To Chloe and me? The whole thing collapses. Everybody loses."

"Behind closed doors he was a drunk, Shel, apparently a violent one. Only two people in the world could have put a stop to that, the two people who were in there with him. Jesus, Shel, at least Chloe had the sense to talk to—"

Her thumb found the phone's "end" button and she pressed it hard. Like she needed his lecture. Again, Shelby found herself listening to the rush of blood in her ears. She knew Starke would focus on finding the truth. But why was he fixating on the wrong truth?

When she could breathe again, Shelby felt a familiar gravity pulling her toward her office down the hall. There'd been countless nights of her life during the last couple of years—nights when her husband was gone or out whoring or too drunk to stir—when its force was irresistible, when she followed it desperately alone and unthinking, like a moth drawn to the licking heat of flame. Shelby still knew the routine. She stepped to the left side of the hall as she passed the framed family portrait they'd had made when Chloe was six, because the hardwood floorboards on the right side had a noisy squeak. She lifted up while turning her office doorknob, because Paul never did get around to oiling that hinge. The light switch for the overhead was on the left, always on, and if she'd wanted light she could have twisted the silent dimmer knob and entered her former sanctum with no one the wiser.

This time she didn't want light, and wasn't at all sure she wanted to go in again. She peered into the murky space. The only one who'd used the office lately was Chloe, who knew she was allowed in only after homework was done and her bedroom was picked up. Her daughter's world—her online world, anyway—was always waiting on her mother's computer, and Shelby understood the attraction better than most. But the only times Shelby went into the room anymore were when she wanted to snoop a bit, to make sure her daughter's social media life was under control, to peek over Chloe's shoulder as she chatted and Instagrammed and Snapchatted and explored her electronic universe filled with countless seductions. Chloe was just old enough to appreciate the incomparable thrill of danger.

Shelby sipped cold coffee at the threshold. Across the room, their new desktop PC crouched in shadow, in sleep mode, just like her daughter. Its only sign of life was the pale green eye of its power indicator, and its stare was relentless.

Her phone vibrated silently in her hand. She recognized Starke's number.

"You were way out of line," she answered. "My family life is none of your goddamned business."

"Shel?" His voice had calmed. "We're still waiting for final word from the coroner."

"What's that supposed to mean?"

Starke cleared his throat. "How'd you know he was shot?"

6

News traveled fast in Los Colmas. Bad news traveled faster, and now, farther. In the grand central nervous system of Southern California, the little foothill town had always been an insignificant node, a once-remote settlement of second-generation immigrants and city refugees who could lead off-radar lives assured that, no matter what happened there, the wider world wouldn't much notice. But things changed as the place was colonized and gentrified by refugees from the great metropolis to the west. Money brought with it a new ethos. The newcomers wanted good schools, safe streets, *security*.

Kerrigan stood outside the city manager's office, not nervous exactly, but curious. The first call had come from a reporter in Riverside; the second from San Bernardino. She'd had her assistant refer both callers to the department's public information officer. That was SOP. When a news producer from the ABC affiliate in Los Angeles phoned, though, it kicked things up to a whole other level. Now her new boss wanted to see her. Any dead body demanded answers. The body of someone as prominent as Paul Dwyer? The media's feeding frenzy was underway.

She'd only had a few conversations with Douglas Buckley outside of regular staff meetings. He'd offered her little more than chit-chat, but he'd seemed sincere in welcoming her to what he called "the city family." She'd come for complicated reasons, first of which was wanting a fresh start, but knew there'd be a suffocating intimacy in a small-town government where the thirty-one employees were led by a man who, like many of them, had never worked anywhere else, and whose massive insecurities presented as insufferable arrogance. She hadn't ignored the red flags; she'd just decided, all things considered, she could handle it. Still, nothing about the next fifteen minutes was going to be enjoyable.

Buckley's secretary stood up from her desk, peering through the wide window of the manager's office. "Looks like he's off the phone, sweetie. Go on in."

Sweetie? Kerrigan let it slide. This time.

Buckley was seated at his desk, shoulders squared to an open file folder. He read through glasses that clung to the tip of his nose, and didn't look up until she'd sat in one of the two godawful purple-and-chrome chairs.

"Well, hello," he said, as though Kerrigan had arrived unexpectedly instead of being summoned.

"You wanted to see me?"

Buckley stood, stepped around the desk, and closed his office door. Back in his chair, he removed his reading glasses and offered a relaxed smile. "Looks like you've got the hottest case in Southern California. Just a glorified missing persons situation when this started three weeks ago. Now it's not."

"Not by all indications, sir," Kerrigan said. "I've handled my share of high-profile murder cases in LA, though, before I came here."

"So you're comfortable with it?"

"Completely."

Buckley creaked back in his desk chair. He was maybe forty, good-looking in a Crossfit-training kind of way. He'd risen steadily through the ranks without distinguishing himself, but without ever screwing up badly enough to derail his ambition to become city manager. The council had rewarded him with the job three years before. She'd heard he was twice divorced, and she wasn't surprised. He was the kind of guy who had his suits specially tailored to accentuate his broad chest and pinched waist.

"We don't get many of those around here, you know. Murders outside of the bad areas, I mean." He let a meaningful moment pass. "If you're in any way sheepish about what this may bring, the media interest, the pressure, all that, you just let me know. Because we certainly have guys here who've been around this community a long—"

"I believe, sir, I said I was completely comfortable with it."

Buckley nodded, unflustered. "So you did."

"Anything else?"

The city manager slipped his reading glasses back on and leaned toward the open file on his desk. "You've already read up on this one, I know."

"Not a lot to read until this week, sir. Wife reports him missing three weeks ago, but no sign of foul play at the house. No body turns up, but nothing to suggest Paul Dwyer was still active during those three weeks, either. No contacts. No attempts to get money from their accounts. No credit card traces. Absolutely nothing until they found him in the pond."

"So you think he's been dead the whole time?"

Kerrigan nodded. "Condition of the body bears that out, I'm told."

"And the wife's reaction?"

"A little stunned. Not surprised, just stunned."

Buckley pushed away from his desk and leaned back in his chair. "I knew Shelby in high school. Nice girl back then. Good family. Not wealthy, but solid. She was bound for glory, though. A climber."

Where was this headed? "Had you kept in touch?"

Buckley shook his head. "Saw her around. Kids' ballgames. Grocery store. That's about it. Don't know much about her. Didn't know the husband personally, just by reputation. Older. Second marriage. Not a nice man, I hear. Maybe he had some enemies?"

"One for sure."

Buckley's smile seemed genuine.

"What can you tell me about her?" Kerrigan asked.

The city manager leaned back and stared at the ceiling. "It's funny how high school still defines us, all these years later. It may not be right, but reputations do stick, don't they?"

"So," she said, "freak, geek, goth, or jock?"

"Shelby was—" He was a man trying to jam an ill-fitting piece into a puzzle. He turned it every which way, then gave up. "I wish it was that simple. You're right, most of us fell into one of those categories in high school. Shelby just seemed more complicated than that."

Kerrigan noted the familiarity with which he used Shelby Dwyer's name.

After a pause, Buckley said, "Librarian."

"Librarian?"

Buckley nodded. "You know on TV commercials, where there's a mousy-looking woman in glasses with her hair up in a bun. And then she uses the right shampoo or something, and the glasses come off and she shakes her hair free and, vavoom, she's Katy Perry? Except with Shelby, back then anyway, I never knew her to take off her glasses or shake her hair loose. Way too focused and ambitious. Driven, really. But she could've. Does that make sense?"

"Beautiful but not showy?"

The manager shook his head. "One of those girls who sized you up, made an immediate decision about your value to her, and looked right past you if she thought you were a waste of her time. Like she knew she was going places, and you could either help her along the way—or hold her back. We all knew even then that she wasn't like the rest of us. That's just a perception from an old jock, of course. I could be wrong."

"Did she look right past you?"

Buckley smiled. "Shelby was after way bigger game than me."

"Paul Dwyer?"

"Ultimately, him. Yeah. But someone like him, for sure."

"Good student?"

"Couldn't say. School records would tell you that, if you think it's important. Always wanted something bigger, though. Better. I'm sure she saw Dwyer as a way to get that. Wasn't a long courtship, as I recall. She graduates college, then wham, bam, suddenly she's started a family with this very wealthy, much older guy."

Kerrigan nodded. "Always pays to know who you're dealing with."

Buckley leaned forward, put his elbows on the desk. "Anything useful from the scene?"

"The forensic stuff's a little odd. You heard about the anchor, right?"

"Old computer monitor, busted screen. What do you make of that?"

"It's heavy," she said.

"Anything else?"

"I figure we're looking for somebody who's had a lot of computers. The old equipment tends to stack up as you upgrade. I know it does with me. So this old monitor was sitting around the house somewhere, and came in handy when the time came to weigh down the body."

"Doesn't exactly narrow it down much, does it?" Buckley said. "Somebody with an old computer?"

"No sir. But it's probably a guy."

"We know that from statistics."

"Beyond that. Has to do with the location of the body." Kerrigan leaned forward as well and sketched a crude map on the desk with her finger. "Just two ways up to that pond. Both are at least a quarter-mile hike, with some steep parts."

"Used to party up there," Buckley said.

"Seems like everybody around here did. It didn't change much until ten months ago, when the development started. It'd take a strong guy, or more than one person, to get a body up that climb, not to mention lugging that heavy monitor. May even have taken a couple of trips."

"That assumes Dwyer was killed somewhere else and brought there. It assumes he didn't get caught up there by someone, something weird and random. Or maybe he was taking a look at his development project from up there? What if he walked up there willingly with someone who turned out to be his killer?"

"With a heavy computer monitor?" she said.

"Two could carry it easier than one."

"But does that make any sense to you?"

Buckley sat back. Kerrigan did the same. For a long moment, the room was tense, airless. She knew his reaction to her pushback would likely color her career here.

"Good point," he said. "Guess that's why I'm not a cop."

"For whatever it's worth," Kerrigan added, "Detective Starke tells me the crime scene folks sifted the pond pretty well. No bullet found."

"If you're right about when he was killed, though, the site had time to degrade."

"Bullets don't disappear. So I think he was killed somewhere else and dumped."

Buckley steepled his index fingers beneath his nose. "Nice work so far, chief."

"Thank you."

The city manager stood and stepped toward a mirror on the wall behind his desk. The man actually began to preen. "Let me deal with the media on this," he said. "You just stay focused and keep me in the loop as things develop."

Buckley walked to his office door, but didn't open it.

His hand was on the doorknob when he spoke again. "Just curious. The wife. Shelby. Think she knows anything?"

Kerrigan chose her next word carefully: "Yes."

"Because?"

Because. Because. "I don't know, sir. I know a lot of women like her, I guess. She strikes me as someone with something to hide."

Buckley fixed his eyes on hers for long enough that she felt uncomfortable. Without another word, he opened his office door and stepped out of her way.

7

The automatic doors of the Foothill Village Health Center slid open with an institutional whoosh. Starke stepped into the vestibule and, with his free hand, picked up the handset of a telephone on the table to his right. Through the second set of glass doors, at the far end of a long and joyless corridor, he could see Glenda Mendez pick up, spot him, and wave.

"Didn't expect you, Ronnie," she said. "Not today, at least."

Had she seen the news? Was his name in the report? "I've got ten minutes between things, G. Just wanted to check on him. Everything OK?"

"About the same. I'll buzz you in."

The doors slid open. Starke stepped from the stifling heat into the cool, antiseptic-smelling interior of the facility where his father had been housed for the past three years. The old man's journey to what he called "the lockup" began with a fire in his condo. A neighbor had doused the flames with a kitchen extinguisher, and the damage was minimal, mostly just a light char to the stove and the vent fan above. No, he was not cooking something, Dad had patiently explained to the young Los Colmas cop later sent to investigate. He was simply drying his bath towel.

In the oven.

At 475 degrees.

The patrol officer later approached Starke at work. "I don't think your dad's OK," he told him, and that turned out to be as accurate a diagnosis as any. By then Starke already knew his father's occasional eccentricities had become something else, and his doctors made it official later that year: early-onset Alzheimer's. The diagnosis ended a legendary Los Colmas law enforcement career, one that most assumed would have led Tommy Starke to the department's top job, maybe beyond. In time his father would get a hero's funeral, but until then Starke could only watch him slide deeper into dementia's abyss.

The move to this care facility was unavoidable, and difficult. Three years ago his father was still lucid most of the time, and as strong-willed as ever. In three years, he'd still never taken his toiletries out of the battered leather Dopp kit in his tiny bathroom, as though this was just a short motel stay. It was especially hard because he was still managing pretty well in the condo at the time, at least until the Arby's incident. But Starke knew it was time to move him the night Dad wheeled his F-150 into a nearby fast-food place, strode to the counter, and ordered an Angus Steak sandwich and a chocolate shake. He was wearing only a pair of knee-high black socks.

Starke pushed open the door to room 169. His father

was dozing in a recliner positioned directly in front of the flatscreen TV. The angry voices of his favorite national news shouters echoed off the room's bare white walls.

"Just me, Dad," he said. "Ronnie."

The old man's head shot up. The front of his ball cap read "No Spin Zone." He looked confused.

"Your son," Starke reminded.

He stepped across the room and poked the mute button on the remote. Room 169 was suddenly, weirdly quiet while his father tried to ID the intruder.

"You don't live here," the old man said at last.

"No, but I came to see you. Make sure you're doing OK."

Starke set a crumpled paper bag and a small Styrofoam cup on the rolling food tray and wheeled it across the room. He parked it between his father and the TV, and set up a folding chair directly across the table.

"Bear claw," Starke said, sitting down. "Maple. You like these."

"Says who?"

"I bring you one every day."

"Oh."

"And a coffee. Black, two sugars. Careful, it's hot."

His father reached for the bag, unrolled its top, and stuck his nose into the opening, sniffing like a sommelier. "Winchell's," he said.

"Still the best."

Cops and doughnuts, Starke thought. So much more than a cliché.

"Feeling OK today, Dad?"

"Hell no."

Starke smiled. Same answer every time. "So normal then?"

His father smiled back. "Wiseass. But who let you in here?"

"It's Ronnie, Dad. Your kid. The cop."

While his father seemed to consider this, Starke reached for one of the massive hands resting on the rolling table. His father offered it without hestitation. Starke pulled it toward him, and at the same time ran his other hand up the old man's bare forearm. The skin was dry and scaly, as usual, but worse because of the Santa Anas.

"Itching still a problem?"

His father nodded. "I think there's spiders on me. They need to spray."

Starke set the hand back where he'd found it, stood, and crossed the room in three strides. In the bathroom, next to the leather shaving kit, he found the pink, value-size squeeze bottle of baby lotion he'd brought three days before. He squirted a big dollop into his left palm, grabbed the comb, and returned to the folding chair. He set the comb down and slowly rubbed half of the lotion into one leg-of-lamb forearm, then the rest into the other. Tommy Starke's eyes were fixed on the gentle movement of his only son's hands. When Starke was done, he sat back.

"Better?"

"Better."

"The lotion's from the pink plastic bottle in your bathroom. It'll help with the itching. Use it. Or have the nurse use it. When you run out, I'll bring more."

"OK."

Starke picked up the comb, leaned forward, and ran it through his father's silver hair, parting it on the left in the same way it was parted in the black-and-white photo in the department's Hall of Heroes shrine. When he finished, Tommy Starke pulled the bear claw from the bag and set it beside the bag on the rolling table. He took a bite of the maple-flavored sugar bomb, closed his eyes, and chewed. After he swallowed, he looked down at the coffee cup.

"What's this?"

"Your coffee. Like you like it."

The old man pried the plastic lid from the coffee cup and took a delicate sip.

"I was a cop," he said at last.

Starke nodded. "One of the best."

"And you're a cop?"

"Detective, Dad. I made detective."

"No shit?" Big grin. "Detective?"

For a moment, Starke sensed a connection, maybe even a hint of pride in his father's voice. But he knew it was probably an illusion. He watched him take another bite of bear claw, chew, swallow, and sip. By the time their eyes reengaged, the moment had passed.

Tommy Starke picked up the remote and aimed it at the TV. His unraveling mind had moved on, and Starke long ago stopped taking it personally. The room filled again with outraged voices, and after a quick kiss to the top of his father's head, Starke slipped quickly and quietly out of the room. With a quick wave to Glenda, he stepped back through the automatic doors, back into the heat.

By the time he reached his unmarked Crown Vic, sweat was beading on his forehead, and he was thinking again about Shelby Dwyer. He had a delivery to make, and aimed the car toward her big house on the hill.

8

Shelby curled her bare toes over the edge of the pool at the center of the backyard. The reflection staring up at her was the same slim blonde she'd been three weeks ago, the same woman who'd danced through life with looks she knew could get her most anything she wanted, but one who suddenly felt like she was standing in quicksand.

How did it get this crazy?

I did *not* kill my husband, she reminded herself. Mistakes in judgment were made. An intimate trust betrayed. A terrible thing happened. But murder? Never. Paul's killer was… somewhere. Probably somewhere close. She knew that much, and would give anything to be able to tell what she knew. Except her family's reputation. Except her daughter. Except their lives. Those were the stakes, and since there was nothing she could do for Paul, silence seemed less of a sin. It was the only thing keeping them safe.

Goddamned Ron Starke had no idea.

A hot breeze rippled the water, and Shelby looked up.

Not even midmorning, and already it felt like a furnace. A wind like this, in this area, carried a familiar and unmistakable threat that she felt in the hot prickle at the back of her neck, in the dryness of her eyes. After thirty-nine years in Los Colmas, her entire lifetime, she'd stopped counting the number of wildfires, the frenzied evacuations, the scarred ridges and canyons, the endless waits to see if firefighters were able to stop it, turn it, drown it. A Santa Ana wind after a long, dry summer was a fuse. There was menace in its dry crackle.

Shelby tried to remember: Were the Santa Anas blowing the summer night a year ago when Paul, drunk again, tried to kill her and Chloe, when he'd held a gun to her head on their kitchen floor and pulled the trigger? She'd seldom challenged him about the drinking, about the women. The night she reached her limit and threatened to leave him, Chloe heard her screams and came running. Paul looked up, drew a bead on their daughter, and squeezed the trigger again.

They were alive only because Shelby had emptied the gun before she confronted him. His intentions that night were clear. In that rare moment of defiance, though, standing terrified with her screaming daughter, she knew things would never be the same between them and Paul. It was just her and Chloe from then on.

Now Paul was dead. Shelby had to admit an ambivalence about it. She felt as much relief as pain; scar tissue is always less sensitive.

"Mom?"

Chloe's voice was husky from sleep, but there was more to it, an edge of concern.

"Morning." Shelby wiped her eyes and spoke without turning around.

"What's wrong?"

When she did turn, Shelby saw her only child standing in the kitchen doorway, her long blond hair pulled into a lazy knot behind her head. Ramones sweatshirt. Paul Frank sock-monkey pajama bottoms. Hello Kitty bedroom slippers. A walking billboard of conflicted adolescence. Their fourteen-year-old Golden retriever, Boz, stood faithfully at her side.

"What makes you ask?" Shelby followed Chloe into the kitchen and watched her open the cupboard. Chloe grabbed a bowl, stopped by the silverware drawer for a spoon, pulled a gallon of non-fat milk from the fridge, and arranged it all on her side of the café table that was big enough for the whole family now. She poured a grotesque mound of Lucky Charms into the bowl before rooting into the box for more marshmallow stars. She evenly distributed the ones she found, then sloshed so much milk into it that much of the cereal tsunamied onto the tabletop. The sound of intense chewing quickly followed. Chloe closed her eyes as she ate.

Shelby took the chair across from her daughter, she reached across the table and lightly touched Chloe's forearm.

Chloe opened her eyes. "What?"

Shelby had rehearsed this moment a thousand times in the past three weeks, but now the words wouldn't come. Chloe studied her face. Shelby tried to speak, but Chloe beat her to it.

"It's Dad, isn't it?"

Shelby looked away. She knew she shouldn't. She couldn't help herself. "They found a body. Yesterday."

Chloe returned a spoonful of cereal to the bowl and wiped her mouth with a napkin.

"That's all we know at this point," Shelby said.

"It's him."

"They're pretty sure, but they're still doing tests."

"Where'd they find him?"

"Not far from here." Shelby's own words chilled her. Because of what they implied. "Off Spadero Road, where Dad was building those new houses."

"Near Shepherdsen's?"

She nodded, surprised by her daughter's instant familiarity with the place where for decades local kids her age got together to drink and swim and grope in the dark.

Chloe said nothing, didn't move a muscle until she picked up her bowl and walked it over to the sink. Running water. The roar of the DisposAll. She set the rinsed bowl in the draining rack.

"What else?" she asked, turning.

"We should know for sure pretty soon. But they did send someone over this morning to let us know. Maybe they know more than they're saying. I just don't think they'd send someone over here if—"

"It's him." Chloe held up her arm. The soft blond hairs on it were standing on end. "I feel it."

Shelby felt it, too. She crossed the room and pulled her daughter into a hug. Chloe's head dropped onto her shoulder.

"You OK, kiddo?"

"Fine."

Shelby stroked her daughter's blond hair. "I'm not."

"Me either."

"Tell me what happened, Mom."

Shelby hated lying to her daughter. She'd never gotten used to it. But what choice did she have? She shook her head. Again. "No idea. Maybe the police will find something."

"I'd just like to know, even if it's bad. Promise you'll tell me everything."

Shelby pulled away far enough to look her daughter straight in the eyes.

"Promise."

9

Of all the precautions Shelby took in the days after, the one thing she wished she could do differently was the thing she least understood. She'd used computers for years, but what went on behind the tidy façade of her machine's inscrutable brain remained to her a mystifying puzzle. She'd been told different things by different people, each who claimed expertise. Reformatting the hard drive destroys everything. Or it destroys nothing. Once wiped clean, everything is lost. Or anything is retrievable. She had never been sure.

And so, the morning after Paul's body turned up, she waited in her car just outside the Silicon Recycler, the only storefront computer discounter in Los Colmas. The place opened at ten, even on Sundays like this. She'd left Chloe at St. Lawrence, where her daughter volunteered to herd rowdy kids in the playroom every Sunday. Her dashboard clock read 9:56 as she parked across the street. She recognized the owner as he unlocked the front door, wondering if he'd recognize her, a one-time customer who three weeks before had traded in a high-end iMac for a refurbished PC. Even if he did, so what? She was just looking around. The questions she intended to ask were innocuous, meant only to put her mind at ease.

At 10:02, the owner flipped the sign and propped open the front door with a brick. Still, Shelby waited another two minutes, just to seem casual.

The place smelled of tobacco and cardboard. Cartons were stacked everywhere, representing the cramped store's entire inventory of refurbished desktops and laptops. A dozen or so computers were set up and operating on shelves and folding tables around the perimeter.

The owner grunted some sort of greeting, but otherwise paid Shelby little mind.

"Just looking," she said.

The man glanced up from his magazine. "For?"

Shelby shrugged. "Just looking."

He stepped into the narrow aisle. He seemed friendly, but wary.

"A laptop," Shelby said. "But I'm not ready to buy. Just trying to see what's out there, what it might cost, that sort of thing."

The owner sat back down and smiled. "You need help, you ask, OK?" he said in a soft accent, probably Persian.

Shelby made a show of perusing the laptops on display. She fingered the touchpads of a few, typed some gibberish on a few more to gauge the keyboard action, pretended to study the various screens for readability. Then she got down to business.

"Your sign says you buy used computers?" she asked.

The man couldn't have looked more confused. "Still, yes, of course."

Still. So he remembered her. "Of course," Shelby repeated.

"You come here last month, no? The Apple trade-in, I think, right?"

"Good memory," Shelby said.

"For some people."

The man blushed suddenly, convincing Shelby it was a reflexive comment and not a pick-up line. Either way, she wanted to push on.

"So what happens to the computers you buy from people?" she asked. "Just curious."

The owner seemed to relax. "Flip them fast," he said. "Today, hot; tomorrow, junk. That's computer business. The longer it sits, the less I make. If I don't sell here, I wholesale to a buyer who sells parts."

"The one you bought from me was still pretty new. So I'm assuming you sold it?"

The man shrugged, clearly not interested in checking his records for her.

"I reformatted the hard drive. I think that's what you call it, right? But you told me you check all that, clean them up, before you sell them, right?"

"Clean them?"

"You know, make sure all the files and programs are gone, and all that?"

"Oh yeah."

"And that's pretty foolproof? You make sure the whole thing is empty before you sell it? I mean, people keep their whole lives on those things: finances, pictures, things they've written. I'm guessing most people are careful about that."

The store owner shifted on his stool, set his magazine down. If Shelby had to guess, he looked wary again.

"I don't check everything. Just stuff I'm selling here, see? I wipe the drives on those, like I told you. But if it's going to another retailer or my parts guy, I don't bother."

"No?"

"Not my problem."

Shelby felt a disorienting ripple. He'd assured her he planned to sell her computer intact, and would purge its memory before doing so. Why hadn't he mentioned the other possibility back then? If he'd sold it whole to another store or wholesaled it to the parts dealer, what truths might still be out there, embedded on its silicon chips?

"No, not your problem," she said.

"Why? You need something on that computer?"

"No, no, I just—"

"Because I do remember now. We booted it up right here, to check it. The hard drive was clean. And you had CarbonCopy on the keyboard plug."

He'd mentioned it at the time, but Shelby had no idea what he meant. This time she probed. "CarbonCopy?"

"Keylogger hardware." He shifted on his stool and looked away. "You didn't install it?"

Shelby shook her head. "Maybe my computer guy did, or my husband. Why? What does it do?"

The man looked seriously uncomfortable. "You should ask your husband."

When he said nothing else, Shelby asked him again.

He leaned forward and dropped his voice a little.

"Maybe a mom or dad wants to see what teenage boy or girl is doing on computer. Porn sites. Facebook. Like that. Or somebody wants to know what husband or wife is doing, maybe? CarbonCopy records keystrokes and stores it in a secret place. So you have a suspicious husband maybe? Maybe he wants to know what you're up to?"

"And that was on my computer?"

The store owner nodded.

"So it was still on there when you sold it?"

He shrugged. "Not my problem."

Shelby felt dizzy, nauseous. She glanced at her watch, as though suddenly remembering an appointment. "Whoa. Late." Her voice sounded hollow, like she was talking from the bottom of a well.

"Wait. No laptop today?"

"I'll come back. It's just—" Shelby tried her best to smile. To pursue her next question, to ask if it was possible to track that old computer, to find out what it remembered, would be to tip her hand. She managed, "Not today," as she turned toward the door. She heard the owner's, "You come back anytime," but she already was lost in dark thoughts, trying to remember if she'd been smart enough to buy the new computer with cash.

10

The owner folded his magazine once again, set it aside, and studied Starke's open shield wallet, matching the ID photo to the face. The detective offered him the same artificial smile he'd given the department's photographer the day the picture was taken.

"I run clean shop," he said. "No problems with Silicon Recycler. Straight up operation."

"That's what I hear," Starke said. "Friend of mine bought from you a while back. He was very impressed. I'm in the market for a new laptop myself."

"Ah, so you're shopping then, officer?"

"Well, not today."

The owner handed back Starke's wallet. "Everybody want laptops, nobody buying today. How you expect me to stay in business?"

When Starke parked on the street in front of the Dwyer home forty-five minutes earlier, Shelby was just easing her white Jag from the driveway and turning right toward downtown Los Colmas, if you could call its collection of strip malls and discount stores a downtown. He'd come to tell her what the coroner had told him: Dental records confirmed that the body in the damp muck of Shepherdsen's pond was Paul Dwyer's. He had been shot once in the head, and was already dead when someone sunk him into the pond. A pale manila envelope the size of an index card waited on the passenger seat of the Vic. The tiny lump at its center was a wedding band with beaded edges and the initials of Shelby and Paul Dwyer, the one that had required an indelicate amputation to extract from the swollen folds of skin on Dwyer's ring finger.

Starke thought it best to bring only the ring.

He could have come back later to let Shelby ID it. At that point, it was just a formality. Instead of turning around, though, he'd watched the Jag move away down the block. On instinct, he followed at a discreet distance. Shelby's daughter was in the seat beside her. They'd stopped briefly at St. Lawrence Martyr, their church, where Shelby dropped Chloe off. Then she'd driven directly to the town's only used computer retailer. She was there before it opened, waiting for it to open, actually. She took nothing in, and brought nothing out.

"So why you show me your badge just to shop?" the owner asked.

"OK," Starke said. "You got me there. But I only have a couple of questions. Nothing complicated, and you can just say no if you don't want to answer. Deal?"

The owner nodded.

"That woman who was just in here?" Starke said. "She's a regular customer?"

The man tensed, just enough to let Starke know the question made him squirm. "She's in trouble?" he asked.

Starke gave him his most noncommital face. "I didn't say that." He smiled again. "I'm just curious."

"Ah, so she is your friend then, no? You could just ask her, if you're curious."

Starke shook his head. "Got me again, Mr.—"

The owner pushed a business card across the counter: "Jason Samani—Silicon Recycler Inc."

"I'm curious in a professional way, Mr. Samani," he said, tapping his badge, "but it's all very preliminary. And you don't have to talk to me if you don't want to. It's just that any help you can give me might clear things up. Just be between us for now, understand?"

The owner nodded.

"So, you've dealt with her before?"

His answer came an uncomfortable half-minute later. "Once. A sell-buy maybe three weeks ago. Lady had a good machine, desktop, sweet iMac."

He gave Starke a model number. It meant nothing to him, but he wrote it down.

"Thing is, she wants to switch to a PC," Samani said. "That's rare. But I find her something pretty decent. That's it."

"But she came in again today? Was there some problem with the computer you sold her? That's why she came back?"

"No, no. Thirty-day guarantee. Any problems, I fix," he said. "No, today she wants something else. A laptop. She knows my deals. She comes back, see?"

Starke looked at his watch. How hard should he push? "She sure didn't shop long this morning. She was here when you opened, and stayed, what? Ten minutes. Fifteen, tops? And she left empty-handed, so I know she didn't buy."

"People do that. They come in. They look. They leave."

"I guess that's true," Starke said. "That's why it's called shopping, right?"

"This one looks around, asks some questions, then she goes."

An awkward moment passed. The owner flipped a page of his magazine without looking at it.

"Questions?" Starke asked. "About laptops?"

No answer.

"I mean, that's what she was asking about then? A new laptop? Gigabytes? RAM? Wi-Fi? Those kind of questions?"

The owner shrugged.

"*Not* those kind of questions?" Starke asked.

The man stood abruptly. He reached into his display case and began rearranging the items there—an already neat collection of computer components. When he was done, he closed the sliding display-case door with more force than needed. Its woody *clack!* echoed over the stoic hum of nearby machines.

"You seem nervous," Starke said.

"Not nervous, no, no. Busy."

Starke looked around the store. No one else had come in. "I'm sorry to interrupt you at work."

"No problem, OK? But I have many things to do."

Nervous people hate silence. They often fill it with words. So Starke waited.

Samani fussed until he ran out of things to straighten on the counter. Finally, he couldn't stand it any more. "Her old computer, the Apple she sold me. She asked about that, about where it went from here. Did I resell? Sell for parts? Those kind of questions. Happens sometimes."

"Really?"

"People don't reformat the drives. Lazy, you know? Or they don't understand how to do it. They sell to me as is, then remember something on it they want or need. Or they worry they left numbers on it."

"Numbers?"

"Bank accounts. Credit cards. *Numbers*. But not just numbers. Letters. Spreadsheets. Work things. Browser histories. Personal things. Suddenly, too late, they worry. They come back and ask if I can find their old machine, or to make sure I wipe the drives so nobody can get their numbers."

"So she was asking about her old computer? About whether you still had it, or if there might be anything on it she wanted back, or needed, or didn't want somebody else to see?"

He nodded.

"And I suppose you reformatted her hard drive and everything?"

Samani shook his head. "Apples I sell to an Apple guy. These Apple people, they don't mix with PC people."

Starke knew that was true. There are Pepsi people and Coke people; Burger King people and McDonald's people. In terms of tribal loyalty, Apple users were somewhere between La Cosa Nostra and Scientologists.

"But you say she switched? From an Apple to a PC?"

"That's why I remembered her, yes. Very unusual."

"So you don't still have the computer she sold you?"

The owner gestured to his shelves. "Not an Apple in the store."

Samani would have business records, Starke thought, and he could subpoena those if he needed them. At the moment, he was operating on pure hunch, listening to a faint voice in his head. Why would Shelby sell a killer iMac for a PC that arguably was less of a machine? Why would she come back to the store later worried about what might have happened to the machine she'd sold?

"Mr. Samani," he said, "thank you. You've been a help, and I want you to know I appreciate that."

The store owner's shoulders relaxed, and a smile creased his face. "So now you buy laptop?"

Starke shook his head. "I've got your card. When I'm ready, I'll be back. Promise."

Samani extended a hand, so Starke shook it. The owner held the handshake a beat too long before leaning across the counter. He lowered his voice: "Tell me, please. The lady's in trouble?"

"Thank you again, Mr. Samani," Starke said, extracting his hand. "You have a great day."

Back in the Vic, he cracked open a window to let the radiant heat escape. The sun was well up now, hot as hell. The first beads of sweat were rising when he picked up the manila envelope, opened the clasp, and let the Dwyers' marital promise tumble into his open palm. It was hard and unscratched, and he could tell right away it was, at best, 12 karat gold.

11

These were the roughest times. Weekday mornings. Chloe at school. Their air-conditioned house as closed and airless as a confessional. Home alone with little to do except ignore the answering machine filling with calls from well-meaning staffers from the company and the foundation, enterprising reporters, and the few friends who'd heard the news. Bunkered in, Shelby knew she'd be prey to her demons.

And so, almost against her will, she found herself creaking down the hall toward her office. There was no logic to her caution, since she was alone, but she walked as quietly as she could, avoiding the squeaky floorboard on the hallway's right side, lifting while turning the doorknob. She twisted the overhead light's dimmer knob on the left and stepped into her office.

It was awake.

Chloe usually shut down the computer when she signed off each night, or at least left it in sleep mode. Shelby had asked her to do that, for so many reasons. But this time she'd left it on after checking her Facebook account before school. The Windows desktop glowed bright and inviting across the room. The icon for its web browser stood out like a beacon.

No, she thought, even as her feet moved, even as she closed the distance between herself and the portal into that other world, a world where things had gone so wrong, a world from which she'd fled numb and horrified and determined never to return. She hadn't even been tempted. But this time, she was going in for a different reason.

No, no, no, no, no.

She lightly touched the back of the desk chair, but it spun halfway around, offering her a seat. The keyboard and mouse were an arm's length away. She stepped closer, watching her right hand move toward it like something driven by instinct, something apart from her body and the controlling influence of her mind. Her fingertips found the smooth back of the mouse, and she watched her hand settle over it like a nesting bird. The device disappeared into her palm, familiar and unfamiliar at the same time.

She rolled it around the mouse pad without looking at the screen. It felt different than the Apple she'd loved, the one she'd imagined more than once as an electronic version of Eve's forbidden fruit. When she finally looked at the screen, the pointer was hovering above the browser icon. Coincidence? Fate? Her right index finger moved to the mouse's clicker, and she felt a rush-prickle of anticipation— still, even after everything.

She clicked once, highlighting the icon. A second click would bring it alive. A second click would start her down a path. She knew where it would lead, needed it to take her there. Back to him.

No!

Shelby yanked her hand back, a reaction almost like a spasm. For a moment she wondered if she'd been shocked, if a thunderbolt of current had been hurled from some other realm, traveled though the wires, into the computer, into her fingertips. Her heart pounded in hammer-like bursts.

She backed away from the computer, one step, another. Then she stopped, realizing how suddenly alive she felt, how vital life seems when every nerve is sandpapered raw and the body feels everything, how nothing else is quite so elemental, so primitive and scary and thrilling.

No!

Shelby could still hear the nagging voice in her head as she sat back down and touched the mouse again. Her hand shook. The room started to spin. She pushed herself away from the desk and stood, unsteady. *Not now,* she thought. *Too soon.* If she did this, she knew she'd need to be ready.

12

Why Shelby Dwyer's life diverged from his, Starke couldn't say, even if he knew precisely when. They were both homegrown in Los Colmas, both ambitious, and both very much infatuated with one another, if only for one summer. If every man forever carries the mark of his first love, for him it was Shelby, whose lithe young body he'd committed to memory. But that was two lifetimes ago, hers and his, and now he was standing across the street from one of the most spectacular residences in San Bernardino County. Shelby's house was twice the size of his entire apartment building, and it had never been more clear to him that they'd taken different roads. She'd sped away from that summer and ended up here. Him? Just an unpleasant bit of roadkill along the way, and he knew better than most the kind of cold calculations Shelby had probably made to get where she wanted to go.

But now, suddenly, he was driving.

He'd spent much of the morning talking to the Dwyers'

neighbors, if people who lived behind the electronic gates of adjoining mansions could be considered "neighbors." He'd known it would be a waste of time—this wasn't the kind of street where lives intersect during block parties and yard sales—but with Kerrigan riding his ass, he was making sure to cover every base as quickly as possible.

He flipped open his notebook. Two people had mentioned Craig DeMott, fourteen Via Cumbre. You should talk to Craig, both had said. He seemed to know Paul.

Starke walked a few gates down and found the massive wrought-iron barrier between fourteen Via Cumbre and the lesser world. A small keypad and an intercom stood to his left on a matching iron post. He buzzed, and a woman's voice came back: "Yes?"

"Good morning, ma'am. I'm Detective Ron Starke from the Los Colmas Police. I'm hoping to speak for a few minutes with a Craig DeMott. Do I have the right address?"

"Let me see if he's in," the voice said.

Seconds later, Starke heard a subtle click in the bushes to his right. The massive gate rumbled slowly sideways along its metal track. "Thank you," he said, but no answer came back. He stepped onto the yellow brick driveway and started the long walk toward the main house, but was met halfway by an alpha male in tailored golf slacks and a Ralph Lauren polo. He looked to be about sixty, judging by his silver hair, but with squared shoulders and a broad, powerful chest. Definitely military, Starke thought, probably one of the academies. Grip like a vise, set jaw, no smile.

"I'm Craig DeMott," he said.

"Starke. Ron Starke."

"You know, you're the third cop to stop by since Paul went missing. Already told the others what I know."

Starke nodded. "But now—I'm assuming you've heard today's news about Mr. Dwyer? It's not just a missing persons case anymore."

DeMott nodded. "Damned shame."

Starke liked to stay as low-profile as possible when working a case, and he was concerned that anyone driving past DeMott's driveway, including Shelby, could see them. "Would you prefer to talk inside, Mr. DeMott?"

DeMott made no move toward the house. "You should know in advance that I don't claim to know Paul, or his family, all that well. So I want to be clear on that."

Starke slipped his small notebook from inside his jacket pocket and jotted DeMott's name and address on a fresh page. "That's fine, sir. Anything you can tell me might be helpful to—"

"And I debated whether to even say anything, because it was one conversation months ago, and there was some single-malt Scotch involved, and God only knows if it was the liquor talking, or if there was really something going on. I didn't say anything to the other cops, but that was before. Now, I think I should say something."

"About?"

"I know it was on Paul's mind at the time, and I figured I should at least mention it, just in case."

"That's fine. Sure you wouldn't rather talk inside?"

Again, DeMott stood his ground. This was not someone who wasted time. "Last winter, during the holidays, we had a little drop-by for some of the people on the street. Just dessert and drinks, egg nog, like that. Adults only, nothing fancy. One of those holiday social things my wife thinks are important."

Starke scribbled the relevant details without looking at the notebook, making sure to never lose eye contact.

"I'd played golf with Paul a couple of times—my bank financed a couple of his projects—so we weren't exactly strangers. And our wives have met at charity events. But it was the first time they'd been to our house. I've still never been over there. I'm pretty sure our little holiday party was the only time I ever met his wife. Shelby, is it?"

"Yes."

"Have you met her, detective?"

"I have," Starke said.

"Beautiful woman. Really something."

For the first time, DeMott was dogpaddling a bit, allowing himself to linger on a thought rather than plowing relentlessly forward. Shelby had that effect on men.

"The evening went well, and much later than I imagined it would. People came and went. Paul and his wife stayed quite a while. There was a little tension there, you could tell, just they way he was talking to her, about her."

"Tension?"

"Little things he said. Asides. That's none of my business, of course. After a while, the wives knotted up to talk. The men, maybe six of us, swapped lies till about ten. At one point, Paul and I were at the bar by ourselves. I was pouring him another drink."

Starke stopped writing. "Other people have told me Mr. Dwyer drank a fair amount."

"Couldn't say. But that night, the Macallan definitely loosened his tongue. Maybe it was something that was building up over time, or maybe just something that happened that day. I just can't say. But it was obviously on his mind."

"What was that?" Starke asked.

"Typical stuff for an underserviced man his age. I'm guessing he's early fifties? She seems quite a bit younger. I've been there, detective. You'll see. A man gets to a certain age, he feels it all slipping away from him. And Paul was in the thick of it. So he was muttering about his wife. Things were dead in bed. She'd married him for his checkbook. All the standard clichés. But he also mentioned that maybe there was someone else in her life. Just a gut feeling. He said, 'Women change when it's Big Love. They can't hide it.'"

Starke waited for more. The possibility was intriguing, given what he already knew about the Dwyer marriage. Definitely something he'd want to pursue. He knew Shelby was still trying to give him half-truths and spun sugar at this point; he was convinced she was holding something back. But a drunk husband's confided hunch to someone he barely knew? It wasn't much to go on.

"Did Mr. Dwyer say specifically why he suspected her?" Starke said at last. "Behavioral changes? Suspicious travel or expenses? Telephone records? That sort of thing?"

DeMott shook his head. "It was just a moment. It came and went. Never gave it another thought until Paul went missing. Then yesterday, when I heard he'd turned up dead, and that someone may have killed him... like you said, you never know what might be helpful. I debated whether to mention it to the other officers, but kept it to myself. Then you showed up, and I thought, 'It's the right thing to do. I'll get it off my chest and let the chips fall where they may.'"

"I appreciate that." Starke closed his notebook. "Have you or your wife noticed anything that might support the idea that Mrs. Dwyer had a relationship with someone outside of her marriage? Cars coming or going at odd hours while Mr. Dwyer was away? Anything like that?"

"Not me. I could ask Bebe."

Starke waited again for DeMott to turn toward the house. But he did not. "Bebe's your wife?"

"She's home most days, but usually out by the pool in back. She's never mentioned anything like that, but I can ask her. Do you have a card, Detective—?"

"Starke." He fished a business card from his wallet and handed it over after writing his cell number on the back. "Please do call if you remember anything else you think might be helpful. And if your wife has anything to add, I'll be happy to talk to her as well."

DeMott crushed Starke's hand again. "Keep my name out of the paperwork, Detective. I don't want to come off like a snitch in this, since it may be nothing. I just thought it might be another piece of the puzzle."

"Our conversation will be part of my murder book—that's my case file—but that's not public record," Starke said. "You shouldn't have any problems with the media or anything like that."

"Sure as hell don't need *that* aggravation."

They shook hands again. Starke was turning away when DeMott said: "What's her story, anyway?"

"Whose?"

"Paul's wife," DeMott said, dogpaddling still. "What's her story?"

"I'm not quite sure what you mean, Mr. DeMott."

"She's just...." The neighbor glanced at the Dwyer house across the street. "Well, you've met her. You know."

"She's an attractive woman," Starke said. He was tempted to add, "And single!" but swallowed his sarcasm. Now he was curious about the wife by the pool, the state of the DeMott marriage, the sort of idle amusements that went on among the wealthy denizens of this exclusive hilltop, and just how badly the man standing in front of him coveted his neighbor's wife.

Starke looked at his watch. He wanted to schedule an interview with one of Dwyer's business partners in LA, and had at least two more stops in the neighborhood before he could do that. Plus, Eckel had called twice from the morgue, but hung up both times without leaving a message.

"Thank you, Mr. DeMott. I'll be in touch," Starke said, and with that he headed back down Craig DeMott's yellow brick drive.

13

Starke pushed into the gloom of his one-bedroom cave. Home for the past two years, it still looked like a squatter's tenement.

On the way to the fridge, he glanced at the microwave clock—11:43 p.m. It reminded him how little he'd been able to accomplish that day. He'd be back at it early tomorrow, because he'd promised Eckel he'd swing by before heading into LA.

He brought a Newcastle into bed with him, drinking half of it before logging into his iPad. Someday he'd buy himself a desk and a chair, if only to save his spine. For now he propped both pillows behind his back and leaned against the wall where he'd affixed the only piece of art in his apartment—a clipping of a famous Peter Steiner cartoon from *The New Yorker*. One dog seated at a computer is explaining to a four-legged friend: "On the Internet, nobody knows you're a dog."

His nightly online foray had been his unvarying routine

for more than a year. First stop: The website of the San Bernardino Sun. He scanned the updated headlines and read any local stories that might be relevant to his cases. The identification of Dwyer's body was the lead local story, as he'd expected, but there were no surprises in it. It was accompanied by the corporate-issued head shot of Dwyer looking like a silvered James Bond. Starke scanned other headlines. There'd been a 2:00 a.m. drive-by outside the city's most notorious gentleman's club, Pink Velvet; six wounded. A family in Redlands was looking for its reticulated python, Wiggles, who'd gone missing. A story headlined "Local company donates funds for city park" featured a grip-and-grin photo of Los Colmas City Manager Doug Buckley accepting an oversized check from the president of the city's favored public-works contractor, Esparza & Sons Excavation and Construction.

A headline under the statewide news tab caught Starke's eye, mostly because it was accompanied by a grainy video screen grab that looked like something out of Abu Ghraib prison. The headline beside the image of a hooded figure read: "San Diego torture-death video linked to Mexican cartel."

Starke felt like he'd read the story before, but it was an easy mistake to make, a varation on a theme. Cartel violence—the brutal, animal kind common among men operating without fear of consequence—was spilling across the US border in bloody spasms. Just last month, acting on a tip, DEA agents broke open a fresh concrete pad behind one of the nondescript warehouses in Otay Mesa, the industrial area of southern San Diego where hundreds of similar warehouses are clustered along the Mexican border. Buried four feet below were the decomposing bodies of eight young men, each with a single bullet hole in the back of the head.

"Tunnel rats," the lead investigator had said, and insiders knew what that meant.

The DEA team had concluded as much based on the calluses on the victims' hands and the dirt beneath their fingernails, and because agents later found the so-called "supertunnel" they'd spent their final months digging. It was more than a half-mile long and stretched from inside the Otey Mesa warehouse, beneath the US-Mexico border, and into a similar warehouse in Garita de Otay, an industrial neighborhood in northern Tijuana. The tunnel's sophisticated infrastructure—ventilation ducts, electric lights, a rail system for the easy conveyance of cargo—was a hallmark of El Chapo Guzman's Sinaloa operation. But the grunt labor to build those elaborate projects came from Tijuana's poorest neighborhoods, where Guzman's men recruited strong but desperate boys, always thin and narrow-shouldered, with promises of steady work. The recruits quickly found themselves enslaved by gun-toting goons whose job was to ensure completion of yet another underground drug pipeline. The diggers were fed and housed for months, unable to leave but paid generously, always in cash. But they never saw sunshine again once the digging began, and when the job was done and their captors returned their bodies to the same dirt through which they'd burrowed, their accumulated cash was simply collected from their locker within the warehouse and returned to the same stash from which it had come.

A popular *narcocorrido* in steady rotation on Tijuana radio stations paid tribute to the young men lured into the cartel's tunnels. The English translation of the ballad's title: "The Gopher Boys."

Lately, the criminal organization had been waging war with a competing cartel, and had taken a page straight out of the ISIS reign-of-terror playbook: videotaping its revenge attacks and posting them to the Internet. Starke clicked on the latest headline and the story filled his screen.

A source claiming to be with the Sinaloa group had sent a San Diego TV station a link to a ninety-minute videotape showing the gruesome nail-gun torture of a suspected snitch. The station had dutifully edited that tape into twelve seconds of teasing highlights, including the hooded figure's desperate plea for his family as the nail gun was leveled, finally, at the base of his skull. The Action News Team anchor had delivered the video to the station's viewers with an appropriate degree of civilized outrage and a solemn warning that "even the select contents of this tape are disturbing." He noted that the unedited original had been turned over to authorities, of course, but also noted that a copy of it was available in its entirety on the station's website. Now both the edited and unedited versions were ricocheting around the Internet like a cat on a Roomba, and the station's web traffic was soaring, and the aficionados of righteous online snuff porn were sated for another day.

On Twitter, #sinaloathugs was trending.

Starke marveled that all this was unfolding just a hundred miles from Los Colmas, but resisted the urge to dwell too long on the thought. He had plenty of problems of his own. He scanned the sports headlines, skipped to Dilbert, read his horoscope ("Romantic notions can cloud your thinking. See the whole person, not just the one you want to see."), then checked the weather. Tomorrow's expected high: ninety-three. Four percent humidity. Steady westerly wind moving through the San Gabriel passes from Nevada desert. Fire danger: high.

Next stop: Netflix. He checked the offerings. Too tired to watch anything now, but he felt another binge coming on.

Last stop: the NSA Room. His guilty pleasure. It was a poor man's Ashley Madison—no registration or fees required, no chance of exposure by malevolent hackers—an online sexual swap meet of webcam wankers, one-timers and fuck buddies, friends-with-benefits, and artlessly posted crotch pics; a teeming, twenty-four-hour parade of needy people open to adventure and the sometimes peculiar fantasies of strangers. A fair number of them, he knew, were straight-up hookers. A lurker among the crazies, he pulled down the bookmarks in his web browser and clicked on the link, then typed in his username—DirtyHarry.

He'd long ago forgiven himself for this odd indulgence. Lonely people deserved a little latitude in life, he figured, and there were far more destructive ways to cope with loneliness than this kind of virtual voyeurism. Online, as an avatar moving anonymously through the "casual encounters" party rooms, he'd met countless women who seemed eager to indulge him, or anyone, as long as their fantasies were indulged in kind. Some women just described themselves and their fantasies in their postings. Others offered pictures. He enjoyed the game. He'd communicate with the ones who seemed interesting, just to see where things went. Sometimes they'd play roles. Sometimes they'd just talk, messaging back and forth with no sex play at all. With no strings attached, as the NSA name implied, there were none of the messy entanglements of real-world relationships. The ground rules were clear. No pressure. No pain. Win-win.

It was all he had for now.

Starke finished the Newcastle, set the empty bottle on the floor beside his mattress, and began scanning the bios. He opened one with the subject line "BBW looking for threesome!!!" There was a frontal shoulder-to-navel photo showing two asymmetrical breasts squeezed together by hands with bright red fingernails.

"I'm cute but 25# overweight," she'd written. "I'd love 2 meet a couple or 2 guys for regualr get togetherz. No strings just fun. I'm 5'6", 155, long brown hair that i love pulled, 38DD for reals."

Starke moved on. She sounded like a scam, or a dude, or a pro, or a porn-site bot. Besides, he had no interest in actually getting together. The only posts he responded to were the ones where the poster was interested in having a conversation. That's what he wanted most, the contact.

The beer had left him a little light-headed. He looked at the clock again: 1:42 now. When was the last time he'd eaten?

14

"You're the cop, right?"

Starke glanced over at his father in the Vic's passenger seat, then at the dashboard clock. Just past 2:00 a.m. With the help of a night charge nurse accustomed to their eccentricities, he'd coaxed Tommy Starke out of bed with the promise of carne asada, signed him out, and together they made their escape from Foothill Village. His father was wearing only pajama bottoms, a Cal Poly Pomona T-shirt, his "No Spin Zone" ball cap, and the flip-flops he wore on shower days, but Starke knew it was the only time they were likely to have together in the coming week.

Tommy Starke's memories flared bright at times, but in unpredictable ways. Most of them remained tangled and lost somewhere in his eroded neural wiring. They'd had this same conversation, more or less, a thousand times, and probably would have it a thousand more.

"That's right, Dad. Los Colmas PD. Just like you. Detective now."

"Detective? No shit?"

Starke steered into a discount-store lot. Every local night-shift patrol cop knew their favorite food truck would be parked there between midnight and seven o'clock. Sure enough, two cruisers were idling alongside the hand-painted El Burrito Rodeo. The black-and-whites sat amid a harum-scarum collection of street-racing rice burners, rocking low-riders, and bored Uber drivers waiting for drunken passengers trying to sober up with tacos el pastor after the nightclubs closed. Not far away, a driver clutching his warm, tinfoiled prize climbed into the cab of a massive concrete mixer. This time of night, El Burrito Rodeo was the great equalizer.

"I was a cop," his dad said.

Starke reached over to pat his father's knee. "One of the best."

Before getting out to order, Starke set the Vic's door locks so his father couldn't climb out and wander. Foothill Village insisted he wear an electronic ankle bracelet so he wouldn't stray beyond the Alzheimer's unit. Its pinpoint LED blinked in the footwell of the passenger seat every five seconds, casting his father's flip-flopped feet in a pale red glow.

"Wait right here," he said, looking Tommy straight in the eye. "I'll be over there at the food truck, getting our burritos. You can watch me the whole time."

"Burritos?"

"You like them, Dad."

"Sounds Mexican."

"Carne asada. Trust me on this."

His father shrugged. "Need help?"

"I got this. But you stay here, OK?"

Starke stood backward in the line, facing the car in which his father was captive. For most of the time, Tommy Starke surveyed the dark parking lot with a cop's wary eye. Once he appeared to test the car door. Unable to open it, he seemed to content himself with exploring the swivel-mounted laptop and his walkie-talkie. Starke had moved the shotgun into the trunk for exactly that reason.

By the time he climbed back in, juggling the hot burritos, the old man's eyes were fixed on the bulbous concrete truck parked about thirty yards away. Its mixing cylinder spun slowly, for the moment the only thing moving in the parking lot. Starke set the food on the dash, handed his father a wad of paper napkins, then climbed out again to retrieve the two Cokes he'd set on the roof.

"What's that smell?" Tommy Starke asked.

"Carne asada. You like it."

"Smells pretty good."

"Hungry?"

His father nodded. Starke peeled some of the foil back from the top of one burrito, wrapped the bottom in a few napkins so it wouldn't burn his father's fingers, and handed it to him. "It's a little hot, but you should be OK. Just don't eat too fast."

Tommy Starke stared at the fragrant beef bomb, holding it awkwardly, uncertain.

"You eat these with your hands, Dad. Just hold it by the silver part and go for it."

His father took a tentative bite, mostly tortilla from the burrito's top fold, and chewed slowly.

"Doesn't taste like much," he said.

"Keep going. But the middle stuff's hot. Let it cool a while."

Starke unwrapped his own burrito and took a small bite, mostly to let the molton contents vent. His father watched, doing the same. Steam rose and disappeared in the long, salsa-scented silence. They watched the cement truck's bulbous mixing cylinder in the streetlit parking lot.

"Esparza," his father said.

Starke looked at him, then followed his gaze to the cement truck. As the cylinder spun, the construction company's name and logo, emblazoned on the side, kept flashing past: "Esparza & Sons Excavation and Construction." Their equipment was so common on local roads during the ongoing construction boom that it just seemed like part of the landscape.

"Lot of houses going up around here, Dad. You ever imagine Los Colmas would be a suburb of LA? Crazy."

"Rafael Esparza," his father said.

Starke bit into his burrito and wondered what synaptic connection was taking place inside his father's head. He took another bite. "What about him, Dad?"

"He was *dirty*."

Starke stopped chewing and set the burrito on the dash. His father was glaring at the cement truck.

"Why do you say that?"

Tommy Starke stared ahead, unblinking. Then, suddenly, he looked down at his burrito, as if seeing it for the first time.

"What's this?"

"Carne asada burrito, Dad. But what do you know about Rafael Esparza?"

His father sniffed his burrito. "Smells really good."

The moment was gone, but Starke tried once more. "You know something about Rafael Esparza, Dad?"

"Who?"

Starke pointed at the truck, wondering again how deep that particular rabbit hole might go. Paul Dwyer did business with the Esparzas for years, through two generations of the family. "You seemed to know something about the guy whose name is on that cement truck," he said.

Tommy Starke stared again at the truck, but this time without any intensity. His eyes roamed the parking lot, from the rice burners to the low riders to the busy hive around the El Burrito Rodeo truck. Then he took a big bite of burrito, chewed and swallowed, then just said, "Damn. That's good."

15

Eckel called Starke's cell at six in the morning on Tuesday, and again urged him to stop by. At 6:45 Starke was standing next to the deputy coroner, who was shoveling his breakfast into his mouth from a Thermos. Scrambled eggs. Bacon. Buttered toast. The comforting smells mixed with the cold meat smell coming from the morgue's refrigeration units down the hall. "The wife treats me right," Eckel said with a smile, dabbing a bit of yellow yolk from the corner of his mouth.

"So, just to review, Eck, you have the choice of eating breakfast at home with her, or bringing it here to eat. And you prefer to eat it here?"

Eckel shrugged. "Busy, busy. It's not like I eat in the exam room. Toast?"

"Pass." Starke looked at his watch, still tasting the burrito he'd downed just a few hours before. "Hate to rush you, but I have appointments today. Show me what you wanted to show me."

Eckel replaced the Thermos lid and led him along the linoleum corridor. He stopped at a refrigerator door about halfway down the unit, pulled the handle, and slid out a rack holding the body of a deflated Paul Dwyer. Starke's hand went instinctively to his face and pinched his nose shut.

"He's looking better, eh?"

Human at least, Starke thought. "Let me guess," he said, his voice tinny and sharp. "You had Oswaldo let the air out of him because he asked if he could."

Eckel waggled his eyebrows. "Ve haf a special tool for zis," he said, holding up a sharp pencil.

"Yuck."

Dwyer was lying on his side, rigor having frozen him in the position of a man floating underwater but anchored by his neck. The position, now fully revealed in the body's deflated state, was grotesque. Still, Starke could tell that Dwyer had been a handsome man. He was fifty-four when he died, long-legged and lean, with thick silver hair that in recent photographs swept straight back along his skull, but which now was mussed into a lopsided dull gray cumulus peppered by pond dirt and moss. His skin was pale yellow, the color of a file folder. His face was a gruesome death mask, mouth open, eyes shut, but his jaw was square and powerful, as was his upper body. No belly, even hunched as he was. On top of everything else in his busy life, the man managed to work out regularly, and Starke found himself illogically inspired by Dwyer's corpse, thinking maybe he, too, should make more time for exercise.

"The water did you no favors, sir," Eckel said. "God only knows what evidence isn't here anymore. But there were two things we weren't sure about on the initial look-see, and I wanted to show you before we released the body later today. Appreciate you coming in so early."

Eckel slid the pencil beneath Dwyer's rigid arm until its point was just inches from Dwyer's right nipple. "See those two dark marks?" he said.

Starke pinched his nose tight and bent in close. He could feel his eyes watering, but through the blur he saw two small dark brown marks about the size of houseflies, about two inches apart.

"Stun gun?" he said.

"The handheld kind," Eckel said. "There's three more like it, two on the inside of his thighs right up next to his junk, and one under his left arm. All pre-mortem. Somebody didn't like him."

"Tortured?"

"With malice," Eckel said, holding up what looked like an empty, clear plastic Baggie. "This might explain how."

Starke squinted, then fished his reading glasses from the inside pocket of his sports jacket. With his free hand still holding his nose, he pulled the evidence bag closer. Inside were short strands of what looked like extraordinarily thick blond hairs.

"What *are* these, Eck?"

"Hemp fibers, the kind you find in good strong rope. They were embedded in his skin." Using the pencil, he pointed to a brownish-red discoloration that ran all the way around Dwyer's ankles. Same patterns on his wrists. "He was tied up and struggling. And those burn marks from the stun gun are direct to skin, not through clothing. Roped like a steer. Naked. Zapped. I think you'll agree, Ron, it's probably not the most dignified way to go."

Whoa, Starke thought.

"I'm gonna go out on a limb again," Eckel said. "*Somebody* had some anger issues."

Starke tried to imagine how the killer got a strapping man like Dwyer roped up and helpless. It'd take two, maybe three ruthlessly brutal people to manage it, and that scenario didn't fit anything he'd come up with so far. Just what he needed: more possibilities. But if Dwyer had been unconscious....

"Got a tox report yet, Eck?"

"Tomorrow."

"Any way to know now if he was drugged?"

Eckel shook his head. "I'd just be guessing. Wait for tox. But lemme show you one more thing before you go."

Eckel led him back into the outer office, then through the door into the main exam room. Blessedly empty, Starke noted. The massive computer monitor that had anchored Dwyer's body was sitting by itself on one of the exam tables. It was cleaner now, almost recognizable as the piece of ancient technology that it was.

"Whoever had this was probably a middle-aged tech geek, or got it from someone like that," Eckel said. He tapped the mottled lettering just beneath the screen's broken glass: "Vanguard."

"That's the brand?" Starke asked. "Never heard of it."

"Not surprised. I had Oz check it out. They only made these for two years, back in the early 1980s. Even then, they were so heavy and bulky, they were probably most effective as anchors. Company's been out of business for two decades. So whoever had this was probably an early adopter of computer technology."

"Or somebody that shopped at Silicon Valley garage sales," Starke said. "Maybe it's significant. Hard to say."

"Never know. Just thought I'd mention it. OK? OK."

Eckel stepped to a scrub sink and washed his hands in gooey disinfectant. Starke did the same, holding his breath when he let go of his nose, then pinching it shut again as soon as he had a free hand. When he finished, he followed Eckel back into the outer office. The deputy coroner was already chowing down, steam still rising from the scrambled eggs. Starke didn't want to interrupt again, so he called a nasal, "Thanks Eck," through his fingers as he headed for the car.

16

Shelby moved the unfamiliar mouse, and the sleeping PC blinked to life. It made no sound. She was grateful for that, but wasn't sure why. While Chloe was at school, she'd spent the day wrestling with the endless details of a funeral. Now it was early afternoon and the house was silent. Even after everything, she finally felt ready, compelled, to connect with others—even nameless, faceless others—who made her feel wanted, who could give her what she craved. But that wasn't the only reason she needed to dive back into her online world.

Again she thought, *How'd things get this crazy?*

With a few keystrokes, she created a new account, a new identity. It was easy to do. Now she was Gwen_23. She was twenty-three, with no personal history. If she wanted, she could make her new self beautiful, rich, and powerful without the pain, shame, and endless obligations. The avatar she chose had pouty lips and wore a body suit with just enough cleavage to be inviting but not trashy. Gwen_23 could move through this virtual world without leaving tracks—flirting, seducing, ignoring, whatever—the way Shelby had when she really was twenty-three, but without the messy complications.

As Gwen_23, she also could move undetected onto the trail of Paul's killer. Or at least that was what she hoped.

Shelby knew only a name: LoveSick. She had no idea what he looked like, though his avatar was a white knight. She didn't know where he lived, or what he might do if she ever found him again. The thing that worried her most was the twisted logic of his love. Paul's murder was a gift, he'd written, a heartfelt expression of his profound feelings for her. As he'd placed the gun against her husband's head, she had begged. *No, no, no, no, no. Not this. Please God no.*

He'd reminded her it was what she wanted. All those late-night conversations, the expressed desires. He'd recorded them all, studied them often until he'd finally understood what she'd been saying all along. She wanted them to be together. She'd wished there was a way.

Didn't she remember?

No, no, no, no, no. Those were words. Only words. Fantasy. It wasn't real. Please God no.

In the stunned-dumb moment after her ghost lover pulled the trigger, after countless intimate conversations and shared desires, after unwittingly giving LoveSick everything he needed to know to lure Paul to his death, she'd ended it all with a mouse click, rejected his twisted gift. Rejected him. The horror disappeared, as simple as a channel change. She'd closed her eyes and waited three weeks, hoping to wake from the nightmare. Was still waiting.

Now Ron Starke was asking questions.

What could she tell him? What could she tell a jury? Silence was no longer an option. She had to find a phantom.

Shelby moved the computer's cursor to her web browser icon and stepped off the ledge.

17

Starke eased the Vic to the curb outside the two-story main headquarters of Delgado Construction. For a company working its way out of Chapter 11, the place looked pretty healthy. Its parking lot was filled with top-shelf German cars and the $35,000 work trucks of apparently prosperous contractors and subcontractors. He hoped the place was air-conditioned.

His cell rang as he rolled up the driver-side window. It was Kerrigan's secretary.

"You're gonna have to speak up, Ginge," he said.

"Can't talk long, or very loud. Can you hear me?"

"OK. What's up?"

"You may want to check your personnel file. Not today, or even this week. I don't want it getting back to me. But check it sometime soon."

Starke rubbed his temples. "Let me guess. A letter of reprimand?"

"Here's a tip," she said. "Don't use the word 'fucking' when you're accusing her of something. Did you really?"

Shelby Dwyer knew her husband had been shot before the coroner publicly revealed that detail. How? Starke suspected one of two things: Shelby knew more than she was letting on, or Kerrigan had let slip that information when she notified Shelby that a body had turned up. He already knew his indelicate question to his boss—"How'd she know if you didn't fucking tell her?"—was going to be a problem.

"Maybe. How bad is this?"

"On the Richter scale, it's about a 3. Her notes are pretty mild. But I thought you'd want to know."

He wasn't surprised. On the other hand, the nagging suspicion he'd had since Kerrigan took over the department was suddenly a real concern: The chief was building a case to get rid of him. He'd been passed over for the job she now had, the job his own father had once seemed destined to hold, and he was an attitude problem waiting to happen. From her perspective: Why was he still even hanging around? From his: What choice did he have? His resume was "on file" at cop shops all over Southern California, but his phone wasn't ringing. He thanked Ginger for the heads up.

"You didn't hear it from me," she warned.

"You're a good friend, Ginge. I'm in Torrance now, FYI. Back this afternoon."

Starke stepped out into the sweltering heat. The car's AC was busted, just like the one at his apartment, and he'd hoped maybe LA's South Bay would be cooler than the Inland Empire. He was wrong.

"Morning," he said, setting his shield down for the receptionist. "I'm here to see Mr. Delgado."

The woman checked her book. "Detective Starke. Yes. Just have a seat."

The reception area was chilly compared to the inferno outside. Take your time Mr. Delgado, he thought. Take your time.

The night before, Starke had prioritized his schedule. He had two people he needed to talk to right away, contractor Robert Delgado in LA, and Dwyer Foundation President Deacon Beale in Riverside. Based on what he'd found so far, the Delgado interview seemed like the more intriguing possibility.

The one-time Dwyer Development contractor had engaged in a bitter public feud with Dwyer for much of the preceding year, including lawsuits. Dwyer's big LA project—a massive cluster of glorified tract homes marring the last open space along the Palos Verdes peninsula—had been a decade-long scrum of local outrage, conservancy protests, and labor strife. In the middle of all that, one of Dwyer's "community liaisons" had been caught leaving a Redondo Beach hotel room that had been booked by a member of the powerful California Coastal Commission, and a video of her walk of shame became must-see YouTube viewing among the project's opposition. The fallout derailed the entire project for a year, during which Dwyer Development stopped paying contractors whose crews and equipment were idled, including Delgado's. One court filing alluded to a colorful threat Delgado made when confronting Dwyer at a job site, all within earshot of his subs: "You'll die first, because I'll yank your heart out through your asshole, asshole."

Delgado seemed like a promising lead. Beale could wait.

A cannonball with legs suddenly burst through the back-office door. Short, maybe five foot five, and nearly as round as he was tall, Delgado had a pencil-thin mustache that reminded Starke of 1980s-era Wayne Newton. He was finishing a conversation with someone behind him, handing a stack of rolled blueprints to a toady scuttling alongside, and simultaneously extending his hand, practically pulling Starke up off the couch where he'd been waiting.

"Can we make this fast?" he said by way of greeting.

Starke followed him through the back-office door, around a corner, and into a private room that looked less like an executive office than an on-site construction trailer. Delgado collapsed into leather chair and rolled it forward, folding his beefy forearms on the desk in front of him. Starke claimed the chair across from him and took out his notebook.

"I didn't kill him," Delgado began.

"Come again?"

"It wasn't me. But only because somebody beat me to it."

Starke studied the man's eyes. If he had to guess, what he saw there was pure, unbridled glee. He scribbled a note to that effect. "You're talking about Paul Dwyer, then?"

"I hear he had a family and all, may God strike me dead. But the guy tried to ruin me. Not an accident. Not bad luck. He just flat out fucked me in the ass and left me for dead, and it's taken me the better part of a year to get this company back on its feet. So do I really care?"

"Do you?"

Delgado sawed an imaginary bow across a violin's

strings. "I hear somebody shot him right here," he said, pointing to the side of his own head. He smiled. "And they say there's no justice."

Starke scribbled another note. "Just to be clear, Mr. Delgado, you're saying that Paul Dwyer deserved to be shot in the head?"

Delgado suddenly looked nervous. "Don't get me wrong."

"Maybe I misunderstood then."

"No love lost between me and Dwyer, understand," Delgado said. "I knew his reputation when I went into business with him. Can't blame him for *my* stupidity. I never should've agreed to his terms, because it put us in the toilet and he knew that. I didn't kill him, though."

"So you said. I don't recall asking that question, but I'll note your response." Starke waited. "Maybe you can just tell me where you were and what you were doing on the date Mr. Dwyer disappeared."

Starke gave him the date. Delgado leaned over his desk and flipped back through the pages of his desk calendar. "ASH," he said. "American Society of Homebuilders. It's an annual thing. Three days in Vegas. I left the day before he went missing, got back a day or so later. I remember now, because I was at the Hooters Resort when my office called. They'd heard Dwyer was MIA and wanted to put me in a good mood. I was halfway there, anyway. Ever stay at the Hooters, detective?"

"Sorry."

"Real Vegas, baby. They got one of them mechanical bulls. Bikini bull-riding contest every Saturday night. High-rent poon." He winked. "All you can eat, know what I mean? That's where I was when I heard the news."

Starke couldn't get a handle on Delgado. He had guile, or was totally without guile. Hard to tell which.

"Here," Delgado said, tossing an unsealed envelope across the desk. "I was just putting this together for our controller."

Starke pulled a stack of receipts from the envelope. Airline tickets. Restaurants. Bars. Coffee shops. Cabs. Convenient, Starke thought. An entire alibi in an envelope.

"Executive International?" Starke asked, holding up one receipt. "The escort service?"

"Whoa!" Delgado snatched it out of Starke's hand before he could object. "I'll take that one."

Starke copied the words "Executive International" into his notebook. It was all he'd had time to read. Delgado fed the receipt into a shredder beneath his desk, its whir a dead giveaway, then smoothed the diverging rails of hair along his upper lip.

"Musta got mixed in with the others," Delgado said.

"Of course."

Starke shuffled the paperwork in his hands. The largest receipt, printed on 8.5 x 11 paper, was from the Hooters Resort. The stay dates covered a three-day span during which Dwyer disappeared and apparently was killed. Starke made a note to check with Southwest Airlines and the American Society of Homebuilders to verify that Delgado had actually been in Vegas and present at the conference all three days.

"Could I get copies of these receipts, Mr. Delgado?"

"Why not?" The cannonball stood up, took the receipts back from Starke, and disappeared into an adjoining room. Through the open door, Starke could hear the copy machine.

Delgado was back within a minute. He handed Starke the copies he'd made.

"Bikini bull-riding, eh?" Starke said.

"Sweet. Skip those overpriced new joints like the Bellagio or Aria. When in Vegas, go 'boner' fide Vegas, if you ask me. Two-buck shrimp cocktails and margaritas. Fifty-buck rooms. Free porn 24-7. *That's* Vegas, baby." Delgado looked at his watch. "So we done here?"

Back at the car, Starke rolled down the Vic's windows to let it cool down before climbing in. Something about Delgado's story wasn't quite right. He could confirm, or refute, the alibi with a few more phone calls. At least he'd nailed down his story—a productive morning so far, and still not even eleven.

He had two more stops to make before getting back on the crowded freeway. First, he wanted to visit the new LAPD. headquarters. A friend of his dad's in the personnel department owed him a favor. And as long as he was downtown, he figured he might as well stop by the county clerk's office, where the civil court records were kept.

Kerrigan had said she'd never met a woman without secrets. He might be fighting for his job, and wondered if maybe she had a few of her own.

18

Shelby had been online all morning, and for hours the night before. She'd again added LoveSick's username to Gwen_23's friend list, hoping he'd log on and approach her, but so far, nothing. Now she was biding her time checking the newsfeed on her Facebook page, remembering back to the moment seven months before when it all began.

She'd been escaping anonymously into this electronic universe for a while by then, always late at night, when Chloe was asleep and Paul was either gone or passed out drunk. Especially then. Computers were a mystery to him, just another reason for her husband to suspect her, control her, rage at her. He didn't have a clue about her online life, but he clearly found it threatening in ways that secretly thrilled her. But it was just easier when he was gone or asleep. At least then he couldn't hit her.

She'd been a lurker, at first, presenting herself as a generic, genderless avatar called XYZ. She learned to navigate the virtual world without drawing attention to herself, a silent witness to the flirtations, flame wars, couplings, and uncouplings of her fellow travelers. But after she created a new persona, LonelyMrs, and chose a somewhat more noticeable avatar, her online life began to change. She met the usual creeps and users, but also other women with secrets much like her own. After a while, she felt comfortable enough to confide in them, and found companionship and solace among those with stories like hers. Connections were easy to make, easy to break. Once in a while, she'd start a conversation with another woman who seemed to be leading a parallel life, and it always helped to know she wasn't the only one living a lie with someone like Paul.

Sometimes, she connected with men. She could play that game, too. Most were scammers, just hoping for a good fuck, real or virtual. But not all of them.

She'd connected with LoveSick by accident. He'd misdirected a message to her. She'd replied to point out the error, in case the message was important. He'd thanked her, made a joke, and a conversation began. Eventually, he invited her to join him in a private chat room. Going along reminded her of the incomparable thrill of following a college date back to his dorm room for the first time. She wasn't sure where it was going, but liked the idea of not knowing. She'd let herself fantasize for the first time in years.

They began regularly slipping into the world's private rooms, just the two of them, to talk. During one late-night conversation, he'd let slip the reason he'd chosen LoveSick as his screen name: *can't seem 2 stay on the horse, and falling off hurts 2 much. you?*

Her little-white-lie response surprised them both:

Probably the same, with the scars to prove it. Show you mine if you show me yours?

That upped the ante.

It was like he already knew her, had known her for years, a lifetime. They'd chat online for hours, sometimes until after 3:00 a.m., until her wrists ached from typing. About everything. About nothing. Food. Wine. Sports. Parents. God. He shared her faith that life could be good again. He understood how women thought, and why men grew angry with age. He said he had no kids, but listened tirelessly to her bragging about Chloe. For once, Shelby knew, she'd begun a relationship based on something other than her looks; he never once asked for a photo, nor did he offer one. *i see u in my mind*, he once wrote, *and for now that's enough. just not ready for anything real.*

So they'd kept talking. And talking. The more comfortable she got, the more she told him about her life. Not all at once. A hint here. A detail there. The town where she lived. The name of her parish priest, whose memorable homilies she sometimes related during their late-night talks. Chloe's private school. Her developer husband. His drinking. The violence. The endless charade of her public life. Her profound love for Chloe. He said he understood the bond between women who share a secret.

Then one night eight weeks ago he confessed he was falling in love with her. *impossible for us, I know*, he wrote. *i know ur committed to ur marriage, even after what he's done to u.*

Only then did she realize that she, too, had fallen in love with him, or at least the idea of him. She'd told him so. But she also realized how little he'd really told her about himself, even while seeming to tell so much. She knew what he thought about everything, how he'd react in any given situation. But she couldn't think of a single specific detail of his life. She should have known then that something was off. Within days, empathy transformed into intimacy. Her confessor quickly became her fantasy lover. He was wicked good with words, and she found herself urging him to narrate their online lovemaking each night as she slipped her hand inside the waistband of her panties. When she described her fantasies to him, she imagined him, wherever he was, bringing himself to the same joyful release she came to expect every time she logged on.

In time, she'd let herself imagine, let him imagine, a day when Paul was not part of the equation. A day when the accumulated pain and secret shame of her life simply vanished, and she could start life over in a parallel universe where there was no Paul, there was only him, and her, and Chloe, and a chance for real happiness for the three of them. For Shelby, that was the most seductive fantasy of all.

All we need is a magic wand, she remembered writing, *and the pain would disappear.*

say the word, he'd answered, *if that's what u want.*

More than anything.

Shelby shuddered at the recollection. To a jury, she thought, that would sound like a plan.

Then, with the sudden ping of her buddy list notification, there he was.

LoveSick: *been a while, lonelymrs.*

Shelby bolted upright in her chair. He hadn't even bothered to change his username. And how had he recognized her as Gwen_23, and with her entirely new avatar? She pulled in closer to the computer, aware that, if the whole thing unraveled, he wouldn't hesitate to use her own words against her. Shelby put her hands to the keyboard.

Gwen_23: *I'm terrified.*

She hated herself for admitting that. But there it was. They were her first words to him since the killing, when she'd signed off: *You've got no idea what you just did, you stupid, stupid fuck.*

LoveSick: *u should be terrified. they're after u.*

He had always been talkative. In his clipped response, she felt his rage at what he must have seen as a betrayal. She tried a different tack.

Gwen_23: *How did you know this was me?*

LoveSick: *i know everything about u. so long.*

Gwen_23: *Wait. Don't.* Shelby was typing fast. *We need to talk.*

LoveSick: *u get what u want from me, then… nothing? u vanish from the net? after everything we said, everything we did… your life got better. what abt mine?*

Gwen_23: *My life is shit.*

LoveSick: *ur life was shit before. that's what u told me. that's why u wanted out. now you're out. deal with it. and keep ur mouth shut. just hope nobody gets close or u'll really know what shit is—u stupid, stupid fuck.*

God damn, Shelby thought. God damn.

Gwen_23: *What does that mean?*

Shelby waited through a long electronic silence, and eventually shot a panicked look at the computer's clock—12:40. Chloe would be home soon from her half day at school. She'd completely forgotten. Before she turned away from the screen, LoveSick posted his reply: *shouldn't that daughter of yours be getting home about now?*

19

"Don't screw me on this." Dan Damian handed Starke the thick file folder filled with the photocopies he'd been making for the past fifteen minutes. "It's my ass if you do. You know that."

Starke nodded at his father's old friend. "We're square now, Danny. I really appreciate this."

"Nothing in the file but promotions, commendations, and awards. Not what you'd call dirt. So what's she to you?"

"My new boss." Starke winked. "It just pays to know who you're dealing with, that's all. So hard to suck up when you don't know the details."

Damian, head of the LAPD's records division, grinned. "She ain't bad-looking, either. Not many official department photos I'd call smokin' hot."

Starke winced. "Hadn't noticed. You'd have to meet her to understand."

"I hear you. Got two exes like that."

Starke flipped open the file then closed it again, a reflex

to pass an awkward silence. Damian leaned back in his creaky desk chair and sipped from a bright red coffee mug imprinted with the warning: "Just back the fuck off until this cup is empty."

"How's your dad?"

"Same."

"Fucking nightmare, is what that is. So sorry. But I know how proud he'd be of you."

"Appreciate that."

What else was there to say? Starke tucked the file under his arm and reached across the desk. Damian's grip was firm and sincere, but he held Starke's hand a beat too long. Starke knew what was coming next.

"Can I ask you something, Ronnie?"

"Anything, Dan."

"Rosaleen. You ever figure out what happened there? No note or anything?"

Starke shook his head. "Dealing with it the best I can, Danny. Every day hurts a little less."

"Hope you're doing OK."

Starke nodded, and Damian let it drop. But he thanked him for asking.

In the car, he set the copied contents of Donna Kerrigan's LAPD personnel file on the passenger-side seat, on top of a folder containing copies of what he'd seen at the clerk's office an hour before—the paperwork from Kerrigan's divorce case. The Vic was an oven after forty minutes in the sun, but he opened all four windows and started to read.

Dan had put her LAPD photo on top. Starke wasn't sure he was capable of ever seeing Kerrigan as "smokin' hot," but Damian was right about everything else in her LAPD file. She'd been a rising star from the moment she got out of the Los Angeles Police Academy. Her rank advanced steadily during her seventeen years on the force, from patrol cop to desk sergeant to lieutenant. She'd been commended for bravery twice, and the letters accompanying those awards were effusive about her cool in the face of danger. The *Times* had done a feature story about her behind-the-scenes role negotiating the release of a hostage during a SWAT action five years before. She'd even served a psyche-busting stint in the Internal Affairs Division, one of the requirements for a top department job, and was cited for her extraordinary professionalism during her tenure at IAD. Kerrigan's path seemed clear, her LAPD future seemingly unlimited.

But she'd walked away a year ago, right after the split with her husband. She'd left it all behind to start over, running a small, understaffed department in a distant if growing suburb struggling with resources. Why?

Starke opened the other file, a collection of eye-glazing legal motions, lists of communal property, house-sale paperwork, and negotiation transcripts spanning the year it took Kerrigan and her ex to dissolve their nine-year union. They'd finalized the deal just two months ago. Guy's name was Richard Holywell, electronics manufacturer, now living in Santa Monica. They'd had a nice place in Echo Park, a crushing mortgage just like everybody else in town, a little equity, some savings, a decent collection of midcentury furniture and "late-century antiques," whatever that meant. No surprises, really. He could have been reading about any one of a million other walking wounded on the vast trading floor of love and loss in the LA basin. Starke flipped more quickly through the docs, looking for one in particular: The original filing. Divorces happen for all kind of reasons. Starke knew that. But he wanted to know more about the flesh-and-blood woman behind the professional juggernaut that was Donna Kerrigan. It was fast becoming a matter of self-preservation.

Whoa.

Abuse? Intimacy issues? Infidelity?

The words seemed to leap from the page. Starke read more closely. As they got down to nut-cutting time on the property division, she'd claimed "emotional and physical abuse" during the entire nine years they were together. He'd countered with "an unwillingness to become intimate," and her "possible infidelity with a person or persons unknown." He also alluded to an incident in which she discharged a department-issued gun inside their home during an argument. The bullet grazed his shoulder. "Mr. Holywell sought medical help, but declined to press charges," his attorney wrote, "though that could change."

Kerrigan's ex was playing hardball.

Starke flipped through the remaining documents. In the end, neither Kerrigan nor her former husband offered evidence or details to support the various accusations. Maybe there was something to them, or maybe it was just the lawyers talking, pressing any advantage they could find or imagine. If true, though, the gun incident was the trump card. If they'd decided to split, and if Kerrigan had been convicted of felony assault, California's fifty-fifty community property laws would go out the window. She'd have been lucky to get the clothes from her closet. Even a public accusation would have derailed her law enforcement career. *That* was leverage.

He closed the divorce file. If Starke's new boss was railroading him out of a job, was there anything in either folder he'd be willing to use to fight back? He tried to imagine doing so, but decided he couldn't. He even felt bad about prying. Just a little.

20

The hiker stopped at the mouth of Esmeralda Canyon and looked up into the hills, sipping cool water from her Nalgene bottle. Breathtaking, she thought, even though she'd walked the canyon many times before. She pulled a small digital camera from the side pocket of her daypack and raised it to frame the scene.

An ancient California oak rose in stark relief about thirty yards ahead of her. It was the only thing other than rock outcroppings that stood more than three feet high in the lower part of the canyon, which ran like a wide scar down the foothills of Mt. San Gorgonio. Day hikers like her who trekked the three miles from Los Colmas often used the tree as a stopping place, taking refuge from the harsh summer sun to rehydrate or eat a sack lunch. Much wine had been drunk beneath the oak. She'd made love once in its shade.

Every year, after the winter rains, the springtime canyon was carpeted by lush wild grasses and sprays of orange and red wildflowers, which gave refuge to countless rodents, rabbits, and rattlesnakes. That was when it was most spectacular. But she preferred it now, in October, when the oak was surrounded in every direction by high wheaty groundcover and crisp chaparral that had been drying in the sun since the last spring rain, to a color the water conservation naggers called "California Golden." By this time of year, and especially this year, the canyon looked like it had been covered by a giant, rumpled rug. The mighty oak stood at its center.

It was a beautiful tinderbox.

She raised her camera and zoomed in and out until the golden canyon perfectly framed the tree, but she never pressed the shutter button. She knew only that she regained consciousness on her back with a disorienting ringing in her ears.

She later read other hikers' accounts of the lightning strike on her social networks. The bolt that obliterated the 170-year-old oak came from a clear, cloudless sky shortly after noon when the air temperature was ninety-eight degrees, the humidity two percent, and a steady westerly wind was gusting to fifteen miles an hour. The tree exploded in a flash, cleaving nearly in two as the strike scorched its way down the trunk. The biggest branch, measuring forty feet from end to end, was ablaze before it hit the ground. Embers from its impact bounced and rolled away into the potent kindling around the tree.

The relentless wind fanned those embers into tiny flames.

21

Starke didn't call ahead. He wanted to catch Shelby Dwyer off guard at home. Traffic from LA had been light. It was only 3:40, and he had no other interviews scheduled. He rang the buzzer at the end of her driveway gate.

"Please go away." Sounded like the daughter.

"It's Detective Starke, Los Colmas Police," he said.

Another voice answered: "Ron?"

"Shelby, it's me. Can I come in?"

"Are the reporters gone?" she asked.

Starke looked around. "Guess so."

The gate rolled silently to the side, then closed behind Starke's car as he drove onto the property. He parked in one of the spaces to the right of the house, next to Shelby's Jag, a convertible bullet, so he wouldn't block the circular drive. Shelby didn't come out to greet him. She took forever, in fact, to answer the door after he rang the bell. When she did, it was only after staring a long time through the peephole. When she finally unlocked the heavy door and peered out through the narrow opening, her eyes were red, her face blotchy.

"Nobody followed you in?" she said.

"Sorry to drop by like this, but I had some questions as we move forward."

"Can it wait until after the funeral tomorrow, Ron? Bad day."

"Afraid it can't, Shel. Thirty minutes? That's all I need."

She swung open the door, and Starke stepped into a subtly elegant entryway, one with none of the ostentation of the faux-Mediterranean mansions that Paul Dwyer built for LA's upscale refugees. It reflected what he immediately recognized as Shelby's exquisite taste, the kind that also reeks of self-assurance and money.

A blonde girl was standing beside Shelby, but she stepped confidently forward to shake his hand. Her mother clearly had the dominant genes in the family. The girl looked exactly like Shelby had looked during their summer together nearly twenty years before.

"You must be Chloe," he said. "I'm Ron Starke, with the police department. Your mom's told me a lot about you."

"Likewise," she said.

He looked at Shelby, then back at Chloe. "I'm sorry about your dad."

"The funeral's tomorrow," she said.

"I'm thirty-nine years old," Shelby said. "I'm not supposed to be burying my spouse."

"I know how you're feeling, Shel."

She softened. "I suppose you do. I'm sorry."

Starke shifted his eyes to other parts of the house. "Thanks for letting me in. Can we sit somewhere and talk?

I just want to go back over a few things we covered when we spoke a week or so ago, before… all this. When Paul was still missing."

Chloe padded down one of the hallways leading away from the foyer, her slippers scuffing along the floor. Shelby led him through the kitchen, and he caught himself watching the sway of her still-slim hips. She had a personal trainer, he guessed. There was probably an exercise room full of Nautilus equipment somewhere in the house.

They walked across a massive patio to a table overlooking the pool. Two towering palms rose from one deep corner of the lot, their fronds rustling high overhead in the hot breeze. The lawn surrounding the pool was immaculately trimmed, and the gardens had been planned by a precise and discerning eye. Starke had been in spa resorts that weren't this well barbered. An ancient golden retriever dozed in a shaded patch of grass, looking up briefly as they approached. Its face was a mask of white, and it managed only a single wag of its well-groomed tail.

Shelby offered nothing to drink, just took a chair at a glass-topped patio table beneath a wide, dun-colored umbrella. He sat across and slid a small manila envelope to her. She pinched it open and her husband's gold wedding band tumbled into her palm.

"Recovered with the body," he said. "Is it Paul's?"

She dabbed her eyes with the tissue in her hand. She nodded and put the ring back in the envelope. It lay between them like grenade.

Starke took the notebook from his jacket pocket. He flipped back to its first pages, to his notes of their conversation a week before, when he'd first heard her story of the night her husband disappeared. She had first told it to a responding officer three weeks ago when she reported Paul missing. She told the same story to him last week when it became a murder investigation and he took over the case. He wanted to hear it again. He still couldn't get past the most nagging question of all: How had she known Paul was shot that day when he'd spoken to her by phone?

"Shel, one more time," he said. "Walk me through that first night Paul when didn't come home."

"Again?"

"Again. Sorry. I wouldn't ask if it wasn't important."

Shelby took a deep breath and squeegeed a single tear from the corner of one eye with a manicured and polished fingernail.

"I was home alone," she began. "That was typical. Chloe was out, overnighting at her friend Ashlyn's house. Paul was always out at some function or another. Mostly business. Not always, but usually."

Starke spotted the opening. This was new territory. She'd confided her marital problems to him on the phone, but now he was looking her in the eye with a notebook in his hand. Somewhere along the line, Shelby Dwyer had made a calculation. This was the first crack in the façade.

"What about when it wasn't business?" he asked.

Shelby's voice was rock steady. "There were other women. I knew that. There had always been other women. I just learned not to ask. So it was just me, home alone and walking on eggshells like I always did, hoping he'd come home and go to bed and I'd have an uneventful night."

Starke looked up from his notes. "You realize this

account is a bit more detailed than the one you gave me last time."

"You asked me to be completely straight with you, so I'm being straight. I'm sure you'll be careful about how you use this information. It's irrelevant, but honest."

"Thank you. Shel, I hope you understand why I need to ask this next question: has there been anyone else in *your* life, romantically?"

Her smile was sad. "Not really."

"Clarify that for me."

"I've never understood how people our age have time for affairs. I'm Mrs. Paul Dwyer, Ron. Between the foundation work and everything else that goes along with that, and raising my daughter, it's a full-time job."

"So, nothing?"

She shook her head. "You know I'm a flirt. But no, nothing."

Starke penned her answer into his notebook as she watched his hand move across the page. "Do you think your husband ever suspected you of having an affair?"

"Constantly. He wasn't a particularly secure man, wicked jealous sometimes. But I never gave him any reason to suspect."

Starke let his silence work on her, but she offered nothing more.

"OK, Shel," he said finally, "when was the last time you saw Paul?"

"That morning when he left for work. I know he had a busy day planned, because he was complaining about it. I heard from him about four o'clock when he phoned to say he wouldn't be home. He was meeting someone for dinner, no idea who. I didn't ask. So with Chloe at school and then at Ashlyn's, it was just me the rest of the day. I worked in my office for a couple of hours after that, then turned in a little after midnight. I—"

"Can I ask what you were doing in your office for those couple of hours?"

Shelby shifted in her chair. "Mostly e-mails. Foundation stuff, mostly."

"And that involves what?"

She smiled, but it was sad more than anything else. "Finding ways to give away Paul's money. You'd be surprised how much work it is."

Starke jotted a note. Again, he caught her watching his hand move across the page.

"Anything else?"

She shook her head. "Can't think of anything."

Starke read from the notes of his previous interview. "And you said you woke up around 4:30?"

"That's right."

"And your husband wasn't home?"

Another sad smile. "Like I said, I'd learned not to ask. Frankly, those were the good nights around here."

"So he didn't come home at all?"

Shelby shook her head. "I called his office after breakfast. He wasn't there, either. Hadn't even checked in. Now *that* wasn't like him."

"But you didn't call it in until late that night?"

"You have to understand, my husband didn't feel like he had to answer to me. I didn't demand it, and he didn't feel the need to explain where he was, or who he was with, or when he'd be back."

"Did you call anyone to ask about him?"

"I gave you those names before."

Starke checked his notes. "I see it now. Sorry. His attorney, right? And his partner in the Villa Cordera project. And who's Skip Bronson again?"

"Paul's CFO."

"He's running the construction company now, right?"

"Right."

"What's he like?"

"Loyal," she said. "With Paul from the start."

Starke jotted another note. "Any reason to think—"

"No. Just, no. You'd have to know Skip to understand, but there's no chance."

Starke would check him out anyway, but put him way down on the priority list. With Dwyer dead, Bronson had slid effortlessly into the boss's chair to command an enterprise that generated millions of dollars each month and included the kind of perks accorded Roman emperors. Pumping Shelby for more information seemed like a waste of time. "So nobody had seen Paul or heard from him since?"

She nodded. "It took me all afternoon and evening to track them all down. I didn't get worried until late that night. Two nights in a row would have been unusual, unless he was traveling, and he would have told me if he was out of town. So that's when I called the police. I didn't want to alarm anybody, but I thought maybe I should, just in case."

Starke laid his notebook on the table and set his pen beside it. "And there was no indication after that that your husband was still alive? No phone calls to anyone? No credit card expenditures?"

"Nothing. Until Saturday, when I was notified of his death."

Time to confront it, Starke thought. "Shelby, the other day when we talked by phone, after you'd been notified, I asked you how you knew Paul had been shot."

Did she tense a bit? He waited, but she just glared across the table at him.

"You didn't answer," he said.

"That woman, the police chief, must have told me."

Starke leaned forward. "That's the thing, Shel. She didn't know, not at that point. The reason I didn't handle the notification was because I was at the morgue that morning. I saw the head wound, but me and the two guys from the coroner's office were the only people who knew about it at the time you were notified. I didn't fill in the chief until later, long after she spoke to you."

Shelby Dwyer stood. "You need to leave." The look she gave him could have melted the elastic in his boxers.

Starke kept his seat. "You never answered the question."

"This conversation is over," she said. "Please go."

"Can I ask why?"

Shelby put her hands flat on the tabletop and leaned down. Her eyes were wet, and he noticed a slight tremble in her lower lip. She said: "I'm not having this conversation without an attorney."

22

Starke briefly considered stopping as he passed Emerald Hills Cemetery, which was just off Spadero Road on his way back from Shelby Dwyer's. Rosaleen was never far from his mind, and thoughts of her crowded out everything else as he steered back toward downtown Los Colmas. He'd marked her grave with a simple stone carved with her name: Rosaleen Tierney Starke. No birth or death dates. No epitaph—what was there to say? But he didn't stop. He hadn't been back since he'd buried her. It was just too hard.

Suicides were always a mystery, but some were more mysterious than others. He'd concluded in the two years since he found her on their bedroom floor that the most painful deaths were the ones that were flat-out impossible to explain. Why couldn't she have had a history of depression? Why couldn't there have been logical clues, dots to connect, that helped those who loved her understand the sad end of her life? Why no parting note that spoke of her private pain? Afterward, during the worst of it, he'd even wished she'd died in a car accident, or been the victim of a street crime. At least then he'd understand what had happened. He'd have some focus for his rage.

Instead, he wondered.

This was his hell.

A screaming fire truck snapped Starke back to the moment. It closed in dangerously fast, nearly sideswiping him as he hugged the inside corner of a tight curve. Its siren surged and faded, and he watched it disappear from his rearview mirror just as quickly as it appeared, headed for the San Gorgonio foothills just outside of town. His heart was still pounding minutes later as he parked in front of the Silicon Recycler. It was nearly six, and he hoped it was still open.

Jason Samani was at his post, reading a magazine behind the counter. The owner looked up and smiled as he entered. "Laptop! You come back, Detective, like you said! Good, good. Thank you."

Starke was starting to feel guilty about not buying something. The guy was as sincere as he was eager. "Not today, I'm afraid."

Samani's face fell. "Too bad. Good deals today."

"I do want to ask you about something, though," Starke said. "An old piece of equipment, a computer monitor. Vanguard. Ever heard of that brand?"

The store owner laughed. "Jurassic era," he said. "So you're a collector?"

"Just curious."

"But why?"

Starke went stone-faced. He'd withheld from the Los Colmas PD news release any description of the anchor used to weigh down Paul Dwyer's body. It was a detail only the killer would know.

"Just trying to find out more about this particular brand of monitor," Starke said. "You mentioned collectors. Anybody in town who might own something like that?"

Samani waved his hand like a man swatting flies. "The company died, many, many years ago. I'm surprised any still exist. Maybe one turns up at a swap meet or something?"

"So they're rare then? Does that mean they're valuable?"

Samani laughed again. "Only for target practice maybe. They were shit, even brand new."

Starke tried another tack. "Are there collectors in town who might know a little more about them?"

Samani shrugged. "Maybe."

"Know any names?"

"Sure you don't need a laptop? I give you special police department deal."

"As soon as I'm ready to buy. Promise. So, any collectors around here?"

Samani sighed. "There's a club. Eric might know." He opened a drawer under the display counter and rummaged around. He came up with a business card and pushed it across the counter. Starke read it: "Los Colmas Computer Collective." There was a street address, an e-mail address, a Twitter handle, and a name.

"Eric Barbaric?" Starke said.

"Geek god," Samani said. "Stays on top of things around here. Maybe he knows something?"

Starke copied the contact information into his notebook. "That's a real name?"

"Good customer, Eric. Buys and sells with me all the time, not like *some* people who just talk, talk, talk."

"Point taken." Starke closed the notebook and thanked Samani for his time.

"Eric's an Apple," Samani said.

"Beg pardon?"

"Before, when you asked about lady who sold the Apple? Eric's my Apple guy. He buys. He sells. Maybe he still has it, or knows something?"

"I'll sure ask him," Starke said, and stuck out his hand. "Thank you. I hope we can do business someday."

Samani shook, but there was no passion in it. He turned his back and returned to his magazine even before Starke left the store. No more time for talk, talk, talk.

23

Donna Kerrigan stuck her head into Starke's tiny, doorless office. He looked up from his dinner—a half-eaten, hours-old meat bomb from the El Burrito Rodeo truck.

"Taking off?" he asked.

She didn't answer. "The funeral's tomorrow. One of us should go, to show the flag. I think the community should see us there."

"I'm told it's a private burial," he said.

"Graveside service is. The Mass and the country-club reception afterward is an open house. What's your schedule?"

Starke had spent the evening making calls. He'd booked the next day solid, with follow-ups on the interviews he'd already done, and fresh interviews with practically every remaining name in his notebook, from Deacon Beale, the head of the Dwyer Foundation, to Skip Bronson, the Dwyer Development CFO and a long-time whoring partner, to Eric Barbaric, the geek god.

"Tomorrow's nuts for me," he said. "I just don't see—"

"Then I'll go," she said. "St. Lawrence Martyr. Hope you're OK with that."

Starke thought for a moment. He wasn't OK with it. Clearly, though, she'd made up her mind. "Just give Shelby Dwyer a wide berth," he said. "I talked to her a few hours ago. She's not cooperating any more without an attorney."

"Interesting." Kerrigan stepped fully into the tiny space. It was crowded with one person. With two it was oppressive, even if it was someone you didn't loathe. "Was that your suggestion?"

Starke folded the burrito remains into its paper wrapper and dropped it into his trash can. When he stood up, the office shrank to half its size. "By which you mean?"

His boss backed up a step. "Please tell me how the conversation evolved," she said, "and how it ended with her shutting down."

"I was pressing her on something, and she reacted."

"Pressing her on what?"

Starke forced himself to wait before answering. They'd covered this ground before, and covering it again was only going to aggravate the situation. But what choice did he have?

"Somehow, between the time you arrived at her house for the next-of-kin notification and when I talked to her a couple of hours later, she concluded that her husband had been shot before the body dump. The first time I asked her how she knew that, she didn't answer. So I asked her again."

"You wondered before, rather rudely, if maybe I told her," Kerrigan said. "Let me be very clear on this, detective: I did *not* tell her. How could I? You were still at the morgue finding the bullet hole at the time."

"I realize that. But *somebody* told her."

"Or maybe she found out some other way. What if she knows more about this than she's saying?"

"I'm looking into that."

"Thank you."

He could see her mind shifting into management mode. How to defuse a tense situation with an employee?

"There's a fire," she said. "You've been busy, I know, so I wasn't sure if you'd heard."

"I knew something was up."

"Lightning strike in one of the Gorgonio canyons. County fire's working it pretty hard. Forty percent contained as of an hour ago, but a wind shift could complicate things. Things can change fast this time of year. Hope for the best."

"Yep."

"Back at it tomorrow, then," she said, turning to go.

"Yep."

Starke had one more thing to do before heading home. He tugged an unlabeled file from the corner of his desk, the one containing Kerrigan's divorce papers. He scanned the documents until he found the street address for Richard Holywell. He ran a crisscross and came up with a phone number. He ran a DMV check and came up with a photo. He printed both out and tucked both pages into the file. Prying into her personal life still made him uneasy, but he was more convinced than ever that he was fighting for his job, maybe his professional reputation. He didn't want the police union rep going into that fight unarmed.

24

From his spot on a ridgeline about a mile from the inferno's leading edge, the fire captain knew this one looked like trouble. It was hard to tell from down on the line, where he'd been directing the effort to contain it for the past two hours. So he'd driven up here in a San Bernardino County Fire rescue vehicle for some perspective. He was standing on the truck's hood, walkie-talkie in hand.

The scene before him was familiar and strange at the same time. There was something beautiful and surreal about a wildfire at night, and he'd seen a lot of them in his nineteen years as a firefighter. The Santa Anas usually slowed after dark, but they were still whipping this one and it was growing fast. It'd spread through greasewood and scrub oak from the canyon where the lightning struck, and within the past hour had reached a fifty-acre stand of Coulter pines that had been dedicated as a memorial to the four firefighters who lost their lives in the 1969 El Piñon Fire. Pine bark beetles were the main problem. The little bastards thrived during drought, and had devastated hundreds of thousands of acres in the San Bernardino National Forest. They'd eaten their way through more than half of the El Piñon memorial trees. Brown as rusted nails, the dead ones stood side by side with their still-green-but-doomed compatriots that somehow had also survived the drought. In ten years, if nothing changed, the whole national forest would be the same color. He'd had work crews clearing the dead trees almost nonstop for three years, and they hadn't even made a dent.

He lifted the walkie-talkie. "It's bad, Carlos," he said. "It's moving away from the point of origin in three prongs, north, west, and east. Main problem is west, down in the memorial grove, so for now let's focus any extra resources there. Over."

His line commander's voice crackled back. "Couple of Riverside crews just got here. That's where you want 'em?"

"Fast as they can get there. We got to stop it there, or else there's nothing but dried trees clear into Riverside. Read me?"

"Got it. Hang on."

He climbed down from the truck's hood. Carlos forgot to take his finger off the communicator's "talk" button, because for a moment he could hear him directing the Riverside crews. The flames were getting brighter at the western edge of the ribbon of orange as the fire worked its way through the memorial grove's tinder. There, they roared hundreds of feet in the air. Their light defined the column of dirty white smoke that rose thousands more feet into the night sky. His eyes followed the column of smoke up, up—shit.

"Carlos?"

"Go ahead."

"I'm looking way up high, and it looks like the wind up there is shifting. It's pushing the smoke east."

"East?"

"Maybe it's nothing. I'll check with the weather folks and keep an eye on it."

"An offshore wind, if that's what it is, actually might help. Lot less fuel in its path if the wind pushes it that direction. Over."

"Roger that, Carlos. Less trees, but more houses."

The endless housing tracts and treeless new neighborhoods around Los Colmas might be easier to defend, he knew, so Carlos was right. On the other hand, he still hoped they were wrong about the offshore wind shift. One of those tract houses was his.

25

Shelby had checked the driveway gate, double-locked the front door, tested all the windows upstairs and down, slid bar locks into all the sliders, loaded Paul's handgun and put it in the drawer of her bedside table, and set the house's sophisticated alarm system. She'd offered Chloe the chance to sleep with her in her king-sized bed—quietly locking the bedroom door behind them—using the argument that they needed to be together on the eve of Paul's funeral. In truth, she knew they were being watched. He knew their routines.

"Mom?"

"Yeah, baby?" Shelby stroked her daughter's hair as she lay curled beside her in the dark, under the pillowy down comforter Shelby used year-round because the house's air-conditioning blew so cold.

"I think Dad had a secret life. Like maybe he was a spy or something. Or in the Mafia. Or a fugitive. I think that's what happened."

"You think so?"

Shelby felt Chloe shift up onto one elbow. "People like you and Dad always have secret lives. That's what me and Ashlyn think. There's things you never tell your kids. Like you really did smoke weed when you were in high school. Like you hooked up a lot before you got married. Like you'd still like to party and dance naked once in a while except you don't because you're worried what the neighbors would think. Admit it."

Shelby laughed. "You never stop making mistakes and learning, that's true. You do things as you grow that sometimes you regret, and you don't necessarily want the world to know about. I know I'm still screwing up. That's just life."

Chloe laid her head back down. "Spare me the Big Lesson. You're such a *bore* when you do that."

Shelby put an arm around her daughter's thin shoulder and pulled her close. "Maybe what happened to your dad isn't what you're thinking at all. You'll see at the funeral tomorrow. He had a lot of friends. Personal friends. Business friends. Golfing friends."

"Girlfriends?"

There was no point in lying; Chloe already knew the answer. She'd overheard their arguments, watched Paul bully her, helped her mother brush makeup onto her bruises on too many mornings after. They'd cowered together on the floor the summer night she'd finally challenged him and Paul pulled the gun.

"Yes, girlfriends," Shelby said.

"Did you hate him for it?"

"Sometimes."

"You put up with it, though?"

A year ago, before Shelby had secrets of her own, the comment would have cut her deep. Not now. "We all make choices," she said. "I chose not to make it an issue in our marriage, because my family means too much to me. I couldn't risk that."

"Dad's the one who was risking it, Mom. He was the one perving around. What'd he think, you were stupid?"

Shelby pushed Chloe away and rolled over. She felt the tears coming. "I did make it an issue once, and you saw what happened. Think it was worth it?"

Neither of them said anything else. A minute passed, maybe two. "I was so scared, Mom. He meant to kill us both. I saw it in his eyes. I hated him."

"Me, too, baby."

It was late and their conversation was lagging. The gaps were getting longer.

"They won't be there tomorrow, will they?" Chloe asked, rallying. "At the funeral."

"Who?"

"The women Dad was fucking."

Shelby flinched at the word. "I wouldn't know them anyway."

Chloe rolled away and pulled a pillow to her chest. Within minutes, Shelby heard her daughter's breathing fall into a deep, steady rhythm. Good to know at least one of them would sleep tonight.

Alone with her thoughts, Shelby's mood darkened. What had she told LoveSick? What hadn't she? She'd poured her heart out to him in the past few months, since he'd professed his love for her. Not just her fantasies, but the details of her life, of Paul's life, of Chloe's. Paul's routines. Her routines.

He knew so much. He was close. The only thing she knew about him for sure was that he'd already killed without conscience, and that he was smart—smart enough to know she was the only person who could ever link him to Paul's murder. Smart enough to set her up as an accomplice.

Whoever he was.

26

After a few Newcastles and his late-night browse through the NSA Room, Starke was, by ten the next morning, interviewing the "executive escort" who'd been with Robert Delgado the night Paul Dwyer went missing. He'd cadged the name of the service from the receipt he'd glimpsed at Delgado's office, run that through a friend at Las Vegas PD, and come up with incorporation papers listing the owner's name. Turns out, the owner owed the Vegas cop a favor, badda bing, badda boom—Miss Congeniality called him back.

"You had a client a little more than three weeks ago, a homebuilder from LA named Robert Delgado," he said. "There was a convention in town. This ringing any bells, Luscious?"

"It's Lucy," she said. "When I'm off the clock, sweetheart, I'm Lucy."

Starke could hear a mournful opera playing in the background, the soundtrack of high culture. Vegas, Starke thought. Gotta love it. "OK Lucy, this would have been sometime on—" Starke looked up the date that Dwyer disappeared and read it to her. "The gentleman in question says he was in Vegas that weekend, and his story checks out with the people who ran this convention. He was definitely in Vegas. But I'm told he slipped away from the group on Friday night, and I suspect he was with you, probably between about ten and midnight."

"Busy weekend, you know," she said. "Homebuilders is one of the big ones."

"You might remember this guy. About five foot five, 230, with kind of a pencil-thin mustache that—"

"Oh yeah, yeah," she said. "Sawed-off little dude. That mustache. Dressed like a Havana tourist. Jesus."

Starke made a note. The convention's keynote dinner that Friday night was black-tie only. "Define 'Havana tourist,' please."

The background aria was building like a storm as Lucy rummaged for details. Starke imagined her with her eyes closed, sifting the faces and body parts of a busy convention more than three weeks ago. How many that weekend? How many since?

"Guyabera. White shoes. Cigar."

Starke stopped her. "No tux?"

Lucy laughed out loud. Actually snorted. "Seriously? He'd look like an eight ball in a tux."

Starke was struck by how vividly she remembered Delgado. "How long would you say you were with him?"

"He got the full hour," she said. "Made an issue of it, in fact. Finished in ten minutes, but didn't want me to leave.

He wanted to talk. Whatever. So I just listened to him brag about himself for fifty minutes and watched the clock."

"And this was in his room at the Hooters hotel?"

"I usually won't work there. Hooters gets your less-enlightened types. But the request came in for a real redhead, and that's my thing, and money's money. I remember he made a big deal about the hotel, like it was big-time Vegas. 'Free porn,' he kept saying. 'Three channels!' Like that would be a huge turn-on for me."

She seemed to have Delgado's personality nailed. "Do you remember what time you left his room, Lucy?"

"Late. After midnight, I'd guess. I walked through the casino to get out, so there'd be video if you want to check."

True, Starke thought. But he still had no idea when Dwyer actually went missing. He was last seen at his office around 7:15, and Eckel's best guess was that he'd been shot within forty-eight hours of that. If he could narrow the time frame, the video might be important in terms of confirming or undercutting Delgado's alibi.

"And you're sure this was that Friday night?" he asked, reading her the date again.

Her pause was long enough to be uncomfortable. "I think maybe it was Saturday. But I remember him, for sure."

"Saturday? Not Friday? You're not sure about that?"

Another pause. "I know you want me to say I'm sure, but I'm not. Busy weekend, like I said."

"The day is pretty important, Lucy. Friday versus Saturday."

"I wish I could be sure. But I'm not. I'm sorry."

Starke buried his face in his free hand. He'd held the Executive International receipt for a moment before

Delgado snatched it back and shredded it. He flipped back to his notes from that conversation, but found only the corporate name. No date. But he still had options. The lobby surveillance tapes. And if Executive International was legit enough to offer receipts to clients planning to write off its services, there'd be a discoverable duplicate somewhere if other evidence pointed to Delgado.

"Lucy, thank you for helping with this," he said. "I think that's all I need for now."

In the background, the unfamiliar aria reached its crescendo. "I remember Mr. Eight Ball, for sure," she said. "And it was definitely sometime during Homebuilders."

"I'll try to run that down on my end, Lucy," Starke said. "I'm actually surprised you found him so memorable."

Lucy laughed again. "One thing I'll say for the little Napoleons: They tip well."

27

The pews of St. Lawrence Martyr were mostly filled, with the late arrivals standing along the perimeter. They had all come for Paul, whose polished oak casket was parked at the front of the center aisle, barely visible beneath the massive spray of fresh gardenias on its lid. Shelby dabbed a tear with her crumpled tissue and looked out over the congregation from the lectern, hoping words would come, noting how the people representing each facet of her husband's complicated life seemed to clump together.

Skip Bronson and the company's executive staff and their families gathered to her left, toward the front. Behind them sat the Dwyer Foundation staff and some of its most notable beneficiaries, including its executive director Deacon Beale and the presidents of the two local colleges and a local hospital that the foundation so generously funded. To her right, Shelby saw her parents seated with Paul's stoic widowed mother, neighbors, friends from church, Chloe's school counselor and a few of her friends, as well as several of Paul's most trusted bankers, architects, and contractors. She recognized Oscar Esparza, head of the company that for years had done grading and infrastructure work for Paul's major projects, and a major foundation donor. A scattering of people she didn't know well watched from the rear of the church, including the ice-cold Los Colmas police chief who'd brought her the news four days before. She sat alone.

"Thank all of you for being here for us," Shelby began, "for me and Chloe. Your friendship and support means the world to us. I'm sure it would have meant the world to my husband."

She stopped for a moment to collect her thoughts. "You know, Paul was so grateful to you all for helping him realize his vision over the years. He saw his work as one extended partnership, and considered it his privilege to be a part of that. His name was on the company headquarters, so he got the credit, but he'd have been the first to tell you, as he often told me, he was just part of a talented team. I want to thank you all on his behalf."

She turned to the young priest who'd said the funeral Mass. "Father David, thank you for your words of comfort and hope. They were lovely. Really."

Shelby considered sitting down, even turned away from the lectern. Then she stepped back to the microphone and squared her shoulders. There was an elephant in the room, and it felt wrong to ignore it.

"Paul was a good man. You all know that as well as I do. He deserved better. That's all. He just—" Another glance at the priest, a forced smile. "I know we're supposed to forgive. We all need forgiveness. I'm a work in progress right now. I just hope God bears with me."

Shelby heard sniffles and a rustle of tissues from the pews. She had no idea what to do next, so she stood mutely to the side and waited until Father David stepped to the microphone. He thanked everyone for coming, asked that they keep Shelby and Chloe in their prayers, and invited the immediate family to accompany Paul to Emerald Hills Cemetery for a short graveside service.

Six pallbearers moved down the center aisle toward the casket. Shelby had chosen them carefully—Skip Bronson, Dwyer Development's interim chief executive; Deacon Beale, the foundation's CEO; the two college presidents; and Paul's two younger brothers. At the funeral director's command, they took up their assigned positions, three to a side.

An elderly gentleman with an usher badge touched Shelby's arm. "Would you like to greet your guests at the back of the church, Mrs. Dwyer?"

She nodded.

"We'll need you to follow the casket then. Are you and your daughter ready?"

Shelby put her arm around Chloe, who'd held her tears throughout the Mass, and focused on the open door at the rear of the church. They fell into step behind the rolling casket. Chloe quietly greeted family and friends as she walked. Toward the rear of the church, she leaned into a pew and hugged a young man Shelby had never seen before. He was dark and tall, well over six feet with the shoulders and chest of an athlete, sitting with Oscar Esparza. For a moment, Shelby flashed to Chloe's comment from the night before, about people having secret lives. But she stayed focused, facing straight ahead, concentrating on the task at hand.

The receiving line was going to be the toughest part, the struggle to look all these people in the eye. She offered another silent prayer to St. Jude as she turned and waited in the vestibule for the guests to file out.

The rest was a blur of handshakes, hugs, sad eyes, and requests to "let us know" if she and Chloe ever needed anything. No one mentioned the murder. When the young man Chloe had hugged shook her hand, Shelby asked, "And you are?"

"Mario Esparza," he'd replied. "I—"

"From school, Mom," Chloe interjected. "A friend."

"My family worked with Mr. Dwyer. My sister, too," he added before moving on.

By the time the last guests were gone, Paul's casket had been loaded into the hearse waiting at the curb. It was trailed by two limousines, doors open. Shelby urged Chloe, Paul's mother, and her parents into the lead car and started to join them.

"Mrs. Dwyer?"

The voice was familiar. Shelby considered walking on, not turning around. She did, though, and greeted the police chief with a forced smile. Just the two of them remained on the church steps. "Thank you for coming, Chief—I'm sorry, I've forgotten your name."

"Kerrigan," she said, extending a hand. "Donna Kerrigan. On behalf of the city, I wanted to be here to extend our deepest sympathies."

Shelby offered a limp handshake. This time there was no compassion in the woman's eyes, no hint of goodwill or empathy. Nothing personal, Shelby knew, just business. "Nice of you to come," she said. "You'll let me know if there's any progress in the investigation, won't you?"

Kerrigan delivered her answer without a smile. "Certainly, Mrs. Dwyer. And of course, if you have more information that might be a help to us, you'll make sure to let us know?"

"Of course."

Car doors thumped shut behind her, and Shelby turned. Only one door, in the lead limo, remained open. She felt no need to say goodbye as she descended the church steps to join her daughter and the others for the ride to Emerald Hills. She gave only a moment's thought to the single, dense cloud that hugged the horizon. It hung there, dirty white, in the bright blue sky to the west.

28

Barbaric *was* his real name. Starke found him in the phone directory. The listing included a street address, too, and at the moment Starke was standing outside the house on the outer fringes of old Los Colmas, wondering if he had the right place. He'd seen better-maintained meth labs.

The yard was choked with weeds, and at its center was a battered plywood skate ramp. Or at least Starke assumed it was plywood; its sides were covered by skate stickers. The garage door was off its track and hung like an uneven window shade. A pale green Datsun B210, something vaguely Carter Administration, was parked in the driveway. Its rear window was sheet plastic fastened to its frame with red duct tape, and its left front tire was nearly flat. He jotted down the license number out of habit. Even as he did, he smiled at the absurd notion that it might be stolen.

At least there's no pit bull staked out front, he thought, stepping onto the cracked concrete walk that led to the door. The house seemed to throb with the sound of

Metallica blaring from serious speakers somewhere inside. He pounded hard. Harder.

The music stopped, and seconds later the front door creaked open. Starke stood face to face with a young man, maybe twenty, wearing the chinos-and-blue-polo-shirt uniform of a video-rental chain currently working its way through bankruptcy. The chain's logo adorned his chest.

"Hi," the kid said.

He was about six foot three, maybe 160 in his clothes, with the fish-belly-white complexion of someone who spent far too much time indoors. His posture was downright nightmarish.

"Eric?"

"Was the music too loud?"

"You're killing a lot of brain cells with that stuff."

"I'll keep it down. My bad."

"That's not why I'm here, though." Starke offered his ID. "Got a minute?"

Eric Barbaric looked like a squirrel caught in traffic on the center stripe of a wide, wide road. "For what?"

"You're not in trouble or anything." Starke smiled. "You know Jason Samani down at Silicon Recycler, right?"

Barbaric still wasn't breathing.

"He gave me your name," Starke said. "He says you sometimes buy and sell Apple computers around here, and I'm trying to track one down. One in particular. He also said you might know if there's anybody around here who might collect old tech stuff. So, got a minute to talk?"

Barbaric looked at his black Casio. "I was supposed to be at work, like, ten minutes ago."

"Video Depot?"

"Yeah."

If Starke was reading him right, he looked a little embarrassed. "Can't believe that place is still in business. I used to rent from them back in the VHS days."

"Not everybody has an iPad. Gotta feed the need."

Starke nodded. "Good place to work?"

Barbaric shrugged. "It's a Joe job."

Starke immediately recognized the term—and an opening. He tried his best Mike Myers impersonation: "'I've had plenty of Joe jobs. Nothing I'd call a career. Let me put it this way: I have an extensive collection of name tags and hair nets.'"

Barbaric finally relaxed. Even grinned. "*Wayne's World.* A classic."

"Oh yeah." Starke let a moment pass. "So, can I come in?"

Barbaric swung open the door and led him into a house every bit as ruined as the front yard.

"Nice place," Starke said, stepping over a small, crusted, meat-smelling bowl of dog food.

"My dad's house," Barbaric said, clearing a spot on the couch for Starke to sit. "He died two years ago, so now it's mine."

"Live alone?"

Barbaric nodded. "Just me and Churchill. Dad left me his house and his pug, and no money to take care of either. I hate the dog, but what am I supposed to do?" He looked at his watch. "I really need to get to work, though. Can we make this quick?"

"Sure thing," Starke said. "I'm looking for this one computer that someone traded in with Samani a little more than three weeks ago, Eric. Nice high-end iMac. He buys Apples, but says he resells them to you to refurbish and re-resell, because his customers are all PC people. That right?"

Barbaric nodded. "Maybe a dozen or so per month. Not many. But yeah, I grew up with Apples and make a few bucks refurbing."

"So what happens when you buy one of these used computers from Samani?"

"Wait." Barbaric looked wary again. "This isn't about my taxes or anything, right?"

Starke already had the feeling that any conversation with Eric Barbaric would be an elliptical journey. "Guy's entitled to make a few bucks off the books, far as I'm concerned," he said. "I just want to know what might've happened to this computer I'm looking for."

"I don't sell it myself, I parts it out. Video Depot doesn't exactly pay a sweet wage." He shook his head. "You have any idea what taxes on a place like this run? Effing thanks, Dad."

Starke tried to stay low-key. "You may remember this computer. Big-ass thing. Top shelf. Nothing wrong with it, as far as I know. Just a trade-in, so it was probably in great shape."

Barbaric stood suddenly and walked into what Starke assumed was a bedroom. He returned with a laptop. "What about something like this? It's a thoroughbred. Fast. Elegant."

"No, no, I'm not just looking for any computer." Starke removed his notebook from his jacket and flipped back through its pages. He shook his head. "This one I'm looking for is a desktop, big screen." He found the page where he'd scribbled the model number Samani gave him.

"Oh yeah," Barbaric said. "Had a few of those last month. Sweet machines."

"What are the odds of finding this one in particular?" Starke said. "See, there may still be information somewhere in its memory that could help us on a case. It's important. That's really all I can tell you."

Barbaric looked disappointed. "Must be fun to be a cop."

Starke tried a different tack. "When you 'refurb' a computer, Eric, what exactly do you do to it?"

Barbaric shrugged. "Same as Jason. The nicer ones, I just reformat the hard drives and sell as is."

"Which would erase everything in its memory, correct?"

"Right. The ones with problems I sell as parts to some of the techs I know. So this one, depending on what I did with it, may or may not still have any memory at all. Its hard drive already may be in another machine somewhere. You got a serial number or anything?"

Starke reached for his wallet, opened it, and pulled out a hundred dollar bill. Barbaric's eyes got wide.

"Could you at least check around for me on this?" Starke said. "Think of this as your finder's fee. If you locate it and need to buy it back from somebody, I'll pay you twice what it costs you."

"What if I can't find it?"

"You keep this for your trouble." Starke handed the cash to a very pleased looking young Video Depot associate. He also gave him his Los Colmas PD business card.

"I might need a couple of days."

"Sooner's better," Starke said, "before somebody erases what still might be on there. Like I said, it's important."

"Are you deputizing me?"

"You might call it that." Starke stood up. "By the way, one of the tires on your Datsun went flat."

Barbaric rushed to the front window. He shot a panicked look at his watch. "Noooooooo!"

"Tell you what, I'll take you," Starke said. "I go right by the store on my way back to the office. Might even pick up a couple of flicks while I'm there. Suddenly got a hankering for *Wayne's World.*"

Barbaric grabbed his wallet from the kitchen table and flung open the front door. He grinned. "Party on, Wayne."

Starke stepped outside. "Party on, Garth."

29

Starke had been looking forward to his Wednesday afternoon interview with Deacon Beale, the long-time executive director of the Paul W. Dwyer Foundation. Beale's name had come up twice in early interviews, before Dwyer turned up dead. Both sources had mentioned an unintentionally public shouting match between Beale and Dwyer that unfolded behind closed doors in the foundation's board room.

Both told Starke it was about a woman.

"He's expecting me," Starke announced to the foundation receptionist, after pushing his card across her desk.

He turned around and for the first time absorbed the splendor in which Dwyer's charitable arm operated. Like the Dwyer home, the lobby of its headquarters bore Shelby's understated but elegant design touch. Daylight streamed from overhead skylights that ran the length of the room, giving the space an outdoor feel. Even as staffers moved through the thick-carpeted reception area, it was as silent as a church. The modern architecture provided the perfect canvas for the industrial sculptures that stood against angled walls. For contrast, the curator had hung stunning examples of primitive art along the white walls between the sculptures, adding a touch of humanity. Starke fixated on an oversized mask suspended directly across from where he stood. About the size of a bicycle wheel, it was a collection of tree branches, twigs, and dried, dark brown mud shaped into a face that was both appealing and horrifying. Its one intense eye was made from the dark bottom of a broken beer bottle. It was unforgettable, if a little creepy.

"Sir?"

Starke turned. The receptionist handed him a security badge. "I'll buzz you through. Just follow the corridor to the end, and Mr. Beale's assistant will meet you."

"Pretty tight security, eh?" he said.

The woman said nothing. Starke clipped the badge to his belt and moved on. Beale's executive assistant had the storky, high-waisted legs of a classical dancer. Her face was model perfect, with short brown hair like Rosaleen's that Starke felt the sudden urge to reach out and touch. Starke guessed she was in her early thirties, but there was a timeless quality to her. "I'm Anna Esparza," she said. "May I offer you anything? Water? Coffee?"

Starke thanked her, but passed.

"Then go right in."

Beale stood as Starke entered. He reminded Starke of Dwyer himself, same slim athletic build and silvery hair, same winning smile he'd seen in countless charity grip-and-grin photos over the years. Maybe there was something healthy and energizing about giving away vast sums of money for a living?

"Detective, thanks for postponing this until after the funeral this morning," Beale said. "Shelby asked me to be one of Paul's honor guard, so for that and a thousand other reasons I needed to be there. But that's past us. What can I do for you today?"

Starke began with the simple stuff. Dwyer and Beale had worked closely together for a number of years, first at the company and then at the foundation. Was Beale aware of anyone who might have had reason to harm Dwyer? Was he aware of any unusual contacts or incidents leading up to Dwyer's disappearance that suggested what was to come? Had Dwyer talked to him about any concerns about his safety? Beale seemed to wrack his brain for anything that might help.

"Paul wasn't just a colleague and friend," he said. "He was my mentor. In so many, many ways."

Starke riffled the pages of his notebook back to the beginning, to the first conversations he'd had with people in Paul Dwyer's orbit in the days after he disappeared. From those conversations, Starke also knew the two men, along with executives from Dwyer Development, sometimes partied like Italian prime ministers, hosting "hospitality" bacchanals for key contractors on company projects, and at least one annual "golf" weekend for major foundation figures, all male, at a rented private home in Palm Desert. He doubted any of the guests brought their clubs.

"Let me ask you about something else while I've got you," he said.

"Certainly."

Starke mentioned a date about six weeks ago. "What

can you tell me about a fairly heated discussion you and Mr. Dwyer had in these offices on that day?"

Beale's left eye twitched, but his smile didn't dim. "Sorry, that date again?" he asked.

"Did you have more than one heated discussion?"

Beale pushed away from his desk, crossed the room, and closed his office door. He sat back down, his posture suddenly relaxed. "So that's what this is about?"

"What happened that day, Mr. Beale?"

"I can clear this up very quickly."

"Great."

Beale sat stone still. He seemed to be reconsidering. "The truth," he said. "This is the God's honest truth."

Starke waited.

Finally: "My wife died eighteen months ago. Ovarian cancer. A long, brutal battle. Just hope you never have to go through something like that, detective. It's hell. Pure acid hell."

At least you know *why*, Starke thought, but said nothing.

"Took me a year to come out of it, this deep, deep depression," Beale said. "It was the hardest thing I've ever been through, like thrashing around underwater for a long time, trying to breathe. Then one day I broke the surface. I don't know why, or what changed, but I just somehow knew it was time to stop grieving."

The foundation leader cocked his head toward his office door. "You met Anna," he said. "She's really the only one who had any idea what I was going through. She watched me struggle every day, saw me close my office door for hours at a time. Covered for me on the days when I just couldn't face anybody. And then one day about six months ago, I realized how she'd been there for me all along. She'd given me the space to work through it all without asking a single thing in return. She's just a very special woman. I hadn't even considered another relationship until then, but suddenly there it was."

Starke jotted some notes, still not sure where this was headed. "Just to clarify, then, you've been seeing your secretary, Anna, for about six months?"

"My executive assistant. Yes. She's worked with me here for about three years, but during my years at Dwyer Development I dealt with Esparza Construction—her family's business—for a couple of decades. "

"I guess I'm a little unclear about what that has to do with—"

"Paul, as you may have heard, had an appetite for beautiful women. Surely I'm not the first to tell you that."

Starke acknowledged nothing. "You and Paul Dwyer traveled together quite a bit. For business."

Beale studied him. "We did," he said at last. "Both for the company and for the foundation."

At least twenty seconds passed while Starke waited for Beale to break the silence, but guys like him weren't easily rattled. Starke let it stretch another ten, to make sure Beale was wondering exactly what Starke had heard about their way of doing business.

"Any other questions?" Beale prompted.

"So, you were saying about the women?"

Beale reached for a black mug on his desk and took a sip. "Did Anna offer—?"

"She did. Please go on."

Beale swiveled his chair toward the wide office window

for a moment before turning back to Starke. "Not many people knew about us, meaning me and Anna. We'd told almost no one, because of the awkwardness of the work situation. But Paul knew. I'd told him, and assured him that we were working to find Anna a new position at the foundation so that I wasn't in a direct supervisory role over her. So he was about the only person who did know. And he knew the whole story, *why* I'd fallen in love with her, which is what made him... his behavior, I should say, so difficult to understand. It put me, and her, in an impossible situation."

Now Starke understood. "So he was pursuing Anna as well?"

"Relentlessly. Almost irrationally. Calling and texting her three times a day, trying to convince her to see him. Sending flowers to her here at the office. Why would he do that? To either of us? To Shelby?"

The story fit the generally unflattering profile of Dwyer that Starke was piecing together in the wake of his death.

"But Paul was a man used to getting everything he wanted, right now. He could be flat-out childish sometimes, and God forbid if you had something he wanted. It was no holds barred."

"He had that reputation in business, I know. That carried over to women as well?"

Beale nodded. "It was painful for those of us who worked closely with him. We all know Shelby. We all love her deeply. She was so dedicated to Paul, and remains dedicated to the work of this foundation. There just aren't many like her. Of course, that didn't stop Paul."

"So the argument was about that?"

Beale nodded. "It was about Anna, plain and simple.

I finally confronted him, in the boardroom just off the hallway where you came in. I closed the door and told him he needed to respect her, and me, to understand the difficult position he was putting us in."

"How'd that go over?"

"You can imagine."

"I'd rather you tell me, Mr. Beale."

Beale sighed. "There are at least a dozen people who work along this corridor, besides Anna and myself. The discussion got loud enough toward the end that others obviously overheard. This place stays pretty quiet, so even if no one understood what it was about, the sheer volume probably pricked up a few ears. Then Paul stormed out, so I'm sure it was hard to ignore. There really aren't many people involved in a foundation this size. We're all pretty close."

"At any point did the discussion turn violent?" Starke asked.

"Absolutely not."

"Did Mr. Dwyer make any threats?"

"He said I could be replaced just as easily as Anna could. So yes, I took that as a threat."

"Did you threaten him?"

Beale laughed, but there was an edge to it. "With what? I had no power over him. I'm his *employee*."

Starke let a moment pass. "Mr. Dwyer did turn up dead a few weeks later, Mr. Beale."

Beale leveled his gaze at Starke across his expansive desk. "You don't believe I had anything to do with this, detective. You're smarter than that. I understand why you're here, why you're asking these questions. It's due diligence. But this one's a dry well. What happened happened. I won't deny the hard feelings. But kill Paul? The man who hired me, mentored me? The cash cow of the foundation I oversee? Does that make sense on any level?"

"You've heard of crimes of passion?" Starke said.

"I drew a line," he said. "Paul made clear he was perfectly willing to step over it. But kill him? Why? Anna wasn't interested in his attentions. I knew she wasn't interested. He threw a tantrum. So what if he'd fired me? It wouldn't have been the worst day of my life. Believe me, I've already lived through that."

Starke closed his notebook. Beale's account of the conference room confrontation matched what he'd heard from the foundation staffers who first told him the story. "I'd like to spend a few minutes with Anna on my way out, if you don't mind," Starke said.

"I told her that might be a possibility. She said she'd be willing to talk to you."

Starke stepped through Beale's office door and invited Anna to join him in the boardroom where the face-off had apparently taken place.

30

Starke pulled the heavy door shut while Anna Esparza perched like a hummingbird on the edge of an executive leather chair, picking at a tissue in her hand. A dozen similar chairs rimmed the immense boardroom table with the Dwyer Foundation's distinctive "PDF" logo inlaid in dark wood at its center. A small, pop-up panel at each seat offered a power outlet, USB ports, and whatever other electronic access the foundation's board members needed during the quarterly meetings where they redistributed Paul Dwyer's money to worthy organizations. Starke felt like he'd stepped into some sort of power vortex. The table probably cost more than any car he'd ever own.

"No need to be nervous," he assured her.

Esparza was looking past him, through the room's wide windows and into the reception area. Starke turned just in time to see Beale standing in his office doorway, arms crossed. He wasn't smiling, and Starke was well aware of the lopsided dynamic between a wealthy older man and his beautiful young lover. He reached for the control rod of the window's miniblind and twisted it. Beale disappeared. He did the same with the other two windows before turning his attention back to Esparza.

"Do you feel comfortable talking here, Anna?"

"It's fine."

"Because we can schedule a time to meet outside of the office, if you prefer."

She crumpled and recrumpled the tissue. "I'm just not sure what help I can be. But no, this is fine."

Starke crossed to the other side of the boardroom table and sat facing her from one of the other plush chairs. He thought it might put her more at ease, but her rigid posture remained unchanged. Her eyes tracked him like a wary cat's, at least until he looked directly at her. Then she looked away.

"Esparza's a pretty well-known name around here, Anna. Your family in the construction business, by any chance?"

She nodded.

"Rafael's daughter?"

"Granddaughter. Mario's my father."

Esparza & Sons Excavation and Construction dominated the building trades in Riverside County, not just private development but the lucrative public works contracts that often went along with it. The company dealt in excavation and concrete work, mostly, and Starke knew its trucks and Spanish-speaking work crews were almost always around anytime ground was broken for a public park or housing tract. Rafael was the patriarch of the Mexican immigrant family, rough-trade Americans by way of Sinaloa, who had come to American success the old-fashioned way: bribery, coercion, union-busting, and, when necessary, head-busting.

There'd been incidents and at least one indictment along the way, but nothing ever stuck. For a fleeting moment, an odd thought crossed Starke's mind: #sinaloathugs is trending.

"I'm guessing your family does a lot of business with Mr. Dwyer's development company?"

She shrugged. "I don't really know. I guess."

Entirely possible, Starke thought, given traditional Mexican family dynamics. The old man had died a few years back, but by then he'd handed off his business to favored sons and grandsons, not daughters and granddaughters.

"My brother has been seeing the Dwyer's daughter," she said.

This was news. Starke scribbled a note. "You're talking about Chloe, then?"

Esparza nodded.

"So that would be your younger brother? What's his name?"

"Same as my father, Mario Esparza," she said. Starke penned the name into his notebook and added a comment beside it: "Father AND son." He took a guess. "Your dad's running the business now?"

"Yes."

"And your brother works, too?"

She shook her head. "He's still in school."

"Of course. Right. Any idea how long your brother and Chloe Dwyer have been dating?"

"Do they even call it that anymore? High school stuff, you know."

"But you think there's something between them. Hooking up? Like that, you mean?"

"More than that. I've seen her a few times at my parents'. They definitely run in the same group."

Starke refocused. "So, then, Anna, let's talk about Mr. Dwyer for a minute. Would that be OK?"

Starke wouldn't have thought it possible, but Esparza seemed to tense even more. "I don't really work for him," she said. "Didn't. I work mostly for Mr. Beale."

Starke held up his hand. "Anna, just so you know, Mr. Beale filled me in on your relationship."

Her eyes dropped, and she focused on her tissue again. It was nearly shredded now.

"He also told me there was some tension here in the office, between himself and Paul Dwyer, right here in this room, in fact." He waited for a reaction, but got none. "Can you tell me anything about that?"

She shrugged again. "I wasn't in the room that day, so I don't really know."

"But everyone else in the office seemed to know," he pressed. "I'm told it got pretty loud. And apparently it had to do with you."

Anna Esparza finally looked directly at him. Her eyes flashed, and she dabbed at them with the pulpy wad in her hand. "Mr. Beale told you that?"

Starke smiled. "Just be honest with me, Anna. What was going on? It seems like a pretty complicated situation. I'm just trying to sort everything out."

"Complicated?" she said, her voice trembling. "Complicated. Yes."

Starke waited while she composed herself. Finally, she cleared her throat and spoke. "No disrespect to Mr. Dwyer. I know he's done a lot of good around here. I know how much money he gives away. That's such an honorable thing, and I love being a part of this foundation."

"But?"

Esparza seemed to regain her confidence, but still wouldn't look him in the eye. "He was making me really uncomfortable. Us."

"In what way?"

For the next few minutes, Esparza told him basically the same story Deacon Beale had told a few minutes earlier—how she'd grown to admire Beale as he suffered alone through his wife's long illness, how after Dottie Beale died her admiration transformed, unexpectedly, into fondness for her boss, and then love. How as she and Beale got more involved, Paul Dwyer ramped up his own attentions toward her. "It was a game to him," she said. "Like some weird little competition."

"And you found his interest in you uncomfortable?" Starke asked.

"Intensely. Just the aggressiveness of it."

"Around the office, you mean?

Esparza rolled her eyes. "Here. Anywhere. Once he sent flowers to my apartment. Then to my parents' home. Followed me to my gym."

Devil's advocate time, Starke thought. "And you didn't find it flattering to have the attentions of such a rich and powerful man?"

She glared, meeting his eyes for the first time. "Stalking isn't flattery. Neither is shoving your hand—"

Starke waited for her to continue. Instead, she chewed her lower lip.

"So Mr. Dwyer got physical about it then?" he prompted.

The young woman swiveled her chair to face him, but her eyes went back to her lap. "He was practically humping my leg."

"And you'd made clear to him you weren't interested?"

"Every. Single. Day. I asked him to stop, to the point of being rude. Mr. Beale asked him."

"Do you think that's what led to the shouting match between them? The one everyone overheard?"

"I know it is. Even my father—"

Esparza stopped suddenly and chewed her lip some more.

"Again, your dad is Mario, same as your brother, right?" he prompted.

Esparza's voice trembled when she spoke again. "We were all clear with Mr. Dwyer."

"So even your family knew all this was going on?"

Esparza stood, walked to a wastebasket in the corner of the room, and tossed in her shredded tissue. Starke bore in as soon as she sat back down.

"Your father got involved? Your brother?"

"They knew I was handling it," she said.

"That's not what I asked."

A tear rolled down Esparza's flawless cheek. She brushed it away with a long, perfectly manicured finger and, for only the second time, looked him straight in the eye. "Daddy wanted to talk to him."

"To Mr. Dwyer?"

She nodded. "I told him no. Begged him."

"Did he listen?"

Esparza rolled her eyes. "To me? He's old-school Mexican. What do you think?"

"He'd known Paul Dwyer a long time," Starke prompted. "They do a lot of business together."

She nodded. "Since my grandfather."

"But your father was still willing to confront him about this?"

"Business is business, Daddy always says."

Starke waited before responding. Finally, he said: "But this wasn't business."

"No," she replied. "No, it wasn't."

The comment lay between them until Esparza stood up and nodded toward the conference room door.

"May I go?"

"But Anna, do you know if your father ever confronted Mr. Dwyer?"

She shrugged, opened the door, then asked a question of her own: "Why are men such assholes?"

31

It was an ancient thing, this dog, white-faced and creaky and gentle as a lamb. When it got up from its bed to investigate the footsteps echoing through the empty house, it approached with its tail wagging, its head down, and its untrimmed nails tick-tick-ticking across the stone kitchen floor. It died after a single jolt from the Taser, writhing, frothing, and shitting in a convulsive scramble until its heart simply stopped beating.

The worst part was cleaning up the mess—nothing should dilute the message—then getting the dog and all the stuff out to the pool. The house was huge, but there was plenty of time to work. Shelby and Chloe weren't due home for hours. They were at the catered reception that followed the graveside service. Still, there was a lot to do. Why take chances? Move fast.

First, what to use for an anchor? There was a stunning industrial sculpture in the front hall, no doubt heavy, but maybe too heavy for one person to wrestle across the patio to poolside. It was worth a try. A little test lift and, actually, it was perfect—heavy enough, sturdy, and designed in a way that made it easy to carry. Probably expensive, too. That was a nice touch.

Second, moving eighty pounds of dead-weight dog. It was a cinch compared to Paul Dwyer—now that was an operation, and at night no less—but still a surefire way to work up a sweat. Latex gloves don't exactly breathe.

Finally, the finishing work at poolside. Two unsubtle passes with the duct tape around the dog's muzzle. The poor thing was just the messenger. With a few loops around the legs and a couple of well-placed knots, the hemp rope made a nice harness. The free end fit nicely through a solid ring in the sculpture, and with a double knot there and one more loop around both dog and anchor for good measure, plus a little slack, the whole package was ready to deliver in maybe ten minutes.

Then it was just a matter of shoving the sculpture off the edge of the pool deck. It dragged the limp dog down the angled floor to the pool's deepest point, and within a minute had scraped its way to the low point at the drain. The dog's groomed blond coat stood out nicely against the bottom.

Even so, with everything else going on they might overlook it for days. Eventually it would bloat and rise to the end of the anchor rope and would hang there, suspended four feet from the drain. After a while, the smell would surely bring them to the pool's edge wondering what the hell?

Or maybe they'd realize the dog was missing and go looking. Finding it right away would be the best thing of all. The sooner Shelby got the message, the less likely she'd be to say something stupid.

32

Starke peered into the ordered fluorescence of the Video Depot store, waiting for the end of Eric Barbaric's shift. Barbaric had worried all the way there about how he'd get home.

"Tell you what," Starke had said eight hours earlier as the grateful kid got out of his car. "Since you're doing me a favor trying to track down that hard drive, I'll swing by later and give you a lift home. Deal?"

It was a calculated kindness. The cash he'd slid the kid would at least guarantee some effort on Barbaric's behalf. But Starke needed more than that. He really needed Barbaric to step up. With each interview, the list of people who seemed relieved by Paul Dwyer's death got longer, not shorter. He still was curious about Skip Bronson, the acting head of Dwyer's development company. Now he needed to talk to Anna Esparza's father and brother. Dwyer had been disrespecting Anna Esparza in ways that got people talking. Esparza & Sons had partnered with Dwyer Development for years, decades, and their businesses had grown together into formidible Southern California powerhouses. But dishonoring family? That was something else.

Starke dreaded the idea of going back to Kerrigan with an expanded field of suspects, not a narrower one.

He flashed his headlights as Barbaric stepped out of the store into the parking lot. The kid grinned and jogged over. "Woot!" he said, climbing in. "You came back."

"You sound surprised."

Barbaric handed over a DVD case. Starke read the spine: "Wayne's World."

"Five-day rental," he said. "By Monday at midnight. No charge."

"Thanks."

Starke steered from the parking lot onto the street. It'd been dark for an hour, but there was still an orange glow on the western horizon from the distant wildfire he'd heard was giving the fire crews fits.

"After I dropped you here earlier, I remembered another question I wanted to ask you," Starke said. "Computer related."

"Shoot."

"Ever hear of a company named Vanguard? It made old-style computer monitors, big-ass things, for a while back in the early 1980s."

Barbaric looked out his window at the passing cars. "Dude, like, I wasn't *born* until 1994."

"No, I realize that. I just thought maybe you knew of people who collected old computer equipment and early tech-era stuff."

"You google it?"

Starke nodded. "Found a bunch of websites. The collectors seem pretty organized, even have a 'Computer Collector's Code of Conduct' posted at one. 'I will do my best to find a home for any classic or unwanted computer,' that sort of thing. Serious stuff."

Even in the dark car, Starke could see the contempt on Barbaric's face. "There *are* people like that. I don't *know* anybody like that. I wouldn't *want* to know anybody like that. But sure, they exist."

"But anybody around here? That's what I'm asking."

Barbaric shook his head. "I used to know every wonk in Los Colmas, back in the olden days five or six years ago. That was before the pod people."

"Pod people?"

"The ones in all those phat new houses. They pod two hours into LA every day to work, then pod back because they have to 'live' way the fuck out here," he said. "Some of them may do something annoying and pathetic like collecting old PCs, but I wouldn't know." He snorted. "Never got that, collecting. To have a bunch of stuff just to look at? I mean, what's the point? It's like—you ever watch that big dog show on ESPN?"

"Westminster?"

"Whatever. They have these dogs, I mean, they're good for nothing, your so-called 'toy' breeds—impractical fucking things, you know? Put 'em on a pillow and look at 'em. That's about it."

Starke wasn't sure where Barbaric was headed with this, but he was enjoying the ride. "You sound like a big fan."

"I'm more of a working breeds guy," he said. "Like, you

know, a border collie can practically run your whole ranch for you."

"Uh-huh."

Barbaric seemed to stall, apparently so deep into his metaphor that he'd gotten lost. Maybe he was tired after a grueling eight hours of video slinging.

"And people who collect old computer stuff?" Starke prompted.

Barbaric reengaged. "Same people that own shih tzus. At least the same type. Definitely not *my* type."

"So," Starke said, making a stab at coherence, "to you, computers are like border collies?"

"Exactly," Barbaric said.

"Better explain that to me."

"They're working breeds. They can run your whole ranch. Collectors? I mean, if you want one just to look at, well, what's the point?"

Man, Starke thought, that was a lot of work. He hesitated before asking another question, wondering if there was enough time for another answer during the ride back to Barbaric's inherited house. He took a chance.

"Think there's a way you could hook me into that network of people?"

"Collectors, you mean?"

"Yep."

"Why?"

Starke steered onto Barbaric's street and pulled into the driveway behind the crippled Datsun. He turned off the engine. "To see if anybody around here might be into that. There can't be that many of them. It could be important to this case I'm working on."

"Do I get another hundred bucks?"

Starke sighed. He was running out of options. "Tell you what. You find me some people around here who collect old computer stuff, I'll get you another hundred. This is coming straight out of my pocket, but I'll pay it if you get me some names."

"Deal." Barbaric opened the Vic's door.

"Local names," Starke clarified. "Southern California."

"I like this," Barbaric said. "I'm a hunting breed."

"You still got the card I gave you with my numbers?"

Barbaric patted his pants pocket. Starke could hear a hoarse and strangled rowf-rowfing from inside the house. "Your dad's pug?"

Barbaric slammed the car door, but he bent down and peered through the closed window. He rolled his eyes and mouthed the words, "Toy. Fucking. Breed."

33

Suddenly, it was just the two of them.

Shelby and Chloe had been the center of attention from the moment they awoke Wednesday morning until ten minutes ago, when they bid goodnight to the last of those who stopped by Los Colmas Country Club after Paul's funeral. Some brought food, even though Shelby had arranged a buffet, and most stayed through the afternoon and into the early evening. A few friends asked to speak, and Shelby had been grateful when the affair became an impromptu, good-natured roast. The stories about Paul were funny, sad, wistful. Skip Bronson, the company CFO, lampooned her husband's inability to relax on the golf course. "He played like he drove—fast and always looking to pass whoever was ahead of him. Think NASCAR, but with golf carts." A long-time plumbing contractor recalled Paul's hypervigilant punctuality and his unwillingness to wear a hardhat at construction sites "so he wouldn't mess up his Conway Twitty hair." His long-time corporate executive assistant, Darla, made much of his penchant for loud socks. Shelby was glad Chloe got a glimpse into the man whose business-world persona she seldom saw.

But then it was over, and the last guests gone, and the leftover food packaged and dispatched to the local food bank, as Shelby had asked. Talked out, they drove home mostly in silence. At one point, Shelby brought up the young man Chloe had hugged in church, and who later introduced himself in the reception line. "So that Mario guy," she said. "Is that a thing?"

Chloe didn't answer. By then her daughter was asleep, or at least pretending to be, and remained so until Shelby arrived at the house. She pushed the remote control button on the car's rearview mirror. The iron gate at the base of the driveway began to slide out of the way.

"OK, kiddo, you awake?" Shelby asked.

"Mmm."

"We're home."

"'Kay."

Shelby stopped after passing through the gate, watching in her mirror to make sure it closed behind her. The Jag's brights lit the entire front of the house as the car moved up the drive, then slowly focused down to bright pinpoints as she parked facing the retaining wall that bordered the parking spots, to the left of Paul's black Benz. The interior of the house was already lit, thanks to the sophisticated electronic systems that monitored temperature, light, and moisture, and constantly adjusted them to within the comfort range Paul had specified. She keyed a code into her smartphone's home security app, deactivating the house's alarm system. With all she had to carry inside, she didn't want to be fussing with the keypad beside the front door. She killed the headlights and then the engine.

Chloe opened her door, and the car's dome light blinked on.

"Don't forget the stuff in the backseat," Shelby said. She opened her door, folded her own seat forward, and began collecting the boxes of sympathy notes and personal mementos that people had brought for her and Chloe, things they felt Paul would have wanted them to have. A nine iron borrowed months before but never returned. The photograph of the three of them taken during a ski trip to Whistler. He'd kept it on the credenza behind his desk, and Darla hadn't wanted it to get boxed up and forgotten with the rest of his office stuff. His custom plastic name badge from the Los Colmas Breakfast Club, the goofy, all-male fellowship organization where Paul spent two Saturday mornings a month listening to the latest Viagra jokes and watching some of the city's most respectable citizens perform skits in grass skirts and coconut-shell bras.

"Mom, check this out," Chloe said. "Dad's car."

Shelby put down the armload of stuff and circled around to the other side of the Jag, where Chloe was bent down to eye level with the hood of Paul's Mercedes. It hadn't been moved for more than three weeks.

"I hadn't noticed this before," Chloe said. "Is the air really bad lately or something?"

Shelby bent down as well. "What?"

Chloe swiped a fingertip across the Benz's hood, leaving a dark trail. Shelby examined her daughter's fingertip, which was smudged with the fine gray-white dust that had settled evenly on the parked car's flat surfaces. She swiped a finger across the white hood of her own car, and it came away with the same smudge.

"I guess I didn't notice it on my car, since it's so light. But yeah, must be bad lately, or—" Then she remembered. "Oh, you know what? There's a wildfire over toward Gorgonio. Started yesterday. Heard it on the news. I bet it's ash."

"Great," Chloe said. "Lung cancer."

"We'll be fine inside." Shelby cocked her head toward the Jag's back seat. "Make sure you get everything. I want to go through it all tomorrow."

The western sky was oddly bright, but Shelby was grateful for the recessed lights that lit the Tavertine stone of their front walk. Her arms were full and she didn't want to stumble in the dark.

"Mom?" Chloe said from just behind her.

"What, baby?"

"I don't know…. Listening to everybody today, hearing all those stories about what a swell guy Dad was, didn't you just want to get up there and tell the rest of the story? Maybe he was all those things, but he was a lot of other things, too."

"Yes, he was."

"So?"

"It was a memorial service, Chloe, not a trial."

"But they made him sound like such a saint. Didn't you want to tell them about the rest of it, the crap he put us through, about what happened last summer?"

Shelby groped for an answer. Paul had walked away from that horror show on their kitchen floor and never mentioned it again. Only Shelby and Chloe knew. When they reached the front door, Shelby turned to face her daughter. "It's not up to us, or anybody else, to judge him now."

Chloe studied her eyes. "That's what you were talking about after Mass."

"What's that?"

"When you were talking about forgiveness. How you hope God will bear with you, because you're not ready to forgive. You weren't talking about forgiving whoever killed Dad. You were talking about Dad."

She was partly right. "I was talking about both, I guess."

"I knew that."

"You're the only one who does." Shelby leaned closer and kissed her daughter's forehead. "And no one else ever needs to know."

"I don't get why are you're protecting him like that."

"I'm not protecting *him*, baby," she said. "See, whoever killed him…. There's no point in confusing things. Dad was murdered, and whoever did it is still out there. It's important to find that person. But if people thought you or I might have tried to kill him, because of what happened, they'd waste a lot of time and ask a lot of questions that don't really matter. That's why I want to let it be. Let God judge him, and let the police do their job. That'll be the best thing."

Shelby was suddenly conscious of how long they'd been standing at the front door, exposed. He could be watching. She fumbled for the front door key on her key ring. When she found it, she pushed it into the heavy-duty backup deadbolt and stepped into the wide foyer. She set her armload of stuff on a table beneath the hall mirror, and closed the door as quickly as she could. Shelby shook off a disoriented feeling as she did.

She turned the internal lock and gave the door a reassuring tug. She slid the external deadbolt home and set the alarm for good measure. When she turned around again, the same vague feeling settled in. The house seemed emptier, but she couldn't say why.

34

Wednesday must have been a big day at Suds-Your-Duds, because Starke's apartment felt more like an armpit than usual as he stepped through the door and into a wall of warm, damp air from the downstairs laundromat. He set his shoulder holster, shield wallet, notebook, and DVD of *Wayne's World* on the folding table where he ate cereal and takeout. He hung his jacket on the back of the single folding chair.

Someday he'd buy stuff to replace the furniture he'd driven back up to Rosaleen's parents in Ojai the week after they buried her. Most of it was theirs to begin with, but that wasn't why he wanted it gone. It was just a constant reminder of her, of their lives together and what happened, and he didn't need that.

The red light on his answering machine blinked its own language—two quick flashes, followed by a pause. Two messages. Who'd call him here, and not on his cell?

He grabbed a Newcastle from the fridge and rummaged

through a disorganized drawer containing his entire collection of kitchen utensils—four forks, three spoons, one wood-handled steak knife, one German chef's knife, a butter knife, a plastic spatula, and the extra bottle opener he'd gotten for seventy-nine cents from the nearby "Quicker Liquor" store. He opened the bottle and finished half of the ale, then jabbed the "play" button.

"Let's do a quick debrief Thursday morning."

Kerrigan. No hello. No pleasantries. No chit-chat. Just straight to it.

"I'll be in at seven," she said. "Say, seven thirty? Call my cell if there's an issue. Otherwise, see you then."

Perfect. Kerrigan was asking for a progress report, but things were getting more and more complicated. He'd have to explain to her how he'd identified a long list of potential suspects. She might even compliment him on his diligent work. But she'd also realize they were probably weeks away, at least, from any likely breaks. She'd realize her police department might look slow and plodding. She'd imagine the media glare getting hotter as the investigation dragged on. Plus, she'd probably come back from the funeral Mass with a head full of theories that he'd have to run down, wasting more time.

Clearly, with a seven thirty start like that, his Thursday was going to suck. He hit the "erase" button with enough force that the entire message machine slid several inches across the kitchen counter.

The second message began with an apparently confused silence. Then:

"This is Richard Holywell returning your call. Ah, I don't recognize your name, and you didn't leave much of a message, so I'm not sure what you were calling about. But you apparently have my number."

Starke's stomach clenched. It was the return call he'd been anticipating, and dreading. Kerrigan's ex.

The message he'd left on Holywell's machine was cryptic. Just a first name, his home number, and a request for a call back. He had no idea whether Holywell and Kerrigan were still in touch, and he'd sweated the possibility that Holywell would notice the San Bernardino area code and call his ex-wife to ask if she knew a "Ron" from out this way who was trying to get in touch with him.

He also wasn't sure exactly what he thought a conversation with Holywell might accomplish. There was a bit of "the enemy of my enemy is my friend" going on, and he wondered if the bitter Holywell might spew some bile about Kerrigan that could come in handy if she wanted to edge him out of the department. But he could imagine how Kerrigan might use that against him if she ever got wind of it. So his earlier call to the Santa Monica number wasn't exactly part of a plan, more like a no-huddle Hail Mary pass with the clock winding down.

Now he was having serious second thoughts.

Starke retrieved Holywell's number from the file of Kerrigan's divorce papers and picked up his cordless home phone. He set it immediately back down in its cradle. He picked it up again and walked over to the apartment's single window and drained the rest of the ale. He pressed "talk" and heard the dial tone, then hung up.

What could this possibly accomplish? How was he even going to start the conversation? "Hello, your ex-wife got the job I was supposed to get, and she's now trying to crush me like a bug. I hear you might have some dirt I could use against her." Bottom line, that's what it was. And it felt wrong. In all his years of public service, nearly two decades of handling everything from domestic brawls to gang members with guns, Starke had never once done anything to protect himself that wasn't strictly by the book. He'd never once retaliated against anyone who'd tried to hurt him.

This felt different, though. Maybe it was paranoia, but this time his entire career—professional standing as well as personal reputation—was at stake, along with the unfulfilled ambitions of both his father and himself. This time, it was a fight against someone he didn't understand, on any level. Given a chance to possibly defend himself, how could he not?

Because it felt wrong, he decided.

Then he picked up the phone and dialed. He was relieved when it kicked into voicemail again. He left his cell number and hung up.

35

Shelby had lived through a lot of wildfire seasons in Los Colmas, but she'd never seen anything like the gray-white ash that had accumulated on her kitchen windowsill by early Thursday morning as she stood there smoking and thinking. The light dusting of grit Chloe noticed on the hood of her father's car the night before was now thick on every flat surface on her back patio. School had been canceled.

She stubbed out her cigarette and walked to the slider. Her eyes started to itch as soon as she opened it. Then she sneezed. She noticed, too, that the fronds of her towering twin palms were rustling in the opposite direction as the day before. The westerly Santa Anas had reversed themselves and cooled. The hot westerly wind was now blowing east, and blowing hard.

Back inside, she turned on the small flat-screen TV on her kitchen counter and tuned to an LA news station. The inland fire story dominated even there. The images were familiar—helicopter water drops, walls of flame, exhausted firefighters. A fire captain was telling a news crew that a wind shift in the past twenty-four hours had turned the blaze. "Riverside looks safe for now," he said. "The leading edge now is to the east. We're redeploying our resources as fast as we can."

Shelby studied the fire graphic on her screen. The burn area was massive. If it was heading east, Los Colmas was squarely in its path. She made a list in her head, just in case they'd need to evacuate.

First, Chloe and Boz. That was her family now. Chloe would need some clothes and her school work; Boz would need a bag of food, his prescriptions, and his joint medicine. She looked across the kitchen floor, to where an untouched bowl of kibble sat next to his water bowl. Where was he, anyway?

Second, gather the family photo albums and DVD recordings, personal financial records, insurance papers— everything in the fireproof safe in Paul's study just off the foyer. If she'd learned anything over the years of living in a wildfire zone, it was to put the important stuff in the car well in advance, just in case.

Third, reprogram the automatic lawn-watering system. They were set to water before dawn and after dark, because of the drought; Paul had taught her how to override the automatic program to turn the sprinklers on. Their property had a fair amount of defensible space, and leaving the water running guaranteed nothing, but Paul always said it couldn't hurt to soak everything around the house.

No need to wake Chloe at this point. The fire was still a couple miles from Los Colmas, and the next twenty-four hours would determine whether they'd have to leave. She headed for Paul's study. She could at least get the paperwork and family stuff into her car.

As she passed into the foyer, the vague sense of emptiness she'd felt the night before suddenly came clear. Where was "Flight"?

Since she bought it, the sculpture—all heavy metal, link chains, and sharp metal hooks from the killing machines at an Arkansas chicken plant, assembled into art—had sat on a side table in a space along the curved wall of the house's grand entry hall. Because it was so unusual, guests usually noticed it more often than the other pieces in the foyer.

Shelby walked to the empty, four-foot pedestal where it had sat. Where was it?

She looked around. Nothing else was missing, including pieces considered much more valuable. She shivered as a chill swept through her.

Someone had been in the house.

Were they still here?

She climbed the stairs to her bedroom and went straight to the night table where she'd put Paul's loaded gun on that long Tuesday night before the funeral. She made sure the safety was on, slid it into the pocket of her robe, and moved quietly down the hall to Chloe's room. She opened the door wide enough to make sure her daughter was in her bed and still asleep, then pulled the door shut again. She pulled the gun out and clicked off the safety.

Room by room, right hand clutching the gun like Paul had showed her, heart pounding, she moved through the sprawling house, opening closet doors, looking under beds, behind curtains, into showers. She checked the laundry room, the pantry, the wine cellar, the movie room. She worked her way back toward the front of the house, ending in Paul's study, relieved to find no one and nothing else missing or disturbed.

But someone had been in the house.

Shelby thought back to the last time she noticed "Flight." It was certainly there on Tuesday, when Maria last cleaned. She'd noticed her housekeeper tending it with her feather duster. Had it been there when she left for the funeral Wednesday morning? She thought so, but couldn't say for sure. She definitely remembered standing in the front doorway last night, when she and Chloe got home after the funeral, with the uncertain sense that something was out of place. She'd heard that thieves sometimes scanned obituaries and death notices and target the homes of grieving families, knowing the houses would be empty while everyone attended the services.

But how could someone get past their security system?

And why would someone steal a single sculpture, especially one that weighed as much as "Flight"?

For a moment, but only for a moment, she considered calling Ron Starke.

No, she thought. No. He'd ask questions she didn't want to answer. He'd want to know about more than the missing art. He'd ask if she thought it might be somehow connected to Paul's murder. What could she tell him? That the nameless, faceless phantom she'd watched murder her husband was intimidating her into silence?

No. Ron knew her too well, certainly well enough to know something was wrong. He'd see that even the possibility of a connection between this insignificant theft and Paul's murder scared her more than anything. He'd want to know why, and she was afraid she might tell him.

36

True to her word, Kerrigan already was at her desk and on the phone when Starke arrived at seven on Thursday morning. She didn't even look up as he passed her office. The support staff, including Ginger, didn't arrive until eight, so not many people were around except Kerrigan, the dispatcher, and a couple of beat cops pushing paper at the end of their overnight shift.

He'd stayed awake until three preparing his debrief. He'd cued Kerrigan by phone to some developments as they happened, but he hadn't given her a full accounting of the Dwyer investigation since late Monday morning. He'd decided to begin with updates on Delgado and Beale, two of the three names that had come to the fore early on. He'd tell her how he'd tracked the Vegas hooker with whom Delgado said he was spending time the night Dwyer disappeared. He'd recount his conversations with Beale and Anna Esparza that seemed to credibly explain Beale's recent confrontation with Dwyer, but which also raised intriguing possibilities involving Esparza's family. He'd also explain how he was pursuing local computer collectors to see if there was any connection between them and the Vanguard monitor that anchored Dwyer's body.

Finally, he'd give Kerrigan what she seemed to want from him, a demonstration of his impartiality regarding Shelby Dwyer. She'd seemed mistrusting and suspicious that they'd known each other for so long. But he'd tell her how, after following Shelby to the used computer store the morning after she was notified of her husband's murder, he'd set out to verify her story of the night her husband disappeared. He'd tell her how he tracked down Eric Barbaric, who handled the resale of Shelby Dwyer's Apple computer. There was a good chance the machine or its hard drive was still somewhere in the local computer marketplace, possibly intact. If he could locate it, the information embedded in its memory might confirm or refute her alibi that she was working on her computer the first night Paul didn't come home.

He also needed to update her on the toxicology report. Eckel had called his cell at 6:00 a.m. with interesting news.

That was all he had. He'd generated possibilities. He'd planted some seeds. But he needed a break in the case. Soon.

He sipped Winchell's coffee and scheduled his day until the clock said 7:30, then walked to her office. She waved him in just as she was hanging up the phone.

"County fire," she said by way of greeting. "It's coming our way fast. If we have to evacuate over the next forty-eight hours, we're going to need all hands. The coordination plan is a mess. The communications equipment doesn't interface. Christ."

"Good morning," Starke said.

Kerrigan fanned the pages of a thick bound manual on her desk. "I don't know who put together this emergency response plan—"

She stopped abruptly. Did she know Starke had been on the joint police-fire task force that created the plan? His name was on the cover page.

"Never mind," she said. "I need to shift gears. Fill me in."

He filled her in.

Delgado? "Seems like you've checked everything that can be checked on him personally. Nice work," she said. "Even if his Vegas story holds up, could he have hired it out?"

Starke made a note. Contract murder cases usually broke when someone snitched. Chasing down that possibility based on her hunch would be a long, probably impossible process. Still, he added it to his list.

Beale and Esparza? "There could be something there," she said. "Did their stories sound rehearsed?"

"No. And I checked the local paper. There was an obit for Beale's wife, and the dates match up with what he said. My gut tells me the love story part will hold up. But Dwyer was pissing in both of their punch bowls, so I'm still looking at Beale, and her. Plus, her family and its construction business has some interesting connections to the Dwyer family, so I'm running that down, too."

A look crossed Kerrigan's face that Starke couldn't immediately decipher. "Construction business?"

"Esparza & Sons Excavation and Construction. You may know them by reputation."

Kerrigan offered a blank stare.

"Or maybe not," he said. "Local family? Sinaloa roots. Huge in the construction trades around here? Same basic management philosophy as the cartels."

"Meaning?"

"Headbusters. Cross them, and you're in for a world of hurt."

Kerrigan suddenly reached for her inbox and plucked a paper from the top of the pile. Starke had noticed the letterhead when he first sat down. Even upside down, he could clearly read the words DEA Intelligence Report.

"When you said construction—" she said.

Kerrigan focused on the report in her hand. She read the entire thing in silence, all four pages, occasionally nodding as she did. Finally: "I'll be damned."

Starke waited.

"It's an advisory," she said at last. "DEA. Unclassified. Just came across this morning."

"About?"

Kerrigan began to read, even the acronyms, from the first page: "Mexican transnational criminal organizations (TCOs) pose the greatest criminal drug threat to the United States; no other group is currently positioned to challenge them. These Mexican poly-drug organizations traffic heroin, methamphetamine, cocaine, and marijuana throughout the United States, using established transportation routes and distribution networks, many across, or under, the California-Mexico border. They are moving to expand their share, particularly in the heroin and methamphetamine markets. The Sinaloa Cartel maintains the most significant presence in the United States. They are the dominant TCO along the West Coast, through the Midwest, and into the Northeast.

The DEA projects its presence to grow in the United States over the next year."

"Not exactly a news flash," Starke said.

She glared across the desk. "Except then there's this."

She opened her lap drawer, grabbed a yellow highlighter and upcapped it, made a half dozen aggressive strokes across the DEA advisory, and handed it across the desk. Starke scanned the highlighted portions.

> *Based on information developed by a joint task force of DEA and local police agencies, the Sinaloa group has been partnering with established, legal, US-based companies to build and maintain the infrastructure required for the unimpeded flow of supply across the border, including an elaborate tunnel system thought to exist between Tijuana and San Diego.*

Kerrigan interrupted his reading. "The Esparzas have a lot of heavy equipment, I assume? Digging machines?"

Starke saw where she was heading, but something about her hunch struck him as off-key. He'd had the same thoughts after the late-night burrito conversation with his dad, and he'd made a call to one of his DEA contacts. The Esparzas were dirty, alright, and the agency was close to connecting the dots between the family's US businesses and the Sinaloa cartel. Just a matter of time, the DEA guy said. But he also said the Esparzas did legitimate business with a lot of Southern California builders, not just Dwyer Development. It was what made Esparza & Sons perfect for hiding money.

Could there be a criminal connection to Paul Dwyer's company? His charitable foundation? His murder? Starke flashed to the news story he'd just read about the eight dead tunnel rats in Otay Mesa, and the brutal clip of videotaped torture of a rival released by the same organization.

"You saw the reports about the Otay Mesa murders, right? And their latest video?"

Kerrigan nodded.

Starke's doubts crystallized into words. "The Sinaloa boys don't use heavy equipment. Too big. Too obvious. It's less risky to snatch barrio kids to do the work by hand. And when they're done—" He formed his right hand into the shape of a pistol and aimed it at the base of his skull.

The police chief looked away. "Animals."

"It's a big leap to link all that to Dwyer."

"But his development company does business with the Esparzas. And has for years."

"So do a lot of people."

"And Dwyer's daughter—" She stalled, grasping for a name.

"Chloe."

"She has a personal relationship with someone from that family."

"Also true."

Kerrigan stared. Starke scribbled a few fresh lines in his notebook. Her questions were legitimate. Coming from someone else, he might actually have thought them insightful. Not that he'd ever say that.

"I'll nose around," he said. "Even if there's no Sinaloa connection, it's possible they got crossways with Dwyer on some developer-contractor thing. Or the family things."

"You think it's a detour," Kerrigan said.

"No. You're right. They've done business for years, so there's a complicated history. And Dwyer *was* hound-dogging Anna, and her family knew about it. Sounds like her dad may have felt disrepected. It's just a whole new channel of posibilities, and running them down will take more time. I can make more calls."

"Share the load with Susan Garza. Just because you're the lead detective—"

"I get it."

"She's feeling marginalized."

"I *get* it," he repeated. "But if you'll let me finish the debrief, I think—"

Kerrigan sat back in her chair. "Of course."

He flipped back through his notes, mentioning covetous neighbor Craig Demott as a follow-up possibility before offering one last thought, the computer-collector lead.

"Long shot," Kerrigan said.

Long shot? Starke leaned forward. "It's the single most compelling piece of physical evidence we have right now," he said. "That old monitor is rare, there's a limited number of them in existence, and it links directly to the killer. I think it could be important."

Kerrigan shrugged. "Or like I said, it could be something somebody picked up at a garage sale. But you prioritize your time any way you see fit. I assume you're focusing on local collectors?"

Starke nodded.

"What else?"

He sat forward. "Turns out the guy that's helping me track collectors around here handled the computer Shelby Dwyer sold the morning after Paul vanished. I'm working with him to track it down."

Kerrigan stared. "You mentioned that idea before. Seems

like a long way to go to get some marginal information. What am I missing here?"

Starke took a deep, calming breath. "Remember, Shelby Dwyer says she stayed home the night Paul disappeared, worked on her computer for a couple of hours, then went to bed. Then, the next day, she dumps the computer, an Apple, at a local used-computer store and buys a PC. And she goes back to that store three weeks later, after his body turns up, asking about what happened to it, if there might still be information on it, that sort of thing."

"And you're thinking what?"

"Nothing about that story that makes sense to me," Starke said. "Nobody dumps a perfectly good computer to replace it with an equivalent machine. People upgrade, but that's not what this was. And why would she suddenly get paranoid about it after the body turned up? If her old computer is a blank slate, we get nothing. If it's not, though—I don't know. Maybe she created a file or sent an e-mail that night that's time-stamped. That would confirm her story. Or not."

Kerrigan seemed to consider the possibilities. "Interesting," she said, "but flawed. We don't have an exact time of death. He could have been killed anytime between the last time he was seen at his office and—" She closed her eyes. "What was the coroner's best guess again?"

"Two and a half to three weeks in the water."

"Right. So there's a potential three- or four-day lag in the timeline. Knowing what she was doing that particular night, when her husband may or may not have been killed, I'm just not sure that tells us much."

She was right. Starke couldn't fault her for her mind.

"I'm still gonna pursue it," he said. "Paul suspected she was having an affair, remember? When I pushed her about how she knew Paul was shot, she shut down fast until she could call an attorney. It just makes me think the computer could be another piece of the puzzle. Maybe we'll find proof of an affair on it and we can leverage that to open her up."

"Anything new from forensics?"

"I phoned you about the Taser, right? And that he was tied up at some point?"

She nodded. "Got it. Tox?"

Starke flipped to his notes from his last cell conversation with Eckel. "That's new. Just got the call before I came in: heavy dose of sedatives." He paused. "Rohypnol."

"Roofies? The date-rape drug?"

Starke nodded.

"Now there's a switch," she said. "So that explains how the killer got him tied up."

"Roofies dissolve fast," he said. "I'm thinking maybe it started with a drink or two with his killer. Dwyer was a drinker, we know that. Meets somebody he knows for dinner. He gets up to take a piss, comes back to a spiked drink."

"Clear premeditation. That'll be nice to have in court." Kerrigan sipped from her Starbucks cup. "You've checked his calendar for that night, I assume?"

Starke nodded. "Blank. Which actually might tell us a lot."

Kerrigan looked confused.

"We know booze wasn't Dwyer's only vice, right?" he said. "He wasn't particularly conscientious about his marriage vows. But 'evening with mistress' isn't the sort of thing you log into your office calendar. Shelby says he wasn't home most nights. Not many of his nights were 'scheduled,' either."

Kerrigan leaned forward. "Now that's promising," she said. "You're tracking the women?"

"Just got the tox report an hour ago, but I'll start as soon as we're done here."

"Then again," she said, "how does that seduced-to-his-death scenario fit with everything else we know about this? The torture, the execution, transporting the body up the hill to the pond. Does any of that say female to you?"

"No." Starke hesitated, then couldn't help himself. "But we're going to build this case on physical evidence, not guesswork and assumptions."

Kerrigan narrowed her gaze, recognizing her own words as he echoed them back to her. Starke had seen that same look on dogs about to bite. He was glad she let the comment pass, but knew he'd just undone any goodwill his sparkling debrief might have earned. He imagined her putting another note in his personnel file.

"I'll be focused on this fire for the next couple of days," Kerrigan said, her voice even despite what he saw in her eyes. She gave the emergency-management manual a contemptuous little shove across her desk. "We might as well be operating without a plan."

He stared her down. "This isn't the first fire we've handled here, Chief. Some of us have handled a lot of them, and we put everything we learned over the years down on paper. It's all right there, the collected wisdom of people who know this community a lot better than you."

"It's disorganized and unprofessional," she said.

Starke gathered his things and stood up. "You already got the job," he said. "You can stop campaigning for it."

He turned around and didn't look back.

37

Shelby laid the gun on the kitchen counter and fumbled into the space behind her cookbooks for a cigarette. She usually smoked about three a week. This would be her third of the morning.

Through the window above the sink, she surveyed the wide deck, the patio table, and the half dozen chaise lounges rimming the pool, three on each long side. The two towering palm trees stood like gangly sentinels just beyond, the signature of the hilltop estate Paul had dubbed Twin Palms even when it was nothing more than a blueprint. Beyond that, the craggy profile of Mt. San Gorgonio rose in the near distance. She loved this view, even with the mountain obscured by the yellow-brown wildfire haze. She'd designed the kitchen window to perfectly frame it, and envisioned a view much like it long before she had the means to afford it. Now she savored it, maybe for the last time, believing the life she'd imagined was nearly over.

Ding!

The unlit cigarette still in hand, Shelby turned toward the familiar sound of Chloe's phone signaling an incoming message. She couldn't imagine her daughter had gone to bed without it. Chloe usually fell asleep with it in her hand, and often began texting and poking and liking and otherwise digichattering the second she woke up. But the funeral had been a day-long stressor for them both, and her daughter had trudged upstairs exhausted not long after they got home.

Ding!

The phone wasn't on the far counter where they kept the chargers, but Chloe's purse was on the breakfast table. Shelby set down her cigarette and turned off her lighter, the nearest burner on her six-burner stove. The blue flame disappeared back into the vast, brushed-stainless beast.

For the past year, Shelby had tried to walk the difficult line between responsible motherhood and her daughter's need for independence. She made a point of getting to know Chloe's close friends and their parents, occasionally snooped at her browser history on the home computer and her tablet, peeked into bedroom drawers while Chloe was at school. She'd been proud of her restraint the day two months ago when she found a prescription for birth control pills tucked into a pocket of her high-school agenda book. Chloe was, after all, seventeen. But her daughter rebuffed gentle queries about who she'd been seeing, dismissing archaic words like "dating" and "boyfriend" with a contempuous roll of her eyes. Backing off seemed like the right thing to do at the time; Chloe was just following her mother's cardinal rule about avoiding an unwanted pregnancy, a talk they'd first had the day Chloe got her period. But now Shelby wondered.

Ding!

Shelby reached for the purse, a distressed-leather shoulderbag Chloe had picked up on El Paseo during one of their Palm Desert shopping trips. Its mouth yawned open, exposing a knot of teen debris. Gum. Blush. Tic-Tacs. The phone had to be in there somewhere; she could see its touchscreen glowing somewhere near the bottom. Shelby dug in, at one point pushing aside what she first thought was a tube of eyeliner. It was thin and metallic blue, and she pulled it out to take a closer look. It smelled of cannabis oil. An electronic vaporizer.

Christ. When had Chloe started that? What other secrets did she have?

She set the device on the table and continued to dig, finally pulling the phone from the depths. She entered the number of their street address; Shelby used the same password to unlock her own phone. The screen opened to Chloe's Instagram account.

Shelby had sat out that particular phase of the digital revolution. Instagram, Snapchat, Vine, YikYak—who could keep up? But she knew how to scroll.

The just-posted photo had been uploaded by Chloe's friend Ashlyn. Shelby didn't recall seeing Ashlyn at the memorial service, but assumed she was there. The two girls were practically inseparable, and had been since middle school. The photo was taken from the back of the church and captured the awkward moment when her daughter leaned from the aisle into a pew to hug a striking young man, the one who'd introduced himself afterward as Mario Esparza. Ashlyn's typed message was both cryptic and distressingly clear: "**sexyashgirl** wonders if #horndog @

chloedweeb can at least wait til the funeral's ovr to get some? #nympho #domenow"

Shelby scrolled to the next photo, a picture of the ravaged buffet table that Chloe herself had taken and posted at the end of the reception. The photo after that was a shot of the same buffet, untouched and sumptuous, just before the guests began arriving at the Los Colmas Country Club. Despite Shelby's warnings about oversharing in the electronic universe, her daughter was reflexively posting a running commentary of her life, image by image, for god-knew-who-all to see. But Chloe was no different than anyone else her age.

Shelby flicked her finger up the screen and days and weeks of posted images flew past. Unknown friends in high school landscapes. Cryptic messages full of account handles and code and hashtags and gibberish. A shot of a coffeetable in an unfamiliar home, its surface crowded with beer cans, bottles of Captain Morgan rum and Jose Cuervo tequila, exotic glass and ceramic bongs. They told the story of the life her daughter led somewhere off her mother's radar. Shelby scrolled on with a mix of dread and resignation. She'd been a kid once, too.

One of the images jumped out as it flashed past, a glimpse of strobe-lit flesh against a dark background. Shelby stopped and scrolled back, centering the photo on her daughter's smartphone screen for a closer look. Six weeks before, the phone's camera had caught a shirtless Mario Esparza at night. His smile was magnetic, but his hair was slicked and his upper torso glistening, as if he'd just climbed out of a pool. The waistband of his boxers defined the bottom edge of the image, and it was entirely possible that was all he was wearing. Chloe had taken and posted the photo, writing: "**chloedweeb** Oops, #mrmuscles got wet. Mmmmm." Her words were followed by a happy face emoticon, winking.

Seventeen going on twenty-five, Shelby thought. Hoo-boy. She sure hoped her daughter had filled that prescription.

Shelby started to put the phone back in her daughter's purse when a detail from the troubling image stopped her. She looked closer. The smartphone camera's flash had caught the rough edge of something to the young man's left, a pale gray, vertical surface that entered the frame near his hip and bent out of the frame somewhere above his head. Shelby zoomed in tighter. The surface was flecked with sparkles and etched with indecipherable words and initials. She zoomed closer, only to see the details dissolve into nothing. She backed it out and looked again, and immediately recognized the surface as that of a graffiti-scarred granite boulder, the one at a once-remote spot in the foothills where generations of local high school kids had gone to party, the one where so many had memorialized their good times and summer loves.

The one beside a secluded, disappearing pond.

38

Shelby was upstairs looking for Boz when she heard Chloe's scream. She rushed to the window of her bedroom and was relieved to see her daughter standing in her pajamas, alone at the edge of the backyard pool. Her daughter cupped one hand over her mouth and flapped the other arm like a wounded bird. She screamed again.

Shelby prayed as she ran down the stairs.

Ten minutes before, Chloe had stumbled into the kitchen to find the contents of her purse spread across the kitchen table. Shelby said nothing as her daughter calmly gathered up her things and returned them to the shoulderbag. When she was done, all she said was, "Nice, Mom."

"I feel like I hardly know you," she said.

Her only child glared. "About as well as I know you."

To break the standoff, she'd asked Chloe to help her find Boz. His food and water bowls were still full, and that was unusual. For a creaky, fourteen-year-old golden, he still ate well. On hot days like this, he sometimes stood chest deep on the pool steps, or lay in the shallow water on the top step. At his most energetic, he swam a few tight circles and struggled back out to shake. He had a few favorite hidey holes in the house and yard, but Shelby had checked all of them and still couldn't find him. Chloe headed outside as Shelby climbed the curving foyer staircase to check upstairs.

When Shelby rushed up, Chloe's hand was still covering her mouth as she stared into the pool's deep end. She pointed to a golden patch against the pool bottom far below the undulating surface and wailed, "Oh God oh God oh God."

Shelby looked closer. The dog was on its side on the bottom, its long fur shimmering in the late morning sunlight and swaying like a small patch of golden seaweed in the pool's deep currents. A band of gray encircled his white muzzle. She also could see something else beside him, sitting flat on the bottom near the drain. She tried to make sense of it through the wind-rippled surface.

"Oh baby," she said, pulling Chloe into a hug.

Chloe sobbed into her mother's shoulder as Shelby studied the rippling image. When she stopped, Chloe said: "He had trouble climbing the steps the other day after he swam. Maybe with his arthritis he couldn't get out?"

The wind slowed for a moment, then stopped altogether. The pool's surface smoothed. Shelby stood at the edge and felt her world start to spin. Chloe looked down as well.

"What *is* that?" Chloe said.

In that still instant, Shelby knew. It was "Flight," submerged amid a tangle of ropes that also looped around the lifeless body of their beloved dog.

It was an anchor.

Shelby turned Chloe away from the pool and walked her back toward the house. *How the hell was he getting in?*

"Mom? What's going on?"

Chloe pulled away. Tears had left trails down both sides of her face, but sudden anger had replaced grief. "What the hell is going on, Mom? Who would do that?"

Shelby had no answer.

"Who would do that to Boz?"

"I don't know, baby."

When Shelby tried to push on into the house, Chloe grabbed the sleeve of her robe and spun her around. "What aren't you telling me? What is going *on?*"

Shelby stood mute in front of her daughter. What could she possibly say that would make sense of this?

"I'm calling the police," Chloe said.

Shelby stepped between Chloe and the open slider. "You can't."

"Bull*shit*," Chloe spat. "It's the same thing that happened to Dad. This is seriously fucked up."

"Stop. Watch your language."

Chloe stood trembling. Fright? Rage? Both? Her dog's death clearly was hitting her much harder than her father's. "Watch my language?" she screamed. "Watch my fucking *language?*"

"Chloe—"

"You don't want to call the police? After somebody drowns our dog?"

"I can't—"

"You promised me. You said you'd tell me everything." Chloe grabbed Shelby by the shoulders and shook her. "First Dad. Now Boz?"

Shelby's world spun faster. She tried her best to pull away, to run into the house to hide from her daughter's anger, her secret shame, and a one-time fantasy who could enter her life at will, but whose name and face she might never know. There was nowhere to hide, though. Nowhere at all.

She retreated and collapsed into one of the chairs at the kitchen table. Her daughter followed, not bothering to close the slider against the outside heat, and took the chair across from her. Chloe shoved her purse and phone out of the way.

"The truth, Mom. Everything. Now."

39

Richard Holywell returned Starke's latest call while Starke debriefed Kerrigan in her office. He'd turned off his cell, but when he checked messages he found the latest volley of voicemail ping-pong from Kerrigan's ex. The phone number he left this time was different than the home number Starke had in his notes, probably his office, so he knew the next call might actually connect.

Starke gathered his thoughts. Should he return the call again? He retreated to a conference room down the hall that had a door, closed it, and dialed. It rang only once before a woman picked up.

"UltraSharp Digital. Please hold."

He recognized the company name from the couple's divorce documents, but wrote it down next to Holywell's name and circled it. When the receptionist returned, he asked for Holywell.

"One moment please."

The next voice was different, male, but just as efficient: "Mr. Holywell's office. This is Gerard. How may I help you?"

Starke cleared his throat. "Richard Holywell, please. My name is Ron. We've swapped phone messages couple times on his home phone, and he asked me to call him here."

Basically true. There was an officious rustling of papers. "I'm sorry, Mr. Holywell is in a meeting at the moment. May I ask what this is regarding?"

Starke made a choice. He was a big believer in listening to the universe if it was trying to tell him something. He'd felt queasy about contacting Kerrigan's former husband in the first place. Three missed connections was a sign.

"No, no message," he said. "And please tell him to disregard my previous messages. No callback necessary. Would you do that for me?"

"You sure?"

"Yep. Thanks."

Starke felt lighter when he hung up. He'd just have to find another way to deal with Nurse Ratched.

Back in his office, he stared at his notebook for a moment before opening the file containing Kerrigan's divorce papers. Thumbing through the pages, he found one of the early filings that described UltraSharp Digital, Holywell's business. He tried to make sense of the corporate description.

UltraSharp was "a tightly focused Santa Monica-based subsidiary of Pei Lan Electronics," which the document described as "a multinational leader in the field of computer hardware and technology" based in Taiwan. Holywell was president of UltraSharp, but Holywell's phrasing made clear that, in the grand scheme, he considered his company an insignificant node on a far more glorious mother ship.

Funny thing about contesting assets in a community-property state, Starke thought. Men are never more eager to downplay their success. And based on his willingness to resurrect the gun incident at their home, Holywell wasn't shy about protecting his assets.

Starke closed the file, set it in the middle of his desk, and wheeled the task chair around in front of his desktop computer. He pulled up the Google search screen. He was picking up another faint signal from the universe, and wanted to check out a hunch.

40

As Shelby told her story, Chloe sat with her arms folded across her chest, staring into a middle distance between the kitchen table and the cooking island. Even with everything Chloe already knew about the problems in her parents' marriage, Shelby could almost feel what was left of her daughter's remaining teenage innocence crumble and fall away. The story Chloe was hearing now was something she never could have imagined.

"It really started that night last summer, that night with the gun, right there." Shelby pointed to a spot on the kitchen floor. "In my mind, that's the exact place and the exact moment my marriage ended. Nothing was ever going to be the same."

"It never was," Chloe said, eyes still focused on nothing.

"Until then, it had been just a goof, a flirty conversation with this guy I'd met online," Shelby said. "We'd been talking for months, and I could tell he was falling in love with me. I encouraged it, baby, because I needed to feel loved. But that night with your father, that tipping point, that's what set the whole thing sliding."

"I don't get it."

"After that happened, I told him everything," Shelby said. "*Everything*. Dad's drinking. The violence. The other women. How I was sure your dad would've killed us both that night last summer if I hadn't unloaded the gun. I let my anger pour out. He just listened, like he always did. That was the most seductive part of it—he really seemed to care. That's when it all turned a corner. When I was done, he asked me how I wanted it to end. That's when I let myself imagine, let him imagine, a day when your dad was just... not around. I wished there was a magic wand to make the pain go away. He asked if that was what I really wanted. A few weeks later, Dad disappeared."

Shelby saw no need to tell her the rest, how she'd seen the brutal final act on screen, as it happened.

"So you don't know anything about him?"

"You have to understand, baby, for me he was a fantasy. I didn't want details. Reality ruins fantasy. If I knew he was tall or short, or fat or skinny, or rich or poor, then I couldn't create him from scratch. He couldn't be what I needed him to be—this perfect man, always willing to listen, to empathize, to be there for me. I didn't really want to know. He seemed to know that."

Chloe finally turned enough in her chair that Shelby could see her vacant eyes. "So even if you wanted to tell the police, you don't know anything?"

Shelby nodded.

Chloe started to cry. "But all that time you were telling him everything about *us*?"

Shelby swallowed hard. "He knew enough to find Dad. He knows where we live. He knows I'm the only person who could possibly link him to what happened, and he's trying to make sure I don't tell anybody what I know. Which is pretty much nothing anyway. So what would be the point of me telling the police about Boz? Plus, after he did what he did, I said some things.... I made him angry. At least this way—"

Chloe stood up. She was furious in a way Shelby had never seen before. "Mom, he got into our house. The alarm system was on, and he still got in." She pointed through the glass doors out to the pool. "He killed our dog. He could do the same to you if he wanted. To me. He's not gonna go away."

Shelby buried her face in her hands. "I can't believe this."

"Even *I* know not to hook up online with strangers," she said.

"We didn't 'hook up,'" Shelby said, standing so she was face to face with her daughter. "I was *never* unfaithful to your father."

Chloe rolled her eyes. "That's sooo pathetic."

Shelby heard the sound first, the sharp report of flesh on flesh. Chloe's head snapped to one side, then slowly rotated back. Her cheek was red with the imprint of her mother's palm, and only then did Shelby realize what she'd done.

"Perfect," Chloe said.

"Don't judge me. Just... don't. You don't know everything I went through, the way your father treated me, the other women. I was entitled to a few hours of happiness. Even if it was alone at night on the computer in my office. Even if it was wrong."

They were both crying now, both staring across a gulf

of anger and mistrust and fear. Shelby reached for her daughter's face, hoping a gentle touch could ease the sting.

Chloe put her own hand over Shelby's and held it there. "Even—"

Shelby watched her only child struggle to articulate a thought. When Chloe finally did, Shelby wished she hadn't done it so well.

"Even if you hooked up with someone who doesn't even exist?"

41

The website of UltraSharp Digital was far less modest about its role in the world of technology than Holywell had been in his divorce filing. True, it was a small US-based subsidiary of a Taiwanese electronics giant, but that wasn't always the case. Starke was fascinated by the story he found in the site's "Corporate History" link.

Pei Lan Electronics had bought the small US firm only three years earlier, after UltraSharp introduced and began marketing a breakthrough technology that both sharpened and brightened the high-definition screens found in most computers and flat-screen TVs. It was so effective that Dell, Hewlett-Packard, IBM, and other computer makers, along with Vizio and Samsung, immediately licensed the UltraSharp technology and started using it in their own machines. Success made the company ripe for takeover, and Pei Lan swept in with a generous offer that brought UltraSharp under its corporate umbrella. That deal left UltraSharp's long-time management in place, including

CEO Richard Holywell, who founded the company in the early 1990s.

Starke wasn't entirely sure what to make of it. The assets listed in Kerrigan's divorce papers weren't shockingly large, but they weren't exactly modest either. Holywell's company probably fit the profile of a lot of small tech companies that struggle along for years before a breakthrough product puts it on the map. If Holywell was still working, his cut of the deal must not have been enough to bail out. Starke wondered how that corporate drama played into the downfall of Kerrigan's marriage. Was Holywell one of those tech-industry workaholics whose sole focus was his company? Had Kerrigan finally drawn the line after too many late nights alone?

Starke's ringing cell phone distracted him from his sophomoric, obsessive prying. He glanced at the unfamiliar number of the incoming call.

"Detective Starke," he said.

"Hi. It's me."

Starke had no idea who it was until a hoarse and strangled *rowf-rowf* in the background triggered a lusty, "Shut *up*, Churchill," from the caller.

"Eric?"

"I'm telling you: pugs—spawn of Satan."

Starke smiled. "So noted."

"Anyway, I found your thing."

"Which thing?"

"That Apple."

Shelby Dwyer's dumped computer? Damn. Eric Barbaric worked fast. "That's great," Starke said, dampening the excitement in his voice. "Do you have it now?"

"I'd traded it and a couple of monitors to my friend Reg, and he was planning to parts it out to our friend Dirk, but Dirk's girlfriend is this, like, psychopath and took off with his car two weekends ago, so he's been dealing with that and the thing's been sitting in his bedroom all this time. So, yeah."

Starke was completely lost. "But you have it there right now?"

"Yeah, like I said."

Starke had had more coherent conversations with schizophrenics. "Eric, listen to me. Have you tried turning it on? Is there anything on it?"

"Gimme a sec."

Starke waited an eternity, the silence punctuated only by the raspy, two-pack-a-day bark of Churchill the inherited pug.

"Nothing," Barbaric said.

"Nothing?"

"Nope."

Starke heard some furious typing, imagined Barbaric surveying hidden pockets and levels of code he couldn't possibly comprehend. "So basically, you're saying she reformatted the hard drive before she sold it?"

"Looks that way." A pause. "I can keep the hundred bucks, right?"

"Can you show me? I'll run over there now and—"

"Whoa. Hang on."

Starke heard a low, sustained whistle on the other end of the line. He sat forward in his chair.

"Haven't seen one of these in a while," Barbaric said. "Dang."

Starke waited for the start of another loopy detour.

Instead, Barbaric followed up with a single phrase: "CarbonCopy."

"What's that?"

"*Some*body was spying," he said. He hummed the opening notes of the "Dragnet" theme.

Starke wanted to leap through the phone and grab the kid by the throat. Instead, he drew a deep breath and said, "Eric, please tell me what you're talking about."

"It's this little thing. Keylogger hardware. Most people use keylogger software, but this little thing, it's hardware. I've only seen a couple of them, like, ever. But here it is, on the end of the keyboard plug, where it sticks into the box. Just noticed it. So somebody was spying on somebody."

"From the beginning again, Eric. Please. What are you talking about?"

An exasperated sigh. "Say your kid's spending a lot of time locked in his room with his computer, right? You think he's in there scoping out naughtybits.com or something, only you can't say for sure, right? But you don't want him spending all his homework time jerkin' the gherkin, so you decide to see exactly what he's doing in there all day and night. There's two ways to find out. One is a software program. CarbonCopy makes one of those, too. That's called keylogger software. You just install it on the computer and it records every keystroke—e-mails sent, messaging, logins, passwords, chat conversations, web history, screen snapshots. Everything."

The possibilities brought Starke to full attention in his chair. "You're saying that software was on this computer?"

"I didn't say that."

Patience. "Tell me what you're saying, then, please."

"The other way is with keylogger hardware. It's this little thingy, about the size of a flash drive. It's a plug. You plug the keyboard plug into it, then plug that into the computer. It just does its thing without anybody ever noticing, unless they check the keyboard plug, which nobody ever does. Woot! Junior's busted."

"So that's what you found. One of these little spying devices? And it was on this computer?"

"Bingo. Give me a sec and I can check the specs."

Starke hadn't prayed much after Rosaleen, but he found himself giving thanks. He shuddered, suddenly, to think of that potentially critical piece of evidence sitting among the flotsam and jetsam of Eric Barbaric's inherited house.

"Five hundred thousand," Barbaric said.

"Five hundred thousand what, Eric?"

Another impatient sigh. "Keystrokes. That's its capacity. Anywhere from a couple of days to a full month of data, depending. Want me to download it for you?"

Starke grabbed his notebook and shield from his desk. "Listen to me carefully, Eric. I'm leaving now. Wait until I get there. I need to be able to watch what you do with this thing. I need to be there when you do it. So give me about fifteen minutes, and make sure you keep that thing in a safe place until then. It could be very important. Understand?"

"Geez, don't get all CSI on me."

"Just tell me you understand. Tell me you'll wait 'til I get there."

"OK. Geez."

Starke hung up. He was reaching for his car keys when he noticed Kerrigan standing, arms folded, in the middle of his office doorway staring at his computer screen. He followed her gaze across the small space to his monitor, which still displayed the home page of UltraSharp Digital. He leaned across his desk chair, a transparently acrobatic move, and grabbed his mouse. The open window disappeared in one frantic click. Had she seen it?

Kerrigan uncrossed her arms. "Heading out?"

"Shelby Dwyer's computer," he said. "I think we've found it."

He moved toward the door.

Kerrigan stood her ground for an excruciating moment before stepping aside. As he brushed past her, she said, "Let's plan to talk when you get back."

42

They were fighting a killer who didn't exist. Chloe had said it perfectly. Still, Shelby said, they were going to fight. Their house would be their bunker, even if he'd already penetrated it once.

"The driveway gate," Shelby said. "I just called the security company and let them know I'd changed the code. I changed the access code for the house alarm, too. Remember the new numbers?"

Chloe nodded.

"Anytime we go anywhere, the alarm needs to be set. No exceptions. We'll set it at night when we go to bed, too, so the motion detectors are active. Dad put in all this sophisticated stuff when he built the place, and we need to learn how to use it. It's worthless unless we use it. Clear?"

Shelby led her daughter through the foyer to the front door, feeling a sense of dread as she passed the empty space where "Flight" once stood. Chloe seemed to feel it, too.

"We can't leave Boz down there, Mom. We have to do something."

Shelby nodded, but had no idea what to say.

"Two locks," she said, grasping the door handle. A wispy swirl of white ash eddied in on the opening door's air currents. "Internal deadbolt and external deadbolt. I have no idea how he got around the alarm system last time, but anytime we're in the house I want both of these locked behind us. And on the sliders out back, it's not enough to flip the handle lock. Make sure you slide the metal bar into the track behind the door. That way there's no chance it can be opened from the outside."

"OK."

Shelby dragged a toe through the gathering ash as she shut the door. "If we have to leave because of the fire, we'll just find a safe place for a few days and not tell anybody where we're going. The schools would be closed anyway."

Chloe's face had a helpless, hopeless look. "This is so fucked up. What makes you think he'll stop after a few days? This could go on forever."

Again, Shelby had nothing to say, no reassurances to offer her only child. What options did they have? The man who was terrorizing them was no more tangible than the whirl of ash at her feet.

She stepped to her left, to the small table that had served as the base for "Flight." Opening the top drawer, she summoned Chloe to her side. "Dad's gun is in here now," she said. "At night we'll keep it upstairs with us. But during the day, it'll be down here."

Chloe's eyes were wide and disbelieving. "You can't be serious."

"I'll show you how to use it, just like Dad showed me. Just in case."

"Mom," Chloe said, "this is just nuts."

Shelby hit the release and the magazine dropped into her palm. It was filled with .45 caliber shells. "Ready?"

43

Eric Barbaric was standing guard at the front door of his house when Starke pulled up. He was holding the wheezing pug under one arm like a football. As Starke stepped out of the car, the kid grinned the grin of someone who knows he just aced a test.

"Nice job on this, Eric," Starke said. "This could be very important."

"There could be nothing on it, you know. You wouldn't let me check. It could have been wiped, too, just like the hard drive."

Starke hadn't thought of that. He reached out and scratched the walleyed Churchill's forehead. The smoke was complicating Churchill's already difficult breathing. "Why don't we go in and you can show me what you found?"

He followed Barbaric through the minefield of thrashed skate shoes, broken skateboard decks, and unopened junk mail between the front door and the kitchen table. An Apple desktop was up and running on the table, and Starke had a hard time taking his eyes off it. Still, he noticed the gentle way the kid carried the dog to the couch and laid him prone on a dirty cushion. Churchill panted on, his tongue lolling to one side like a pink lava flow.

"You're sure this is the right computer?" Starke said.

"It's the only one I got from Jason that week," Barbaric said, unfolding a Silicon Recycler sales receipt.

Starke checked the date: two days after Paul Dwyer disappeared. "So Samani flipped it right away? He sold it to you the day after he bought it?"

Barbaric nodded. "He doesn't sell Apples, like I said, so calls me right away whenever he gets one."

Starke studied the receipt. "There's no price here."

"I don't buy them," he said. "Do I look like I have the money to buy them?"

"So you have sort of a consignment deal?"

Barbaric shrugged. "What's a consignment deal?"

"He gives you the Apples to sell, and you give him the money after you sell them."

Barbaric straightened and squared his shoulders. "Yes, I have a consignment deal." He waggled his thin eyebrows. "Because *I* have the connections."

"And you just take a percentage of whatever you can sell them for?"

"Twelve percent. Sucks, I know, but better than nothing. I'd sold this one to Dirk, but he didn't pay me yet, because of the psycho girlfriend-slash-car situation, so I just went and got it back from him."

Starke clarified the correct spelling of Dirk's full name and wrote it down in his notebook in case chain of custody ever became an issue. When he was done, he said, "Can you show me this CarbonCopy thing?"

From the far side of the kitchen table, Barbaric pointed to what looked like a small flashlight battery that connected the keyboard plug into the back of the computer. "This thingy just records the keystrokes and keeps a record in the hard drive."

"But you said the hard drive was reformatted."

"It was."

Starke's hopes faltered. "So there's no way to find out what this little device recorded during the past few days this computer was in use."

"There's nothing in the computer." He tapped the machine. "But the data might still be in here." He tapped the CarbonCopy device. "Wiping the hard drive shouldn't have affected this. Of course, I'd know that by now if you hadn't gone all psycho on the phone."

Starke smiled. "I just needed to be here, Eric. Can we take a look?"

Barbaric grabbed a can of Red Bull from the counter and took a long swig. He tapped the can. "Stuff keeps you sharp." Then he pulled a kitchen chair to the keyboard and hit a few keys. He located the CarbonCopy device, which presented as a detachable drive on the computer's connected-hardware menu. With another click, the device's menu popped onto the screen.

"Still works," Barbaric said.

Starke felt his heart rate rise. He imagined the scenario. Suspicious about why his wife was spending so much time online, Paul Dwyer must have decided to find out what she was up to. He was spying on her, and Shelby had no idea. What else could this be? He felt like he was about to intrude into something intensely private, and yet Shelby had unwittingly released it herself into the vast and very public electronics marketplace. He didn't need a warrant.

"The moment of truth," Starke said. "Anything on it?"

Within seconds, they were looking at a screen full of icons:

E-mail Sent
E-mail Received
Web History
Instant Messages
File Operations
Online Chats
Scheduled Screen Snapshots
Empty Cache

"Let's try the first one, 'e-mail sent,'" Starke said.

Barbaric's command brought up a series of about two dozen short e-mails, most of them concluding with Shelby Dwyer's electronic signature and contact information for the Paul Dwyer Foundation. "Does this look like the right computer?" he said.

The hair on the back of Starke's neck stood at attention. He was suddenly aware that this was something he really needed to do with the department's computer forensics guy. "Sure is," he said. "But I think I'm going to have to take this somewhere else to review it, Eric."

"Really?" The kid's face couldn't have looked more disappointed if Starke had snatched candy from his hand.

"Afraid so. Police business. Procedures and all. Can I call you if I need your help navigating this?"

Barbaric nodded, then started sifting through a

seemingly random pile of papers on the table. He pulled a single sheet from a scattered stack and handed it to Stark. It was a copy of the Silicon Recycler receipt that showed what Samani had paid Shelby Dwyer for her computer on the day after her husband disappeared. "Well," he said, "if you take it I'll need to pay Jason. It's a consignment deal, you know."

Starke couldn't see sticking the kid with the cost while his merchandise was in police custody. "How much?"

Barbaric helpfully tapped the receipt specifying the terms of the sale. "Jason made out. Straight trade, this Apple for a PC." He snorted. "Cha-ching! So he's just out the cost of the shit-for-brains PC."

Barbaric studied the specs of the refurbished PC Shelby Dwyer had taken in trade. "He told me he paid $900, and that looks about right." He looked up hopefully. "Plus my 12 percent." The young man closed his eyes, apparently calculating. "That's $1,008. You could round it to an even thousand if you want."

"That's fine, Eric. I'll just give you a personal check. Will that work?"

Barbaric's disappointment at being undeputized faded with a sure sale in hand. "Will that work, Churchill?" The dog wheezed his assent, and Starke turned to retrieve his checkbook from the car.

44

At the card table in his kitchen, seated on his folding chair, Starke stared at Shelby Dwyer's abandoned computer. As he drove away from Eric Barbaric's house, he'd started second-guessing his decision to wait for the department's forensics guy. A deeper dive into the contents of the keylogger device might raise questions, he knew, especially without a witness on hand. But he'd deal with that in court if he had to. To him, exploring the CarbonCopy device seemed a perfectly reasonable next step in the investigation. How else could he know if this was even a relevant piece of evidence?

With a few clicks of the mouse, he began his journey into the final chapters of Shelby Dwyer's electronic life during the days before her husband vanished and was killed.

He brought up the device's options menu, as he'd seen Barbaric do just an hour before. He clicked the "e-mail sent" option and up popped copies of every e-mail that Shelby Dwyer had sent during the period recorded by the tiny hardware spy. He scanned the dates of the e-mails first, concluding that the device's memory had retained about three days' worth of data. Checking the time-stamps on each e-mail, he also concluded that they had all been sent during the day, before 5:00 p.m., and not at night.

The sent e-mails appeared chronologically from top to bottom, with the most recent e-mail last.

Deacon, please make sure the meeting agenda for next Thursday includes time for a brief overview of the Waymer Education project. It'll come to the Foundation as a formal proposal next month. I at least want the board to be familiar with the idea of the project before they see the actual proposal. Thanks. Shel.

The next half dozen were much the same, specific instructions to staffers at the Dwyer Foundation involving initiatives and projects underway. Starke was fascinated. She seemed to be someone in total control of Paul Dwyer's charitable operations, hardly someone plotting his death. But how did the same personality coexist in a woman who apparently tolerated emotional and sometimes physical abuse from her hard-drinking whore of a husband?

One e-mail went to an old friend who'd grown up with Starke and Shelby in Los Colmas. Starke recognized her e-mail address. She was one of the ringleader moms at the high school, and Shelby's e-mail to her involved Chloe's plans to attend a French Club outing at a creperie in Riverside.

Starke scanned the rest. Nearly all involved the foundation. A few were personal e-mails to people whose names Starke didn't recognize. They seemed to involve the mundane details of managing school schedules or children. One was an electronic birthday card Shelby had sent on Paul's behalf to her husband's mother. Another was a complaint to the manager of a local Neiman Marcus store involving a recently purchased pair of Christian Louboutin shoes.

Nothing she e-mailed out during the three days prior to her husband's disappearance seemed in any way relevant to the supposed affair her husband suspected, or to the circumstances surrounding his murder. On the other hand, nothing in the "e-mail sent" file suggested that Shelby had been reading or writing e-mails on her computer the night Paul first disappeared, as she claimed she'd been doing.

Starke hit the "back" button and returned to the menu of icons, clicking on "e-mail received." Dozens of e-mails popped onto the screen, almost all of them unsolicited spam, free stock tips, or scam appeals by unnamed African potentates offering money for Shelby's assistance in transferring vast amounts into foreign bank accounts. CarbonCopy tracked their unceremonious deletion.

Other than the back-and-forth correspondence with foundation staffers, only three of the received e-mails during the computer's final days in Shelby's office were unique or personal in nature. None of them seemed to suggest an ongoing romance or any sort of conspiracy to harm her husband. Again, though, the time stamps on those e-mails did not back up Shelby's claim to have been working on e-mails at home late the first night Paul disappeared. If she had been working on this machine that night, she hadn't been sending e-mails.

The "back" button again took him to the menu of icons. Starke skipped around. He tried "file operations." It was a listing of all the programs and documents that Shelby had used or accessed during her final three days with this computer. Starke couldn't actually access the programs or documents, since she'd purged all that from the machine before she dumped it. Some of the program types were obvious—word processing, spreadsheet software, calendar, calculator. The document titles meant nothing to him. Shelby Dwyer had been a busy and industrious girl, no question, at least during the day.

The "Online Chats" icon brought up nothing. She had electronically chatted with no one during the machine's final three days in her hands.

Her "Web History" log included about two dozen links. Some were obviously irrelevant—a link to *www.neimanmarcus.com*, probably regarding the shoe complaint, and a link to the local newspapers, probably to scan the day's weather and headlines. But one link jumped out, the last one listed: *https://angelquest.net/LoveSick/mygifttoyou/archive*. He clicked the link, but his router wasn't configured for Shelby's computer. He wrote down the web address and double-checked to make sure he'd copied it correctly. He would check that one later on his own computer, just to see what it was.

Starke returned to the CarbonCopy icon menu. The program's default setting was to record a snapshot of the computer's screen every ten minutes when the computer was in use. Starke clicked on the "scheduled screen snapshots" icon.

He scrolled down the sequence of dozens of captured glimpses of Shelby Dwyer's actual computer monitor, each one time-stamped to show when it was taken. Some were simply shots of e-mails in progress, sent or received, many of which he'd seen in full in the "e-mails sent" and "e-mails received" portions of the CarbonCopy log. None of them were from the night Paul disappeared. Others were of web pages she'd been visiting at that particular moment, and he could triangulate the "web history" links to the screen shots and account for most of those.

The last screen snapshot, though, jolted Starke upright in his chair. He slid forward for a closer look at the tight, disturbing color image of Paul Dwyer's face and neck. He had been turning his head violently as the snapshot was taken, blurring the image, but certain details stood out. Dwyer appeared to be bare-chested. His eyes were wide open. His nostrils flared and his mouth was twisted into a disturbing grimace. His elegant silver hair was an unruly mess.

When Starke saw the time and date stamps on the image, he felt the earth move. The image had been captured at 11:14 p.m. on the first night Paul Dwyer didn't come home, during the two hours Shelby said she was working alone on the computer in her office and wondering where her husband might be. That frozen image of her husband's face, blurred by motion, apparently was one of the last things Shelby saw on this computer before she wiped its hard disk clean and disposed of the machine.

Starke stood up, breathing like a man who'd just run a sprint. He crossed the room, turned, and looked at the image of Paul Dwyer again from a distance. He tried to match the cues on Dwyer's face to the forensic evidence, and to other possibilities along the sweeping spectrum of human emotions. He couldn't imagine another interpretation.

The man was being tortured. On camera. While his wife watched on her home computer.

Another thought: Shelby Dwyer had waited almost

another twenty-four hours to say anything to police. And when she did, it was simply to report him missing.

Starke crossed the room again and clicked his mouse, closing the window. He couldn't look at Dwyer's tormented face any longer. Even after it disappeared, he could see it lingering, if not on his screen, then alive like a ghost image on his retinas. He closed his eyes for a moment, trying to erase what he'd seen.

Starke sat down again. He moved his cursor to the last unchecked icon on the CarbonCopy menu. He clicked on "instant messages" and began to scroll through the keystroke transcripts of Shelby Dwyer's final conversations, which she had apparently conducted anonymously as the avatar LonelyMrs. The conversations were all with the same person, LoveSick.

Starke knew right away that Paul Dwyer had been right. His wife had a secret life online. It was immediately clear from the transcripts, too, that her late-night forays into cyberspace involved an online lover. Many of the conversations with LoveSick, recorded during the three days before Dwyer disappeared, were literate, graphic, and highly sexual, alternating narrations of desperately intimate acts. He scrolled to the middle of one.

LoveSick: *i kiss the inside of your thigh, once, twice, then bury my face in the soft flesh there. i've never felt anything softer. i tell you so. you hook your other leg over my shoulder. ur scent excites me. i trace a path toward the intersection of your legs with the tip of my tongue. u moan as I kiss you there. what do you want? say it. i want to hear u say the words.*

LonelyMrs: *Push. Right... there. I press myself to your mouth, and that pressure alone is enough to make me come. I buck and gasp*

and pull your hair. When I open my eyes, I see you smiling and can tell
my weakness pleases you.

Starke closed his eyes, remembering the last time he'd
made love to Shelby Dwyer. They'd taken a bottle of Cold
Duck up to Shepherdsen's pond and swum naked on a
moonlit night. They'd held each other in the cool water and
the warm air, tried to dance in the mucky bottom of the
shallows, hauled out a blanket and explored one another
for hours. That was nearly twenty years ago. He'd made it
his mission that summer to memorize every inch of her, to
commit the sights and sounds and smells of her to a special
place in his mind, forever. It was all still there. So was the
sting of their parting conversation.

Summer had ended with his love-drunk infatuation
intact. Down deep, he knew Shelby's ambitions went well
beyond him. Still, he'd let himself imagine a future together,
and it hurt when she began to pull away. No explanation;
just weeks after that night at the pond, she stopped taking
his calls. When they saw each other around town, she kept
their conversations cold and distant. Months later, when
he'd had enough Jack Daniels to finally demand an answer,
he caught her off guard one evening as she left the small Los
Colmas home-design firm where she was working. Shelby
delivered a three-word answer freighted with so many levels
of meaning and insult and pain that it left Starke gasping for
breath in the parking lot.

"I was pregnant."

He remembered the air leaving his chest in a rush. When
he recovered, he reached for her hand. "Shel—"

She'd pulled away. "And if you tell anybody, I'll say it
was rape."

Her threat hung in the air as Shelby walked away, and they never talked about it again. Within a year, she'd married Paul Dwyer. A year after that, they had a daughter. He didn't hear from her again until two years ago, when she wrote him the condolence note about Rosaleen.

Starke scrolled deeper into the log of conversations. LonelyMrs never said exactly where she lived in Southern California, but there were references to previous conversations. In some exchanges, Shelby seemed grateful for the chance to rant, mostly about her husband. She alluded to the often miserable details of her life—the indignities Paul heaped on her, the threats and intimidation, the egg-shell wait with Chloe every night as they dreaded him coming home drunk and angry. They'd clearly talked about those things before. Starke noticed that, at least in the three days logged by the CarbonCopy device, LoveSick revealed almost nothing. Just listened. To a woman as distraught and alone as Shelby, Starke imagined that willingness to listen might have been what attracted her most.

Each conversation ended the same way, with LoveSick typing: *i love u in a place beyond space and time.* Sometimes Shelby replied with the same.

Clearly, in terms of accumulated keystrokes, this was where Shelby Dwyer was spending her late-night computer time, talking to and making imaginary love to an avatar named LoveSick. Their back-and-forths went on for pages, artful descriptions of extended scenes, whispered desires, moments of explosive passion. It was the end result of an extended seduction, and theirs seemed like the kind of refined passion that Starke recognized from his years with Rosaleen, and which he'd never been able to equal again in life, certainly not during his own online forays. Those were just titillation, another way, along with watching screwball comedies, to get through his loneliest late-night hours. Shelby's conversations with LoveSick were different. All of it virtual, none of it real, but apparently no less satisfying for either of the people involved.

It was everything Shelby had said her marriage to Paul was not.

Did their affair extend into the real world? Starke found nothing on the transcripts to suggest that it did. But he knew better than most that it probably didn't matter.

He found the second-to-last transcript. It was just a straight conversation. No rants. No professions of love. No sex.

LoveSick: *alone?*

LonelyMrs: *As usual. Paul's out. We both know what that means. Chloe's in bed. Why?*

LoveSick: *i have a gift for u.*

LonelyMrs: *A gift?*

LoveSick: *something you want more than anything. u told me so many times. i listened.*

LonelyMrs: *OK, now I'm intrigued.*

LoveSick: *it'll change your life.*

LonelyMrs: *Now THAT would be nice.*

LoveSick: *hoped u'd see it that way. remember that as we move into this next phase.*

LonelyMrs: *Stop talking in code. Next phase of what?*

LoveSick: *of us.*

LonelyMrs: *Meaning what exactly?*

LoveSick: *https://angelquest.net/LoveSick/mygifttoyou*

LonelyMrs: *I don't get it. What's that?*

LoveSick: *webcam. it's live. go there.*

Starke read the final words of Shelby Dwyer's next-to-last conversation with her online lover. Already his skin was electric. The pieces of a grotesque and unimaginable puzzle fell into place. He closed his eyes, and the screenshot of Paul Dwyer's tortured face popped back into his head, a snapshot of terror captured live via webcam. What else could it have been?

The final entry in the CarbonCopy device's circuitry apparently was logged as Shelby toggled between the webcam site and her messaging window. It was an explosion of blurted horror.

LonelyMrs: *No, no, no, no, no! Not this. Please God no!*

LoveSick: *u wanted your life back. remember? u wished there was a way. there is. my gift to you. after this, we can be together, flesh to flesh.*

LonelyMrs: *No, no, no, no, no. That was just words, not real. Please God no.*

The exchange ended with Shelby Dwyer at her keyboard, typing the last words she may have ever typed on this computer. By the next morning, she had wiped its hard drive clean and sold the machine into the Wild West of the electronics marketplace where Starke had found it. Now he was looking at Shelby's final exchange with her patient online lover, the one who listened so well but revealed so little, the one she trusted beyond reason with details of her life offline—her real life.

LonelyMrs: *You've got no idea what you just did, you stupid, stupid fuck.*

Starke immediately booted up his own laptop and brought it from his bedroom into his kitchen. He set it beside Dwyer's computer on his folding table. As soon as his wireless connection was active, he opened his Web browser and typed: *https://angelquest.net/LoveSick/mygifttoyou/*

His apartment was always hot and damp. But that was not why he was sweating as he brought his pinky finger down on "enter."

45

The link took Starke to a simple home page. It contained no images or graphics, only a single hypertext phrase in bright red letters: "My Gift to You." Starke clicked it, and another page appeared. Same thing. Only this time, the red lettering spelled out a date—the date of the first night that Paul Dwyer disappeared. Starke could tell this was a site created for a single purpose in a secluded cove of the Internet, intended for an audience of one.

Starke clicked the date.

Another screen appeared, this one with two hypertext options, "Live Webcam" and "Archive."

The first link was dead. Starke moved his cursor to the other link and hoped, but it, too, brought nothing to the screen. Whoever had posted the video to the Web had since removed it.

Starke sat back. Was that it, then? A dead end? He wished he knew, wished he was smarter about the mysterious world inside these humming boxes. He returned to the CarbonCopy device's main menu and studied the options again. The only one he hadn't yet tried was the last one listed: "Empty Cache." It opened to a list of sequentially numbered files, arranged by date but grayed out. In the foreground was a prompt: "Are you sure you want to delete these files?" Starke clicked on the "no" button, and the list of grayed-out files popped into high-contrast relief.

Sure enough, Starke's own keystrokes on Shelby's computer were being tracked, which he found oddly reassuring. The record could come in handy if he ever had to explain his solo exploration of the machine in court. He scrolled deeper. After his own logged activity, there was a nearly four-week gap in dates. The sequence resumed on the date Paul Dwyer disappeared. Starke moved his cursor to the CarbonCopy log's final entry for that date, and clicked.

The screen suddenly filled with an image, and the video began. No introduction. No narration. Only a tight, static shot of Paul Dwyer lolling his head from side to side, trying to make sense of his circumstances. He looked like a seated man coming out of anesthesia.

Starke leaned forward, felt himself tense.

Behind Dwyer's head was what looked like a solid metal post, about as wide as the basement support pillar in a typical suburban home. Almost no background was visible. Starke knew from Eckel's autopsy that Dwyer's wrists and ankles had been tied with hemp rope. He also got the same impression he had from the screen snapshot: Dwyer was not wearing a shirt. The bottom of the frame cut off at a point just below Dwyer's prominent Adam's apple, and no shirt collar was visible, only bare skin.

"The fuck?" Dwyer said, lifting his head and looking around, trying to find his hands.

Starke heard a movement off camera, the soft rustle of clothing, the scrape of a chair. Dwyer's head bobbled, and he turned toward the sound.

"Where's... who're you? Lemme see your face." Dwyer seemed to be working hard to focus his eyes. "Wha's that?"

Starke recognized the next sound—the crackle-spark of a Taser. Dwyer's eyes shot wide open, then tightly clenched shut. He seemed to convulse. His head turned violently to one side and his face twisted into the same grimace of pain that Starke had seen in a haunting freeze-frame just a few minutes earlier. From the distinctive burn marks that Eckel had found on Dwyer's chest and inner thighs, Starke already knew Dwyer had been tortured with a handheld stun device. He had just witnessed the first jolt.

Within thirty seconds, Dwyer recovered and was completely lucid. The shock had lifted the druggy veil, and suddenly he seemed fully aware he was in trouble. Starke raised the volume on his computer.

"Don't fucking do that again!" Dwyer roared. "Don't you fucking—"

He convulsed again. His head whipped up and smashed against the post. Dwyer held it there, gasped for air, and exhaled a tormented, "ShitShitShitShitShit," like the repeating output of a stuck CD. He recovered more slowly this time. When he did, he looked more scared than defiant.

"What do you want from me?" he said. "Money? Is that what you want? How much?"

His eyes tracked something off camera, a movement

away from him, then back. He followed the movement down toward his lap.

"Please." Dwyer's face distorted in anticipation. "Please no, God don't."

Another jolt. This time, his head bounced off the post and slumped to the left. He was clearly unconscious after the third jolt. The webcam never blinked. The scene didn't change for at least a minute. Starke heard more rustling off camera, then the brief clatter of what sounded like heavy metal on metal. He knew what was coming, even if Dwyer didn't.

Starke pushed his chair away from his computer's screen and stepped back, a reaction more than a choice. Would the horror diminish if he watched from farther away?

The pistol's muzzle and front sight peeked into the top left side of the frame. Dwyer's captor was standing over him, aiming down from about a foot away at a spot just behind Dwyer's right ear. What happened next reminded Starke of the infamous footage of the Saigon street execution of a Viet Cong prisoner. It came without announcement, trial, delay, or ceremony. The single shot snapped Dwyer's head once. It seemed a bloodless act for a moment. Then, a second later, a small red fountain rose from the exit wound on Dwyer's neck as the life geysered out of him. The bullet must have severed his carotid artery.

More off-camera rustling. The screen suddenly went black, the final, haunting image of Paul Dwyer replaced by the bright red question, "Watch Again?"

46

Kerrigan called as Starke was breaking down Shelby's computer. He was about the load it into the Vic to take it down to Los Colmas PD to tell her what he had. He still wasn't exactly sure what it meant, but his next move would be to invite Shelby Dwyer and her attorney down for an interview. While she clearly hadn't pulled the trigger on the gun that killed her husband, she had remotely witnessed it, and sure had some explaining to do.

"How soon can you get here?" Kerrigan said.

"On my way," he said. "Why?"

"Come straight to my office," she said.

"Why?" he asked again, but she was already gone.

He drove slowly, thinking, suspicious. What now? Maybe it was related to the wildfire, an all-hands-on-deck call as the blaze approached Los Colmas. They were a small department, and according to the emergency plan he'd helped write, he knew every cop was pressed into service, even detectives, during a citywide evacuation. He'd been through that drill before. As he steered through town, though, he stifled an even darker thought, the memory of Kerrigan staring at the UltraSharp home page on his computer screen at work. He could only imagine how that might complicate their already impossible relationship.

He patted the center of his chest, feeling for the tiny 2.0-gig flash drive that dangled on a neck cord beneath his shirt. He was taking no chances with what he'd just found.

The squad room was buzzing when he arrived, a pre-fire scramble. Starke focused on the task at hand, moving Shelby's computer and its various other parts from his car, through the loading dock, and into his office. He wasn't about to risk leaving it unattended. It took him twenty minutes, and the whole time Kerrigan watched like a raptor through the glass panels that fronted her office. When he was done, Starke locked his office door behind him and reported to Kerrigan's office, as asked.

"Didn't rush you, I hope," she said.

"I'm here now."

Kerrigan pushed a manila file folder across her desk. Starke flipped it open and practically swallowed his tongue. It was his file of Kerrigan's copied divorce documents. Not a good start. He'd left it on the corner of his desk when he went to meet Barbaric a few hours earlier.

"Before you say anything," Kerrigan said, "I'm going to tell you why I took this from your office."

There was nothing Starke could do or say that would make this any easier. He nodded for her to continue.

"I got a call last night from my former husband in LA," she said. "He said he'd been getting phone messages from someone named Ron in this area code. Since I'm the only person he's in touch with out here, he called to see if I knew anything about it. Naturally I had no idea, and I told him so.

"Then this morning before you left, when I ducked into your office, I saw the website you were looking at. I couldn't help but notice, because I helped Richard build the website and design the home page, back when it was just him and me and a handful of people who understood that someday every computer screen and TV would have an UltraSharp chip inside."

In any other circumstance, Starke would have opened his notebook and scribbled the thought that suddenly crossed his mind. But it hardly seemed the time.

"I put two and two together," Kerrigan continued. "After you left, I went back and found the file on your desk." She offered a weak smile. "But enough about me. Why don't you talk for a while?"

Starke cleared his throat. "Just trying to get to know you better?"

It was a fluttering-duck of a joke. He waited for his humorless boss to shotgun it to earth, but the blast never came. She just stared.

"Alright," he began. "OK." Deep breath. "I had a moment a few days ago, up at Shepherdsen's pond when you questioned my relationship with Shelby Dwyer, when I figured I might be fighting for my job. I always like to know who I'm fighting. It's no more complicated than that. They're public records, but I was out of line. I'm sorry."

"What was your intention, Detective?" she said. "Looking for dirt? Something to use against me sometime?"

"No," he lied.

Kerrigan waved the word away. "Bullshit. Bull. *Shit.*

Reading the file is one thing. But calling him? What did you plan to talk to him about? Our marriage? Our divorce? He's still bitter, you know. I'm sure you could tell that from his court statements. But what the hell business is that of yours?"

"None," Starke said.

"You're goddamned right it's not." She stood up, then sat back down. "Like I need this now. Like I need to be dealing with this bullshit in the middle of a goddamned evacuation."

Kerrigan seemed almost on the verge of tears—the first real emotion he'd ever seen from his new boss. He'd known other people like her, people whose difficulty in relating to others came off as open and constant hostility. The only way they could survive was by living life by their own personal policy manual, where the rules were written and messy emotions were sanitized for their protection. Starke was having trouble holding her gaze, so he brushed an imaginary crumb from the arm of his chair.

When he looked back, Kerrigan's eyes had changed. She'd offered a glimpse of her humanity, then pulled it back. Now he was watching her rebuild the wall behind which she lived, brick by brick, until her policy-manual face obscured the woman behind it. If he had to guess, she was either an adult child of an alcoholic, surrounded for life by thick defensive armor, or a sociopath. When she was done, she pulled her chair closer, put her elbows on her desk, and spoke in her most officious voice.

"I'm placing you on paid administrative leave."

Starke couldn't have been more stunned if she'd reached across the desk and slapped him. "For what reason?"

"Unprofessional conduct," she said. "Digging into my divorce case crosses the line. As soon as the fire danger passes and things get back to normal, I'm going to ask Detective Garza to do the fact-finding. If there's reason for disciplinary action, I'll make that call. But until her report is complete, you're off-duty. Obviously, this comes at the worst possible time for all of us."

"The Dwyer case," he said. "I can't just—not now."

"I'm sorry Detective," she said. "I'll need your murder book, your notes, everything. I take it you located Mrs. Dwyer's computer? That's what I saw you carrying in?"

"I can't agree with this decision," he said.

"I don't expect you to. That doesn't change the fact that it's my call. And I want you off-duty and off the Dwyer case until we know the facts. I promise we'll get Detective Garza to work on it as quickly as possible so we don't leave you hanging. I assume we can count on your cooperation?"

Starke just stared. He'd done something stupid. But paid administrative leave? How was that called for?

"Just leave her computer in your office for now. I'll take care of it, and everything else you turn over. You should have no more contact with anyone involved in the Dwyer case until a decision is made about whether you'll be returned to duty. Is that clear?"

He nodded.

"I'll need your office keys as well," she said, holding out her hand.

Starke stood up, fished the keyring from his pocket, and removed his office key. He placed it squarely in the center of her desk.

"Shield and service piece?" she said.

He laid those beside the office key, setting the gun down with its barrel facing toward her office's far wall. He'd put a band of blue painter's tape around the barrel, to clearly mark it as his among the other identical department-issued weapons.

"This is a mistake," he said. "Please reconsider."

Kerrigan iced him with a dispassionate look. "I've made my decision, Detective. Before you go, is there anything you need to tell me about the Dwyer case that I won't find in your office?"

"Everything's in my office," Starke said.

"You're sure?"

He looked her directly in the eye as he spoke, because he knew he was telling her the truth. "You have everything I've found."

As he turned to go, though, Starke reached up for reassurance. Through the fabric of his shirt, he touched the flash drive that hung like a talisman in the hollow of his chest.

47

At least Kerrigan let him keep the Crown Vic.

Starke was climbing into the driver's seat to head home when he saw Brooks Kaplan jog-walking at top speed across the department's back parking lot, waving his arms. Kaplan was in charge of the department's short-staffed and underfunded crime-scene crew, which at Kerrigan's insistence had spent the past few days scouring the possible access paths to Shepherdsen's pond for evidence of how Paul Dwyer's body was transported to the dump site.

Technically, Starke wasn't allowed to speak about the Dwyer case with anyone involved. So he just waved. And waited.

"Got a sec?" Kaplan shouted from twenty yards away. He closed the distance and put both hands on the driver's-side door. Starke just smiled through the door's open window. "Glad I caught you, Ron. I think we found something. No direct physical evidence, but I picked up some good intel during the search. Maybe it'll help."

Starke adjusted himself in his seat, rearranging his posture to convey full and undivided attention. When he did, he noticed Donna Kerrigan standing at one of her office windows, watching them from above.

"We may have answered the question about which path the shooter took up to the pond," Kaplan said. "The steep Shepherdsen path seemed unlikely, like you said, and we didn't find anything back there. But we did the paperwork and got homeowner approval to search the new homes on that back slope off Spadero Road. We didn't find a lot, but get this—ready?"

Starke offered another encouraging smile.

"True, it's a long quarter of a mile from Spadero Road to get up there. But here's the thing: There's two McMansion's within fifty yards of the dump site. We think the killer got access to one of those properties, the one at 1512 Spadero. Its owners were away the whole week when the body was probably dumped. They'd left vacation notices everywhere— the post office, neighbors, their private security company, Los Colmas cops."

Starke nodded.

"While they were away, their security company notified them that someone had accessed their driveway gate while they were gone. No entry into the house, just the driveway. Know what time? Between 3:12 and 3:47 a.m. on the first morning after your guy was last seen alive. So there's your time on the body dump."

Starke furrowed his brow, but said nothing.

"Thing is, the driveway goes all the way up the hill, and the carport is within fifty yards of the pond," Kaplan said. "So the killer's car would have been well off Spadero Road.

No one driving along Spadero would have noticed anything unusual. And from the top of the driveway, the pond would have been just a little way across private property. In the dark. You don't exactly have to be a master criminal to pull that off."

Starke gave another thoughtful nod. If the killer had mastered the fireman's carry, those final fifty yards would have been a short ramble up the rest of the slope to the edge of the pond, even with two hundred pounds of dead weight. Moving the heavy and unwieldy computer monitor probably would have been the more difficult task.

Before Starke could say a word, Kaplan obliged with a theory.

"And that computer monitor?" he said. "Wheelbarrow. The concrete contractor was still working on hardscape stuff around the property, and his guy had left a big wheelbarrow at the top of the drive. We found track marks from its tire way up near the pond, well away from any of the hardscaping pour."

For a moment, Starke flashed to the odd late-night conversation with his father as they ate burritos in a parking lot, watching an idling Esparza Construction cement truck. *He was dirty.*

"So my guess is that's how a single person could have moved that big goddamned thing up there. Two trips, one carrying or wheeling the body, another to wheel the monitor up there. Wouldn't have taken more than ten, fifteen minutes, leaving enough time to strap him up to the anchor and sink him. Whole thing takes thirty minutes, tops, which fits the time frame from the security company. Just my theory."

Starke smiled. It made perfect sense. He reached through

the window and shook Kaplan's hand. "Brooks," he said, "I need to tell you something."

Kaplan leaned down.

"I'm currently on paid administrative leave and no longer involved in the Dwyer case," Starke said. "So while I appreciate the update, I have to tell you I'm unable to talk about details of the case with you or anyone else involved until further notice."

A look somewhere between disbelief and confusion transformed Kaplan's face. "What the hell's *that* about?"

Starke winked. "Just doing what I've been told. I was asked to refrain from speaking to anyone about the case, and so I can't really say anything to you about it except to say I'm not involved at the moment."

Kaplan realized he'd been had. He smiled. "Understood."

"Do me a favor, Brooks, OK?"

Kaplan nodded.

"Don't turn around when I say this, because we're being watched from upstairs. Just make sure Kerrigan knows I did the right thing here. I didn't speak to you at all about the case, right?"

Kaplan saluted and stepped away from the car. "Not a word, Ron. I can testify to that."

Starke started the Vic. He was off the case, but he had a sudden and undeniable hunch. And nothing was stopping him from detouring past a couple of McMansions on his way home.

48

Private security operations ran the gamut. The best ones worked hand-in-hand with local police, fire, and ambulance services to monitor client properties. They maintained monitoring centers twenty-four hours a day, trained their operators well, and made sure their alarm and notification systems were installed by professionals. The worst ones offered a lawn sign and empty promises.

If Kaplan's theory about the route to Shepherdsen's pond was correct, Paul Dwyer's killer had somehow defeated the security system at 1512 Spadero Road, or at least the driveway gate. Access to the driveway of an unoccupied home gave the killer access to the dump site, as well as the privacy needed to dispose of a body.

It had to be someone who knew the owners were away.

Starke steered slowly west along Spadero Road. All along the ridge above him on his left, massive homes rose in faux Mediterranean splendor, lacking only a view of the sea to conjure an image of the Valencia, Spain, Italy's Amalfi coast, or the hillside homes of the French Riviera. These homes overlooked heavy truck traffic along Spadero Road and the beginnings of a lesser housing tract, one of Paul Dwyer's other works in progress. At the moment, with the approach of Thursday's late-afternoon dusk, that site was a parking lot for the fleet of earthmovers that had spent the day excavating dirt and scraping lots for these bloated American Dreams.

Above Starke, some of the hillside homes covered ten thousand square feet and cost more money than he had made in his entire career. Still, most were jammed cheek-by-jowl on lots no larger than an acre. A startling number were owned by people much younger than him, and the thought of that depressed him.

Starke slowed as he approached 1512 and steered onto the road's narrow shoulder. A massive cement truck roared past with a rush of air that rocked the Vic, the name on its rear mudflaps receding into the distance: Esparza & Sons Construction. It was followed by two more just like it. The builder may be dead, but the building continued. The juggernaut that was Dwyer Development was rolling onward, turning dirt into money, paving paradise, bringing barely affordable opulence to the inland strivers while destroying everything in its path. The company created communities, but almost always gated ones like Villa Cordero that excluded far more people than would ever be included. For the people left outside those gates, hating Dwyer Development and the man behind it was a simple reflex.

He stopped across Spadero at the base of an elegant brick apron that welcomed visitors—or at least those with the iron gate's access code—into 1512's long, elegantly curving driveway. Through the gate, he could see the house up the hill, atop a knoll of fresh green sod. From there it looked like it sat almost on top of the ridge, just on the other side of which was the mud flat that once was Shepherdsen's pond.

Starke stayed just long enough to read the prominent blue sign, shaped like a police badge, that was affixed to a four-foot metal post and stabbed into the landscaping along the property's stucco front wall: KGT Protection. He reached for his notebook to write it down, then realized it was back in his office, locked away with every other scrap of information he'd gathered about Paul Dwyer's murder. He searched the glove box for something to write on, but all he could come up with was the Vic's most recent service report from the Los Colmas PD garage. The Vic's oil had last been changed eight thousand miles ago.

He turned the page over and scribbled himself a note: "1512 Spadero. Access route? Posted KGT Protection." He'd seen a similar blue KGT sign at the base of Shelby Dwyer's driveway when he visited there.

Starke checked the mirror, took his foot off the brake, and let the car move back into traffic. Ahead of him, the setting sun brought the horizon into sharp relief. The column of white-brown smoke that billowed from the approaching wildfire seemed closer than ever.

49

Starke officially began his paid administrative leave with a movie marathon. Now it was nearly 4:00 a.m. and his only entertainment alternative was to watch more movies. Sleep? Not an option.

He stood up and stretched after ten mostly prone hours, startled by the noise level in his joints and cartilage. His body sounded like the finale at a Fourth of July show. *Maybe some time off will be good,* he thought. *Get a little exercise. Start eating better. Use the time productively, you know?*

Before he could seriously consider those possibilities, he sat down again, this time in front of his laptop at his kitchen table. He called up his start page and opened his favorites bar. He briefly considered clicking on the NSA link, but his fingers took him in another direction. In the search box, he typed: "Richard Holywell."

He couldn't shake the feeling that something was left undone about that whole situation. What it was he couldn't say, or why he felt that way, but Kerrigan's relationship with her former husband still felt relevant to him.

The search engine got 107,000 hits. The search took 0.10 seconds. He resisted the impulse to leave it alone.

A lot of the links led to England. There was a local councilor in a town called Holywell that was named Richard Busby. There was a Holywell Music Room at a university there, and an uncanny number of the musicians who played in the music room were named Richard. He narrowed the search: "Richard Holywell UltraSharp."

The search engine got only 43 hits. The search took 0.03 seconds.

The first page of links were to stories in the financial or technology press, apparently featuring the correct Richard Holywell. The results got more scattered on the second page, so Starke returned to the first. The stories there chronicled what he already knew from the company's website. The launch of UltraSharp's breakthrough circuit that sharpened and brightened screens. The company's boasts that its technology was "a major leap forward in visual clarity for portable computing and video screens." Holywell was almost always quoted, usually to the effect that UltraSharp was leading the way into a new frontier of blah blah blah. Other stories described the company's later success with major computer makers, as the UltraSharp chip found its way into countless tech brands, and eventually tablets and smartphones. The more recent stories announced the sale of UltraSharp to Pei Lan, the multinational Taiwan-based electronics giant that wanted to bring the feisty American innovator under its corporate umbrella.

One link took Starke to a year-old consumer review about

a new twenty-four-inch Dell monitor posted on a website for computing enthusiasts. The review mentioned Holywell by name and credited the UltraSharp device inside the Dell screen for its "luscious" picture. "Brace yourself for some hardcore geek lust, gamers and graphics pros," the reviewer wrote. "Dell's monster LCD goes on sale next month!!!!!"

One of the links took Starke to a short profile of Richard Holywell in a tech-industry trade journal named *VisuComp Review*. It was a puff piece, but included a link to a full-color photograph that accompanied the story. Starke clicked on that link, and up popped an environmental portrait of Holywell.

He seemed much like most wonky businessmen, a sort of Woz-goes-to-the-stylist look that seemed to accompany every story Starke had ever read about a tech entrepreneur on the verge of breaking through. What he saw in the background, though, pulled Starke closer to the screen. Holywell was standing in front of a long, low credenza in an executive office. The cabinet was studded with what looked like a collection of massive 1990s-era CRT computer monitors.

50

By dawn, Starke had a plan. He'd thought it through from every angle and decided the downside risks were acceptable. The accumulating evidence in the Dwyer case was pointing him in directions he never could have imagined, and he suddenly understood why Shelby Dwyer had kept silent after watching her husband tortured and murdered via live webcam. It wasn't always easy to know who your enemy might be.

Seated in front of his laptop in the kitchen of his muggy apartment, he reviewed the situation. He'd said nothing to Kerrigan about what he'd found inside the tiny CarbonCopy device on Shelby's computer. It sat with the computer on a desk in a locked office at a police department that was scrambling to manage an approaching wildfire. Because the department's only other detective, Susan Garza, was for the moment charged with investigating *him* rather than the Dwyer murder, its story could remain untold for days, possibly weeks. Knowledge is power, Starke decided, and he was still the only one besides Shelby and her husband's killer who knew about their relationship, and where it apparently had led. He alone had followed the silicon trail to the grisly video still embedded on that tiny electronic spy. He alone had copied that video to his flash drive.

Now it was time to do something with it. He'd considered his options.

Confront Shelby Dwyer with what he knew and force her to cooperate? What would be the point? Because of her ongoing silence, he suspected she may not even know the killer's true identity. Besides, Starke had no official standing in the investigation at this point and was forbidden from talking to anyone involved.

Take the information to Kerrigan? It was still a long shot, but what if her cash-cow, computer-collecting ex-husband was somehow involved? What if Kerrigan was trying to protect him? Or herself?

Take what he had to the district attorney? Even Starke would be skeptical about a guy who suggested that his boss—a boss who'd reprimanded him—might actually be covering up a murder.

No, this was better. He could do it without official standing. It would nudge the crime out of the shadows. It would make what really happened impossible to ignore. Best of all, it might flush the killer into the open. That always involved risk. But he also knew that, with the right provocation, killers sometimes make mistakes.

Starke raised his hands to the keyboard and began.

51

Exhausted and filthy, but with no relief in sight, the San Bernardino fire captain slumped against the side of his rescue vehicle. He'd parked it on a residential street in a new tract called Villa Cordera, about two miles due east of where the fire had started. Advance teams of county police, fire, and rescue workers had already evacuated the tract, and he'd hoped they could stop the wildfire's progress before it could destroy the neighborhood. But two homes on the perimeter street were fully engulfed, and a half dozen more were doomed. If this neighborhood went, it was a short hop over Spadero Road to the much larger new homes that dotted the dry, terraced ridge above.

There was nothing but fuel between the top of that ridge and Los Colmas, where the city's houses were jammed together in a tight, combustible little package.

"Carlos?" he said into his walkie-talkie. "Give me some good news."

He waited, pounding down water from a plastic bottle

as he did. He was dehydrated and hungry, but there'd been no chance to stop since late the night before.

"No good news, Captain," Carlos said. "We've lost the two. We'll redeploy to the north and south sides, see what we can do there. We've had some problems with water pressure."

Typical, he thought. He'd never known a developer to install more than the bare minimum pipe capacity to get a project approved.

"Didn't there used to be a bunch of ponds and small lakes around here?"

Carlos took his time answering. "Used to be. I asked a couple of the guys. Looks like they drained or filled 'em all. You can't build on water."

Christ. "Do the best you can with it, Carlos. The choppers should be back from Big Bear Lake in about ten. Just tell 'em where you want the drop."

He spread his county map across the dusty hood of the truck as a ladder unit whipped past, leaving eddies of smoke and ash in its wake. The fire's heat was generating its own windstorm, of course, making the situation unpredictable and dangerous. The local temperature was pushing eighty-five, almost no humidity. Another day in paradise, unless your job was to derail hell.

He took off his heavy gloves and laid them on the map's top two corners to pin it. He anchored its bottom two corners with his hands. Using the scale at the bottom, he calculated the distance between this tract and Los Colmas. It was a little less than a mile. He also tried to quantify the speed of the wildfire's advance during the past twenty-four hours, when the offshore winds had turned it east and whipped it into the monster it had become.

Without a break in the weather or wind, he figured the fire would be at the edge of Los Colmas by nightfall. He'd need to give the evacuation order there soon. He checked his watch.

It was just past eight o'clock in the morning. By ten, he'd have to decide.

52

"Mom?"

Chloe Dwyer's voice rose above the chatter of the small kitchen TV. The Los Colmas Unified School District had canceled classes for the third straight day as the fire marched on and made the air almost unbreathable. Shelby turned from the kitchen window.

Chloe cranked the volume of a Los Angeles station's midmorning newscast. The word "Exclusive," in bright yellow letters, blinked on and off in the upper left corner of the screen. In a panel across the bottom, the question: "Is a Killer Taunting Police?"

"This is about Dad," Chloe said.

Shelby joined her daughter at the cooking island. They both leaned forward on their elbows, peering at the screen.

"—when KTLA received an anonymous telephone tip this morning that a bizarre video had surfaced on YouTube," co-anchor Golden Vargas-Wong was saying. "That tape apparently shows a cold-blooded murder. Could it be a videotape of the recent unsolved killing of Inland Empire developer Paul Dwyer? Our investigative team has been working hard to answer that question all morning. Brian?"

Shelby moved toward the TV. Chloe grabbed her arm. Hard. "You're *not* going to turn this off," Chloe said.

The screen filled with Paul Dwyer's face, the official company portrait. In it, his hair and confident smile all but sparkled. Brian, the investigative team newscaster, gave the backstory: disappeared nearly a month ago, body found last Friday with a single bullet wound in the head, search for suspects continues.

"And now a bizarre new twist to this ongoing saga," Brian said. "Early this morning, someone posted a video of what could be the actual murder in progress. The man in the video appears to be Paul Dwyer, according to our analysis."

A blurry still photo taken from the video appeared on the screen alongside the portrait of a smiling Paul Dwyer.

The voiceover continued. "Could it be the killer taunting police? We hope to talk to investigators involved in the case for our 'News at Noon' broadcast. In the meantime, the undated tape offers new insight into the merciless nature of the crime. It shows the man whose face resembles Dwyer's struggling and possibly being tortured. It ends with a point-blank, execution-style gunshot. We warn you in advance that even the limited portion of the video we're about to show is disturbing—"

"Chloe, no," Shelby said. She pulled her arm free of her daughter's grasp and reached for the remote. The TV blinked off. "I can't watch that. I won't."

Chloe walked to the TV and hit the power button. The

screen blinked back on. "How do we know it's him? The picture's so blurry."

"It is."

Chloe fixed Shelby with a stare. "How do you know?"

Shelby said nothing.

"Mom, how do you know?"

"I don't. It's just—I don't."

Her daughter turned again to face the TV. "I need to know."

The screen had filled with a grainy image of Paul Dwyer in distress. The clip lasted less than five seconds. Chloe reached forward and turned off the TV again. She raised one hand to her mouth and tears ran down both cheeks.

"Oh God," Chloe said. "The voice—it *is* him. Oh Jesus."

She lurched toward the sink and retched. Shelby put an arm around her daughter's heaving back and turned on the water to wash away the little that came up.

"Nobody deserves that," she said. "I hated him, but nobody deserves that."

"I know, baby."

"You know what he looked like, Mom? He looked as scared as you looked that night last summer."

"Like he knew he was about to die," Shelby said.

Her daughter nodded.

Shelby pulled Chloe into a hug. She stroked her hair and rubbed her back. Chloe let her do it for a long time, for longer than Shelby could ever remember. This was not a kid who stood still for long. Her exuberance demanded constant motion. But when the rest of your world is spinning, you need to just stop, to plant your feet firmly, and hope everything settles. Shelby understood that feeling all too well.

"What are we gonna do?" Chloe said. "How's anybody ever going to find this guy?"

"I don't know, baby."

"Mom, he's been in our house."

They both looked through the kitchen window and toward the pool beyond. Neither had had the stomach to dive down and loose Boz from the weight that was holding him underwater.

"I don't want to stay here," Chloe said. "I want to move away."

"What about school?"

"I don't care, Mom. I'm scared."

"Me too, baby." Now Shelby was crying. She flashed back to the morning when the police chief came to deliver the news that Paul's body had turned up. "Don't leave town, Mrs. Dwyer," she'd said. "We'll be in touch."

Was she about to become a fugitive? Where could they go that no one would find them?

"I'm so sorry," Shelby said.

"You're still not telling me everything. I know you're not."

Shelby took a deep breath. It was time to tell her daughter the rest of it. "I saw it before."

Chloe gasped. "That video?"

"The night it happened, as it happened. He tricked me into watching it. I pleaded with him to stop, to let Dad go. I told him he'd got it wrong. All wrong. But he still—"

Chloe pulled back. "So you knew Dad was dead from that night on?"

Shelby nodded.

"And you never told me?"

"I couldn't tell anybody. How could I? It would have looked like I was part of it."

"But you *were*, Mom."

"No! No, Chloe. I wasn't part of that, of killing your Dad. I would have never done that. See what I mean. If you know I watched it, you assume I was part of it. Anybody would. And *he* knows that. He's using that to keep me quiet. But please believe me, baby, I wasn't. Please. I—"

An electronic chime rang. Shelby held her daughter for a moment more, then headed for the house's foyer to see who was at the driveway gate. From there, she peered through the window beside their bolted front door. Beyond the sweeping stone patio, across the broad lawn, a news van from a different LA station was parked just outside the gate, its satellite antenna already raised twenty feet in the air and its dish pointing toward the sky. A reporter and a cameraman were standing at the gate. As Shelby watched, another news van pulled up and parked just behind the first.

"They're already out here because of the fire," she said. "They must have seen the other station's story. Now they're here. They want to talk to me."

"Mom, what the hell?"

Shelby turned from her daughter and peeked through the blinds. "They'll go away eventually. They will. It's just-- we're just not going anywhere for a while."

She twisted the rod on the louvered window blinds, and the nightmare disappeared, if only for the moment.

53

Starke had unleashed the media monster less than four hours before, and now here it sat, waiting to pounce. He eased the Vic along the street in front of Shelby Dwyer's estate, steering between the six parked satellite trucks from television stations from as far away as LA, Palm Springs, and San Diego—cities where Dwyer Development had significant and usually controversial projects. He knew most were already here to cover the advancing wildfire. But once the webcam video of Dwyer's murder was out there, news directors had redeployed their forces into "victim reax" mode, even if all they could get was a grab-and-go stand-up outside the gate of the Dwyer home. The on-scene reporter could always speculate about what might be happening inside. Even if the widow wouldn't talk, what *might* she have to say about all this?

The camera was always hungry. Feeding time was a frenzy.

He didn't want to stop, couldn't afford being seen

even on the periphery of the Dwyer case. But through the driveway gate as he passed, Starke saw both Shelby's Jag and her late husband's Benz parked just outside the home. He thought again of Shelby, trapped inside by the clamoring horde, the webcam video of her husband's murder still ricocheting from satellite to home dish to TV screen in an endless, numbing loop. She'd seen it once, the night it happened. But had she seen it again on TV? Was it even possible she had not?

Starke parked well down the block, and for the next few minutes watched the scene in his rearview mirror. He knew Shelby wouldn't leave until they were all gone. She had no other choice. There was no point in waiting, so he dropped the gear shift into drive and started to pull away, sure in his gut that the endgame had begun.

Then he noticed something in his mirror.

54

At the far end of the block, well beyond the media vultures gathering at Shelby Dwyer's front gate, an unremarkable white Ford slowed, stopped, and angled backward into an open spot along the curb. Starke watched its arrival in his mirror with a mixture of dread and disbelief. He couldn't be sure, but from a distance it looked like the city-issued car assigned to Kerrigan.

He turned up the volume on the Vic's scanner. The Los Colmas police communications channel was alive with logistical chatter about the evacuation that now seemed inevitable. Kerrigan had to be directing the operation, he knew, but her vehicle was a rolling command center bristling with antenna. She could do it all from her car.

She had parked on the same side of the street at least a hundred yards away, as far north of Dwyer's driveway gate as he was south. His main concern: Could she see him? Technically, he wasn't violating the terms of his administrative leave by simply being here, but he doubted Kerrigan would see it that way if she found her lead detective parked along Dwyer's street after she'd ordered him off the investigation. From where he was, with the media trucks crowding the street between them, there was little chance she'd notice him snugged in behind a bulky news van at the far end of the block. She'd be far more likely to spot him if he tried to drive away. Better to stay put and hope she didn't drive right past him on her way out of the neighborhood.

It was a standoff. He had no choice but to wait. But what was she doing here? She couldn't possibly have had time to review his murder book, or follow the trail of electronic evidence to the CarbonCopy device still attached to Shelby's computer in his office.

Starke checked his watch. Just after noon.

In his mirror, he could see Kerrigan sitting in her car, working her communications equipment, making no move to get out. From time to time, her voice crackled across his scanner. The chief was fully engaged, mustering their small department for a citywide evacuation, calling in off-duty officers, authorizing overtime. But she was also watching the Dwyer home, just like he was. He got the feeling she was waiting, too, maybe for the media circus to fold its tents and move on, or looking for a chance to slip past the clamoring reporters to get to Shelby on the other side.

Starke shifted in his seat and adjusted his mirror, figuring he might be there awhile.

55

Shelby twirled the rod on the louvered blind beside her front door. The slats between the panes opened to the broad lawn and a nearly empty street just beyond her front gate.

It was just before 2:00 p.m. She and Chloe had watched the abbreviated webcam video of Paul's murder replayed on the noon newscasts, watched the frustrated field reporters feed their live stand-ups from in front of their grand estate, listened to them echo the no-comment-from-the-family story line one after the other. Then she'd waited, hoping the urgent need for on-scene fire coverage would divert their attention. Finally, it did. The last of the satellite news trucks was about to pull away.

"They'll be back, Mom."

"I know, baby."

Chloe stood at Shelby's shoulder. Angry and confused, she'd packed a duffle bag, and it sat on the floor beside her. Her arms were crossed. "Can we go?"

"We haven't decided where, Chloe."

"Does it matter?"

Shelby shook her head. "Not really."

Her daughter patted the overstuffed duffle. "Then let's go. I can't be here anymore. I'm not even sure I can be with you anymore."

Shelby tried not to react. She nodded to the duffle. "I'm afraid to ask what's in there."

Chloe looked away.

Shelby peeked through the blinds again. The last TV news truck was gone, but now there was something else, a dull white haze drifting over the entire neighborhood. The fire was getting closer. She was about to hustle Chloe out to the car when she noticed a lone figure walk up to the closed driveway gate. A woman. She carried some sort of flat panel, and shifted it beneath one arm as she reached for the intercom button. Shelby squinted through the smoke.

Chloe was suddenly at Shelby's shoulder. "Who's that?"

Shelby flinched at the sound of the chime. "That police chief."

"Just ignore her."

Shelby twisted the blinds shut. "But she knows we're home. The cars—"

"So?"

"So—" Shelby's lower lip began to tremble. She felt like something caught in a web. "So she'll know we're avoiding her."

"Why do you care?"

The electronic chime sounded again, echoing through the foyer. Shelby turned to her daughter. "I think I'd better talk to her, baby."

"The fire, Mom? We *have* to go."

Shelby looked again. The police chief was back at the intercom keypad, but this time she appeared to be keying in a code. When she finished, the driveway gate began to roll slowly to the side.

Time quickened. Shelby could hear blood pulsing in her ears. The woman was halfway up the driveway, and Shelby could see that the rectangular panel she was carrying was the flat screen of an iMac computer. Each step closer through the drifting smoke brought its details into sharper relief.

Shelby turned to face her daughter and put a hand on each of Chloe's shoulders. "Wait in the car."

"No."

"I said wait in the car, Chloe."

Her daughter again crossed her arms over her chest. "I said no."

"I need to talk to her alone."

"You said no more secrets."

"Baby, please."

Chloe turned and headed for the curving staircase that swept up to the bedrooms. "Fine. I forgot something anyway."

When the knock came a moment later—sharp, solid, unavoidable—Shelby was breathing like she'd just run a sprint.

56

Shelby had a dizzying moment of déjà vu as she swung open the door for the police chief. The first time they met on this doorstep, six days before, Kerrigan had come early in the morning, without warning or explanation, to bring the grim news Shelby already knew. That day, she'd driven right up to the house through the apparently open gate. Now, remembering, Shelby understood. The gate was pointless. The woman could come and go at will.

"You did it again," she said.

"What's that, Mrs. Dwyer?"

"Let yourself in. You know the gate code."

Kerrigan nodded. "It's on file. May I come in?"

Shelby eyed the computer in Kerrigan's arms. "What for?"

"I think you know."

Shelby crossed her arms and stood in the middle of the doorway. "You realize we're being evacuated at the moment."

"Just a few questions, that's all."

"Some other time." Shelby began closing the door.

Kerrigan nodded to the computer. "It's all in here, you know."

Shelby marshaled every muscle in her face into an effort not to blink. "I don't have any idea what you're talking about."

Kerrigan smiled, a withering, condescending, don't-patronize-me expression of raw power. "You recognize this machine, I assume?"

"I'm afraid not."

"No? We have paperwork showing that you sold it the day after your husband disappeared. It took us a few days to find it, but when we did—"

"I'm not going to talk about this now," Shelby snapped. "And when I do, we'll do it right, in a proper setting with my attorney present. Now please, let yourself out the same way you let yourself in. And don't ever come onto my property again unless you have a warrant."

The police chief shifted the computer's weight, and adjusted her grip on it. "I know what happened, Mrs. Dwyer," she said. "There's a ghost in your machine."

Shelby stared.

"You know him, but you don't even know his name. But you know he killed your husband, Mrs. Dwyer. You watched him do it, and that's going to look pretty bad when the time comes to tell this story in court."

Shelby understood the art of the bluff. She searched for a tell in the police's chief's eyes but found none.

"I don't think so," Shelby said.

A weighted moment passed. When the police chief stepped forward, Shelby reflexively stepped back. The woman was just too close. Kerrigan took another step forward until she was standing on the doorstep. Her eyes never left Shelby's, who retreated another step into the foyer. With one foot, Kerrigan closed the front door behind her. It shut with the absolute sound of heavy wood and high-end hardware.

"He's still out there, Mrs. Dwyer. The man who killed your husband. He knows we'll find him, because it's all in this machine. And now we have the machine. It's just a matter of time before we follow the electronic trail right back to him. But right now you have a chance to help us. Help yourself. It starts with telling the truth. The district attorney understands the value of that. Judges and juries, too."

"You need to leave," Shelby said. "Now."

"If I were you, I'd be worried less about leniency than about your situation right now. Because this guy, he knows something else, too. He knows you're the only link between him and the murder. That's not a safe position for you to be in, Mrs. Dwyer. You or your daughter. We both know what he's capable of."

Without shifting her eyes from Shelby's, Kerrigan took three steps to her left and set the computer down on the empty tabletop where an art piece once stood, the heavy sculpture now at the bottom of the backyard pool. There was something too familiar about the way this woman moved in this unfamiliar space.

"I know what it's like to be lonely, Mrs. Dwyer. To be tempted. To be seduced by a fantasy. I understand how things can happen that you never meant to happen. Really I do, and so will a jury. It's the burden of women of a certain age and experience. We want to be understood. We're tired of moving unloved through life, where every day we feel a little less, and a little less, until finally we stop feeling at all. That scares us. So we go looking for a little fun."

Kerrigan set one hand on the iMac. "You found someone you thought could give you what you needed."

Shelby stared at the computer, now certain the police chief knew about LoveSick, had read their online conversations. How else could she understand so clearly?

"Someone," the chief said, "who you thought would love you beyond space and time."

The hair on Shelby's arms stood straight up. Those words. She'd heard them countless times from her secret online lover, the words he used each time they ended their sessions. Now they were coming from the mouth of someone else, someone she clearly didn't know at all.

Only one person understood her so well.

"You're *him*." Shelby raised her voice and said it again. Screamed it. "God damn. You're him!"

Kerrigan's expression didn't change. Her face seemed frozen, hard, but softened by those almond eyes that dipped at the corners. She still looked like someone who Cared Deeply even as her right hand moved to the small of her back. When it returned, it was holding a gun.

"Your husband hurt me," Kerrigan said. "Like I've never been hurt before."

Shelby narrowed her eyes. "My husband?"

"He made promises. He wanted me, not you. He told me so, and I believed him. So I left everything in LA—my marriage, my career, gave it all up to come here, to start over. With him."

"With him," Shelby repeated.

"He said he wanted us to be together," Kerrigan said. "I *believed* him."

Shelby knew so little about Paul's life away from home. That he'd bedded this powerful and attractive woman didn't surprise her, or even that he'd whispered vague and insincere promises to her. She wasn't surprised, either, that this woman let herself be seduced by his power and wealth. But how could Donna Kerrigan, or any woman smart enough to know better, actually buy his bullshit? What kind of desperate fool *believes* a man like Paul?

"He'd never have left me," she said. "Too complicated. Too expensive. You finally figured that out, and you decided to make him pay."

Kerrigan's smile was full of contempt, the gun steady in her hand. "I decided," she said, "to make you *all* pay."

57

Too many coincidences, too many odd choices. Everything was starting to make a sickening sort of sense, even if Starke still wasn't sure how it had all played out, or what exactly was happening at the moment.

As soon as the driveway gate had rolled shut behind Kerrigan, he'd opened his car door and stepped out into the thin veil of smoke that descended over the hilltop street of exclusive homes as the wildfire advanced. The people who lived in the neighborhood's four other houses already had been evacuated. From the streets below, the sounds of emergency equipment and crews rose in a desperate, hopeless clamor. At least two homes down there already were ablaze, and it wouldn't be long before the flames and firefighting equipment blocked one of the two streets that led up to this higher ground.

Starke moved quickly across the road and slid along the high wall of the Dwyer property, edging closer to the closed gate for a peek between the bars. When he leaned around the corner, he saw Kerrigan stepping through the massive home's open front door carrying the single most compelling piece of evidence he'd found during his investigation of Paul Dwyer's murder: Shelby's computer. Then the door closed behind her.

What the hell was happening?

Standing now at the gate, he reached his right hand into his sports jacket for a reassuring touch, thinking now might be a good time to unsnap the strap of his shoulder holster. What he found—nothing—reminded him that he was, for the moment, a private citizen.

He leaned around the wall for another look, but this time his knee brushed against something sharp and metallic. Spiked into the lush soil of the Dwyers' perimeter plantings was a three-foot-high sign for KGT Protection— the same company that monitored 1512 Spadero Road, the staging area for the killer who dumped Dwyer's body in Shepherdsen's pond. Kerrigan had been so *casual* about entering the Dwyers' security code.

Starke checked his watch. Whatever was happening inside probably wouldn't take long. Kerrigan had her radio with her—he'd heard its squawk and crackle as she stood at Shelby's front door—probably so she could continue to monitor and coordinate the evacuation. She had to know that the only escape routes from the hilltop neighborhood would be closed off soon. Within twenty minutes, they'd all be trapped and helpless as the flames moved house by house to the top of the hill. He leaned around the wall for another look, waiting, watching. There was nothing else he could do.

Seconds passed. Minutes. He checked his watch again. Kerrigan had been inside for nearly five minutes.

Then he heard it, even among the uproar of the advancing fire—the unmistakable report of a distant gunshot. Then another. They were muted but familiar, like the snap-sharp thunder of his own Los Colmas PD service piece, but distant and tiny.

The shots came from inside the house.

Starke looked around. He was alone in the thickening smoke and swirling ash. Without thinking, he took a deep breath, reached for the crossbar of the driveway gate and swung one leg up, hooking the instep of his left foot on the same crossbar. Adrenaline carried him high enough to hoist himself over, but the hem of his sports coat snagged on the pointed tip of a vertical iron bar. It slowed the speed of his fall, but only for as long as it took for the fabric to tear away. He landed heavily on the elaborate brickwork of the driveway itself and started to run, peeling the shredded jacket down his arms as he did.

He chose a route that avoided the curving drive, running instead through the sprinklers gurgling without water pressure on the soft pad of lawn along the perimeter wall. It'd take him twice as long to reach the house that way, but surprise was the only weapon he had.

Starke watched the front door as he advanced. There was no rear gate on the Dwyer property, so the shooter had only one way to get out. He hoped he'd moved far enough to the periphery to see without being seen.

When he reached a spot deep into the property, beyond the sight line of the front door, Starke took the chance of cutting across the side lawn, past a sleek fountain, and into the shrubs that stood just outside a floor-to-ceiling ground-floor window on the side of the massive house. Peeking in, he saw nothing but a closed room, a masculine study of some kind, probably Paul Dwyer's office. Nothing inside seemed out of order.

Starke crept toward the corner of the house. He saw three more windows between where he stood and the door, and if he remembered correctly, the one farthest from him looked into the house's sprawling foyer. He dropped to his hands and knees and started to crawl behind shrubs that clawed him as he moved.

The silence from inside was almost a presence, a chasm of questions.

One answer came in a shocking rush the moment he peeked over the sill at the window nearest the front door. Shelby Dwyer was curled into a fetal ball next to an overstuffed duffel bag on the floor of the home's cavernous entryway, the only figure anywhere in sight. He saw a small smear of blood across the light-colored tile, but there was no mistaking the shuddering throes of a gutshot human body. She was facing away from him, pressing her knees to her chest, one hand clutching at her chest. The other hand, stained a deep, rich red, fluttered into the air like a moth, an incomprehensible reflex, helpless and unthinking, desperately grasping for a handhold in a life slipping away.

Shelby Dwyer was dying alone just thirty feet from where Starke crouched in the dirt.

He reached for the cell phone clipped to his belt, but stopped before his fingers could find it. A 911 call was pointless. Every paramedic and fire crew in the city and surrounding counties was busy with the evacuation and ongoing rescue efforts. Los Colmas PD? If Kerrigan had followed the plan he'd helped write, every upright body in the department already was deployed throughout the city to help with the evacuation and to prevent looting.

Even if he'd had options, there was no time. Starke sprang to his feet, climbed onto the carved stone apron outside the Dwyers' front door, and stepped unarmed into a situation that couldn't possibly end well.

58

Shelby's white shirt was a deep, damp red by the time Starke scanned the foyer, realized they were alone, and quietly entered. He knelt beside her and slipped his hand behind her thin neck, the neck he'd nuzzled as a young man, the neck whose softness and scent he remembered even now whenever he thought of Shelby. Her eyes were open wide, desperate, knowing, helpless. She felt boneless, her skin cool to his touch.

One bullet had caught her in the right shoulder, tearing muscle and shattering bone. It was still inside her, since he saw only an entry wound and that was practically bloodless. The real damage was three inches to the left. The other shot had pierced the soft skin above her clavicle, probably as she turned or fell. It exited the side of her neck, nicking the carotid artery as it did. He could see Shelby's still-strong heart pumping the blood from her body in weakening pulses. It coursed down the center of her chest. Her silk shirt was absorbing a lot of it, but there was so much that it already was pooling around Starke's knee.

"I'm here, Shel."

She clutched his arm, her fingers digging into the flesh of his bicep with startling strength.

"Chlo—" she rasped.

Closer? Starke leaned down until his face was inches from hers. Their eyes locked.

"Chloe," she whispered.

The daughter. "She's here?"

Shelby nodded. The effort seemed to wrack her with pain, and she coughed fresh blood from her flooded lungs. The bullet from her shoulder wound had apparently done most of its damage inside. She tightened her grip on his arm as she tried to choke the blood back down. There was nothing he could do. Starke rolled her onto her side, hoping he could at least ease the sensation of drowning. He leaned down again so they were face to face.

"Who did this, Shel?"

She coughed again, caught a quick breath.

"I watched Chief Kerrigan come in, Shel. Did she do this?"

She nodded. "Him."

Him? "Help me understand, Shel."

Another nod. "She's—"

Her words were coming in gasps now, and her grip on his arm was flagging. Starke quickly scanned the room again to make sure they were still alone. He could see Shelby marshaling her strength for one more try. He pulled a blood-matted strand of blond hair away from her mouth.

"She's... him."

Starke rolled Shelby's head so he could look directly into her eyes. "Shel, what does that mean?"

Her eyes were dulling now, a curtain being drawn. Blood was pooling around him on the floor, and the pulsing flow from her neck had stopped. She released her grip on his hand, and Starke thought for a moment she was gone. But when he looked down, her other arm was raised, a finger pointing across the foyer to a small table that stood beside the front door.

Starke bent down to Shelby's face. Her mouth moved, but all that came out was a thick, pink bubble. He touched his fingertips to the side of her neck, a gesture that felt achingly familiar, and searched for a pulse just beneath her ear. He felt nothing beneath her cold skin.

Starke laid her head gently on the floor and slipped his hand free. He stood up, wishing the sound of his crackling joints wasn't echoing through the cavernous entryway. Kerrigan was still here, somewhere.

He tiptoed to the table by the door and quietly slid open the small, single drawer at its center. A cold steel .45 was the only thing inside.

59

The stairway was wide at the bottom and tapered as it curved up to the house's second floor. Starke moved quickly to its bottom step, already in that narrow-focus survival mode where nothing mattered but the moment. He led with the short barrel of the Dwyers' Smith & Wesson. The chamber had been empty when he'd pulled the matte slide, but there were seven single-stack rounds in the magazine. The chamber wasn't empty anymore.

He'd decided to search the top floor first. If Kerrigan had gone upstairs looking for Chloe, he could search room by room and maybe catch her unaware. If she was somewhere else on the property, there was a better chance he could spot her from one of the second-floor windows. The stairway was the only way down. He could watch it as he moved in and out of the rooms.

Polished marble amplified his footsteps as he moved along the curving handrail, aware of his breathing and the pistol's unfamiliar grip against his palm. Halfway up, he looked back. Shelby had died with her knees drawn to her chest, her blonde hair spread like kelp in the blood around her.

The stairs ended perpendicular to a wide hallway that ran the length of the second floor. Starke counted a dozen doors along the corridor, some open, some not. To his right, the hallway dead-ended into double doors that opened into a bright master suite—the bedroom of Shelby and Paul Dwyer. Light poured through what he imagined were wide windows or doors that offered views of the rear, front, and one side of the property. He'd start there.

A minimalist-modern bed stood atop a one-step platform in the center of the room. Without either a headboard or a footboard, it looked like a stage, or maybe an altar, covered by a cream-colored down comforter. At the far end, a mountain of pillows indicated which direction the Dwyers had slept. The setup had a feng shui vibe Starke couldn't pretend to decipher. He was grateful, though. At least no one could hide under or behind the bed.

He stepped into the room, then around the corner so he couldn't be seen from the hall. Shelby's design taste was an advantage. The room's lines were clean and simple, the furnishings spare and well chosen. There were only two possible places in the master suite where someone might be— the his-and-hers walk-in closets on the left, or the marbled bath that opened to Starke's right. His immediate concern, though, was what he could see through the French doors that opened onto a small deck overlooking the backyard.

Smoke rose in toxic eddies from an adjacent home, and one of the tall palms at the rear of the Dwyers' property was lit up like a tiki torch. Its crown was ablaze. As he watched, the wind tore loose a flaming frond and sent it helicoptering down. It snagged on a utility pole and hung from the wire just feet from a gray transformer.

He checked the closets first. Shelby's was the size of the spare bedroom in most homes. It smelled of cedar and perfume, and had custom-made shoe shelves and clothes arranged along the hang bars by color. He raked the gun barrel through some of the clothes, satisfied that there was no chance someone could hide behind them. A dressing island stood in the middle, but it was layered with small drawers—again, nowhere to hide. He circled it, then moved gun first into Paul Dwyer's closet.

It was empty, just bare hang bars and shelves without shoes. Shelby had wasted no time in purging the house of her dead husband's clothes.

The bathroom was palatial, and in its marble embrace he again was aware of the subtle tick and slide of his footsteps and the raggedness of his breathing. He glimpsed his reflection in the wall of mirrors behind the double-sink vanity. He looked like a man emerging from a cage fight. His climb over the spiked gate not only shredded his sports jacket, but also left a gaping tear in the sleeve of his denim work shirt and a nasty-looking scrape in the skin of his upper arm. His eyes had the darting dread of something feral and hunted.

The shower was enclosed in clear glass, and no one was inside. He yanked open the door of a small linen closet, relieved that it, too, was empty. The door to the toilet was open, and that small room was clear as well.

It suddenly occurred to Starke that, unless Kerrigan knew he was in the house, she'd have no reason to hide. There was still a good chance he'd catch her by surprise.

Back in the upstairs hallway he moved quietly along

the wall, keeping his distance from the top of the stairs so he couldn't be seen from the foyer. He tested each closed door along the corridor. At least two of the open doors were bathrooms, both empty. A linen closet. A utility closet dominated by an enormous water heater. A furnace enclosure. He searched two guest bedrooms, each with its own bath, and a room he guessed was Shelby's home office. The hinges of its door creaked as he pushed it open, and he tensed until the noise stopped and he was sure no one had heard. His eyes fixed on her desk, where he saw the personal computer a panicked Shelby had bought to replace her poisoned Apple. Its screen was blank and inscrutable.

In the window frame just behind the desk, the wildfire smoke was as thick as coastal fog. His eyes were watering, even in the airtight chamber of the climate-controlled house.

By the time he reached the other end of the hall, Starke knew the only remaining bedroom had to be the daughter's. Chloe's door was closed. He twisted the knob, tightened his grip on the gun and entered what looked like the aftermath of an Abercrombie & Fitch explosion. Every piece of furniture in the room was covered with jeans, T-shirts, sports uniforms, underwear. Bedclothes were piled in the center of a four-post bed, as if stripped and gathered for laundry service. A plush Guernsey cow the size of a Labrador retriever lay limply atop the wadded comforter and pile of sheets. The floor was a minefield of unmatched shoes, boots, and sandals. Band and concert posters covered the walls—Ramones, Sex Pistols, Kanye, Snoop.

Starke's first thought was that the room had been ransacked.

The bathroom door was open, and from where he stood

he could see it was small and empty, just a toilet, a shower, and a small vanity. Every inch of the vanity's surface was covered with products—hair gels, brushes, straightening irons, a blow dryer, moisturizers, cosmetics, contact lens solution. He realized then that the room had not been trashed, just lived in by a teenage girl. Even if someone wanted to hide in here, where would they find the space?

So the upstairs was clear.

Starke picked his way through the scattered shoes, moving toward the window on the far wall. From there, he could get a quick look at the approaching fire and this end of the backyard. It was slow going. Halfway across the room, he felt his skin tighten. Had he heard something behind him? Felt a shift in the air?

It was an instinct more than a feeling, but he'd always trusted his instincts.

He took two more steps, navigating for room to move. He carefully angled his leading foot to land between an upended Ugg boot and an orange flip-flop. He spotted open floor space just beyond that and aimed his trailing foot for it, hoping his move would be quick and uneventful.

In a fast pirouette, Starke spun and crouched. His eyes fixed immediately on the dark, shivering figure on the hidden side of the open bedroom room. Chloe was cowering, eyes wide. She flinched at the sight of the gun. Her lips began to move, but no sound came out.

He'd walked right past her.

Starke lowered the gun, but otherwise didn't move. He raised his index finger to his lips, silently urging her not to scream.

He needn't have worried. The girl had the vacant, thousand-yard stare of someone slipping into shock.

60

Starke approached Chloe as he might a wounded animal—careful, uncertain, ready to react. If she was in shock, she might lash out, or worse, cry out. If Kerrigan realized they were in the house, the game would change. Any advantage he had would be gone.

He whispered, "I'm your mother's friend, Ron Starke. Do you remember me?"

Same vacant stare.

Starke spotted a half-empty bottle of Arrowhead water on its side amid the rubble on the bedroom floor. He picked it up, unscrewed the cap, and held it out to her, hoping the sensation of cool water on her lips might bring her around. She didn't move, or even look at the bottle. He inched closer, picked up her limp hand, and placed the open bottle in her palm. Her fingers closed around it, a reflex.

"Take a sip, Chloe," he said. "It might help you feel better."

The girl blinked for the first time and looked down, her

eyes locking on the plastic bottle. She took it and raised it to her mouth, then seemed to notice him for the first time. She pressed herself backward into the wall.

"The cop," she said.

"That's right, Chloe. Ron Starke. An old friend of your mom's."

Still the girl recoiled. Her eyes dropped to the gun still in Starke's right hand. Very deliberately, he engaged the safety and tucked the gun beneath his belt at the small of his back, and brought both hands back to where she could see them.

"You're with *her*," Chloe said, her voice rising with fear. Kerrigan?

"The lady cop. You work with her."

"No!" Starke waved his hands, then pressed an index finger to his lips. "Well, yes, but—Chloe, I was outside and heard a gun go off. So I came in and—"

Starke willed away the image of Shelby in the downstairs foyer, curled like a dead flower in a wide pool of her blood. Did Chloe know? Had she seen it too? The look that suddenly crossed the girl's face answered both questions. When she closed her eyes, tears spilled from both and ran down her cheeks.

"What happened, Chloe? Tell me fast."

"She shot my mom, I think."

"Do you know why?"

Chloe shook her head. "She just showed up. We were trying to leave."

At once, they both turned to the bedroom's window. One of the tall palms in the yard was fully ablaze now. They could see its fiery crown just feet from a transformer atop a nearby utility pole. The entire hilltop was enveloped in dirty white smoke.

"Did you see her shoot your mom?"

Chloe shook her head again. "I came up here to get something before we left, and Mom let her in. They were talking."

"Did you hear anything? Like what they were talking about?"

"I was up here. But I heard my mom's voice, yelling. Right before—"

Chloe winced.

Starke waited as long as he could. "Before?"

"I heard the gun. Twice. So I snuck down the hall to see what was going on."

"But what was your mom saying, Chloe?"

"'You're him!'" she said. "That's it. Just: 'You're him!'"

Shelby's last words rushed back into Starke's head.

Kerrigan.

Him?

Jesus.

He said it out loud: "LoveSick."

Chloe just stared.

Starke gently removed the water bottle from the girl's hand and took a sip. "Chloe, this is important. Do you know where she went? The other cop?"

"I heard the back door slide open."

"So she might still be out there, by the pool?"

"Maybe."

Starke patted the girl's forearm. "Stay right here, OK?"

He was about to turn toward the bedroom window when he suddenly was rocked forward into the wall behind Chloe.

He came to rest on top of the girl. His ears were ringing and a rain of double-pane glass was showering them both.

"What the *hell?*" the girl screamed.

Starke covered her mouth, probably harder than he intended. She glared up at him over the back of his hand. When the last of the debris settled, Starke turned toward the window. All that was left of it was an empty frame. Both the blazing palm tree and the utility pole were gone, and an odd calm was settling over the scene. Down the hill, in the distance, he heard the sound of desperate firefighters and heavy equipment on the move.

"There was an electrical transformer," he whispered. "The fire got too close. It must have exploded. You OK?"

Chloe nodded.

He removed his hand. "I really need you to wait here."

Chloe gasped as soon as he turned toward the window frame. "Wait," she said. "There's glass. In your back."

Only then did Starke notice the sharp pain between his shoulder blades. Before he could object, the girl reached out and tugged something from the same place where it hurt. He felt something long and sharp slide from his flesh. She tossed it aside, and it landed in one of her shoes— a blade of glass the size and shape of a kitchen knife. His blood covered the bottom two inches of it.

"The rest is small stuff," she said.

Starke nodded. He took a deep breath, relieved when there was no pain. His lungs were fine, if burning now from the smoke pouring into the room through the shattered window. His heart was pounding, so it was probably fine as well. "Is there a lot of blood?" he asked.

"No."

"OK then."

On his hands and knees, Starke made his away across a cluttered floor now glittering with bits of window glass. He placed his palms gingerly, pulling his weight back whenever he felt the slice and bite of a glassy splinter. His knees were bleeding by the time he reached the windowsill, and he took a few seconds to pick out the bits that cut through his pants and embedded themselves in his skin. Then he pulled himself up on the windowsill and peeked into the yard.

In the smoky haze below, and through the smoke tears burning his eyes, Starke saw someone moving around. He wiped tears on his sleeve and squinted.

Kerrigan was walking away from the house, between the pool and the home's detached garage. She was holding something over her face—a damp cloth to filter out the smoke as she picked her way through the patio furniture and massive potted plants. She entered the garage through a small door on its side. He could hear the snap and crackle of burning timbers in the house next door.

Kerrigan stepped out a moment later with something red and bulky in one hand. When a drifting cloud of smoke cleared, Starke rose up on his haunches and looked closer.

A five-gallon gas can?

She began pouring, tracing a dark trail between the garage and the back door before disappearing inside, still pouring. Starke felt a surge of adrenaline. Time quickened.

"Is there way out from up here?" he asked.

Across the room, Chloe shook her head.

Damn. He had to get her out without sending her through the nightmare of the front hall.

"No, wait," the girl said. "There's a tree at the corner

of the house. You can climb down it from one of the front bedrooms."

"Think you can you do that, Chloe?"

She nodded.

"Go then," he said. "Right now."

Chloe wobbled to her feet. She waited, watching his eyes. "Come on, I'll show you."

"No," he said. "Just go. Get somewhere safe. If you see firemen, go to them. They'll help you."

He looked down into the yard. Kerrigan had been inside for half a minute, but now she was walking backward from the patio. She was bent like a berry picker, holding the open red can as the last of the gas spilled onto the stonework in a second dark trail toward the other tall palm. Its crown had been ignited by the transformer explosion and was shedding sparks and flaming debris.

When Starke turned away from the window, he was alone.

61

With a sudden roar and flash of flame, Kerrigan's gasoline trail erupted. Starke felt a rush of intense heat as he watched from the obliterated second-story window.

Below, Kerrigan stepped away from the rising flames and returned the gas can to the garage where she'd found it. She emerged empty-handed, still clutching a white cloth over her nose and mouth, and again headed across the patio toward the house's back door.

Burning the place to the ground, and with it Shelby's body, was a long shot. The coroner's crew was too sharp to be fooled for long, and Kerrigan surely knew that. But it was her best hope to cover her tracks, or at least complicate any post-mortem on the wildfire's vast devastation. Kerrigan was in a position to control much of that investigation—much as she'd controlled the investigation into Paul Dwyer's murder.

She might get away with it.

The whole sickening story unspooled for him in an instant. There was only one way this all made sense.

You're him.

What else could Shelby have meant? But why?

Starke edged away from the window frame and stood. Chloe's bedroom was filled with smoke now, and he stifled a cough. His eyes stung and tears streamed down his cheeks as he stumbled across the bedroom and through the door, heading for the stairs. He'd have one chance to stop her, to confront her here. It had to be now.

Smoke was rising into the vast airspace above the foyer where Shelby lay dead, darker than the smoke outside and smelling like gas. It billowed from the rear of the house in great hot breaths and rose toward the entry hall's high ceiling. From the top of the stairs, through a small round window in the home's front wall, Starke saw Chloe working her way down the tree she was using as her escape route. He wondered if Kerrigan could see her as well. He waited until, through a first-floor window, he saw the girl jump from the lowest limb and stagger toward the front gate. Then he started down the stairs.

He didn't get far.

Down below, Kerrigan rushed into the foyer. She was focused on Shelby's body, giving it a wide berth, moving around it like someone afraid of getting too close. She clutched the cloth to her face with one hand, and Starke could see now that she was wearing latex gloves. In the other hand, she held a 9 mm handgun with a band of blue painter's tape around the barrel.

His gun.

He watched as she placed the weapon carefully on the blood-slick floor of the foyer, about six feet from where Shelby was curled like a fallen bloom.

He spoke as soon as she stood up and stepped away from the gun.

"Don't turn around," he shouted. He coughed twice as he moved down the steps. "Hands on your head."

Kerrigan, her back to him now, cocked an ear toward his voice from above. Slowly she put her arms out to her sides and bent her elbows, placing her hands on the top of her head. There seemed an odd defiance to it.

At the bottom of the stairs, Starke walked directly into the pool of Shelby's blood and kicked his gun away. It skittered across the floor to the entryway table where he'd found the unfamiliar .45 now in his hands. He stepped forward and pressed its barrel through a ponytail of auburn hair and directly into the soft spot at the base of Kerrigan's skull. With his free hand, he released the leather holster strap on the department-issued 9 mm at her waist and tugged her gun free.

It was as intimate a moment as they'd ever shared.

Starke set the safety and tucked her piece into his belt before backing three steps away. He coughed twice more, trying to clear his lungs even as the smutty smoke filled the foyer. He could feel a wall of heat just behind him.

"Now turn," he said.

Kerrigan didn't move. Said nothing. Starke raised his voice.

"Turn around, I said."

Hands on her head, disarmed, powerless, Donna Kerrigan turned slowly until they stood face-to-face about ten feet apart. There was no apparent fear in her, no hint of shame. Just the same smoldering contempt he'd felt so many other times in her company. She looked him in the eye.

"You have no authority Ron," she said.

He squinted, raised the .45, and aimed directly at the plucked spot between her eyebrows. She didn't even blink.

"Maybe not," he said, "but I do have this."

"Put it down now."

"I know what happened."

"Put the gun down now and I'll keep this out of your personnel file."

Was she kidding? Delusional?

"I don't think you understand, Chief. I know everything."

He paused. "*Everything.*"

"Put the gun down now," she repeated.

Starke shook his head.

"Now!" she commanded.

Starke kept a steady bead. This time, before he spoke, he made sure to smile at her across the moral chasm between them.

"You're LoveSick," he said.

For the first time, Kerrigan blinked.

62

In his nearly two decades as a firefighter, he'd never seen anything like it. The blaze was moving like a runaway train, up hills, into valleys, across inland Southern California's wide, flat plains where tinderbox housing tracts stood like sundried dominoes. It spread in every direction from the point of origin in the foothills, fanned by the winds, a spreading char-black stain of indiscriminate destruction. It had turned more than a thousand homes to ash during the past three days, leaving in its wake only concrete foundations, standalone stone fireplaces, and tiny blue flames where open gas lines marked each home site like a flickering candle.

The captain had brought a crew to this hilltop overlooking Las Colmas to make one last stand. The massive homes here were centered on huge lots. There was defensible space around them. He thought they might have a chance.

But no, the fire was advancing on several fronts and beat them to the top of the hill. Now he could see the battle was lost. The flames had moved from the wooded hillsides, then from mansion to mansion, finally reaching the massive Dwyer estate that crowned the exclusive neighborhood. A palm tree behind the house was crackling dry and lit up by the hot, glowing ash that rose from the burning homes below. As soon as he'd heard the transformer explode, he'd ordered the crew back down the hill.

Smoke rose immediately from the big house, and now he could see flames. There was nothing more they could do but hope the people who'd lived up here were safely down. The road that snaked up the hill was the only reliable firebreak, and their only way up or down.

He lifted his radio. "We're coming down, Carlos. Clear the road for me, will ya? We'll need to get the trucks around that tight curve at the bottom."

He waited a full sixty seconds for Carlos to answer. His drivers were turning the pumper trucks around in a wide cul-de-sac. It was a painfully slow process.

"Carlos? Check in when you can."

Finally the radio sizzled to life: "Little busy here, Cap."

In the background, he could hear the desperate and unmistakable sounds of a horse in agony—the heavy thump and thud of a large animal thrashing and kicking against its enclosure, a keening, deep-chested cry. He'd passed a small stable on his way up the hill, a stubborn remnant of Los Colmas' ranching days. The horse trailers were gone, and he'd assumed the owners had been able to evacuate the stables as the fire closed in. Now he guessed he was wrong.

He lifted his radio again and closed his eyes. "How many were left behind?"

"Just the one," Carlos said. "Burned pretty bad. They got 'em all out of the stable, but left this one outside in the corral, thinking he'd be OK. Heat was too much, though. We're looking for a gun."

The captain opened his eyes. His trucks were turned now, moving down the hill. He watched until they were out of sight.

"We're heading down. Nothing left to do up here. Just make sure the road's clear for us."

He was climbing into his vehicle when he saw something behind him move in the truck's side mirror. He looked closer. A tiny, dark silhouette was wavering down the road behind him, backlit by the smoke and flames rising from the big house. When he turned around, he saw what looked like a young woman staggering from the toxic cloud. She was running like she couldn't see, weaving and tripping and gasping for breath. By the time he reached her, she was on the ground, coughing, barely conscious.

She was a teenager. Where were her parents?

He lifted her head and turned her face so he could see her eyes, which were closed. She gasped for breath like an asthmatic. Opening the valve on his respirator, he placed its mask over her nose and mouth, hoping a jolt of oxygen would bring her around. There wasn't much time, but she needed air before he could move her down the hill.

Within fifteen seconds, her breathing slowed, and her eyes opened. The girl suddenly grabbed his bicep.

He lifted the mask away from her face. "Anybody else up there?"

She tried to talk, but managed only a coughing fit. He replaced the mask until she caught her breath.

"Are more people caught up there?"

His stomach clenched when she nodded.

"How many?"

She held up three fingers.

He needed to get her down the hill, away from the inferno. There was no one else to take her now. But he also needed to move up the hill, into the madness.

"Pumper Five?" he barked into his radio. "Answer me!"

"Go ahead."

"I know you can't turn around," he said. "But send one of the guys back on foot. I've got a girl here, she needs to get down the hill."

He released the talk button and listened. Ten seconds passed. Finally: "Jorge's on his way, Cap. Christ, you're saying somebody's still up there?"

"Jorge can take my truck. I'll have her there and ready to go by the time he gets here."

He scooped the girl into his arms and carried her to his vehicle. He opened the passenger-side door and propped her into the front seat. She leaned forward, put her head on the dashboard, and vomited onto the floor of the cab.

The radio crackled again as he closed the door. "Wait, Cap. What about you?"

He turned and looked back up the hill. Everything was ablaze. The big house at the top was the only structure still standing, but it was fully involved. A thread of wispy black laced through the brown-gray wall of smoke that nearly obscured the house. The fire had found something oily. He lifted the radio again.

"Just get her down the hill," he said, and started to run toward the flames.

"Cap, dammit! There's no time. Tell me what's going on."

He answered before he lifted the oxygen mask to his face, but after he'd made his choice: "Three souls!"

63

"LoveSick."

Starke coughed with wracking violence, then shouted the name again over the dull roar of flame at his back. "You're *him*!"

The muscles in Donna Kerrigan's jaw clenched and unclenched; her eyes had the look of someone whose mask had been suddenly torn away. In seconds, her face registered shock, anger, and a sad vulnerability. Then it reassembled itself into something unmistakable: contempt.

"I don't know what you're talking about," she said.

He nodded to Shelby's body, and lied: "Shelby told me the whole story. Before she bled out."

"Try proving it," Kerrigan spat. "Your word against mine." She nodded to the long-legged table nearby, beneath which sat Starke's gun. She'd dropped it as he watched from upstairs, a classic cop throw-down.

"Your gun has her blood on it. I found it when I got here," she said. "You're the one with reason to worry."

Starke reached into his belt, where he'd tucked her service piece after pulling it from her holster. He forced a smile, fired two shots into Shelby's body, and dropped Kerrigan's gun into the wide red pool between them. He raised his voice. "We'll let forensics sort it out."

He cut his eyes quickly to the left. Shelby's computer still sat on the foyer table. He'd backed up the contents of the CarbonCopy device to his flash drive, but—was there still a way to get the machine out of this inferno?

Kerrigan noticed him looking at it. She looked almost smug. "There's nothing on the hard drive. She wiped it before she sold it."

Starke played his trump card. "It wasn't on the hard drive. It was on a keystroke logger plugged into the back. Everything, the conversations, the video—it was all in there. I found it. I leaked it."

Kerrigan blinked again.

The smoke was so thick now he could hardly see the second floor. The house's grand staircase ascended into a dirty cloud.

"You've got nothing, Ron. Put the gun down. Now."

He was running out of time. "It was all online, all anonymous. You sucked her in, made her an accomplice."

Kerrigan gave him a deathly stare.

"I've read the chat transcripts. I still don't know why you killed Dwyer, but I know you duped Shelby into watching him die, so she couldn't tell the truth even if she wanted to. You made sure she knew just enough to make it seem like she was part of it."

"Shut up!" Kerrigan was breathing hard now, her chest

heaving as the smoke thickened and he piled her lies at her feet. "Stop it now!"

"I know how you dumped Paul's body by yourself. You had access to security company gate codes."

Kerrigan was shaking.

"That computer monitor belonged to your ex, didn't it? He'd fucked you over in the divorce. Why not a little payback for him, too?"

She screamed—a hoarse, guttural howl. Barely human. An animal sound. A raw purging of rage. It echoed through the vast space around them, louder even than the roar of flame and the crackle of burning timber.

"I know *everything*," Starke shouted.

Despite the smoke, Kerrigan's breathing slowed. She seemed suddenly calm, looking at him with the resolve of someone who'd made a decision.

"Enough," she said. "This ends now."

It wasn't a threat; he could tell that from her tone. More like she was asking a favor.

"Turn around and open the door," he ordered. "Get clear of the house."

"No," she said. "It ends right here. You know the policy. About provocation. About threatening moves."

Starke studied her, his finger tensing on the trigger. She had a plan. He felt the sudden, sickening realization that he was part of it.

"Don't," he said.

Her eyes shifted to her gun, which lay where he'd dropped it. Slick with Shelby's blood, her service piece was one lunge away. Kerrigan was measuring, calculating. If she went for it, he knew she'd lose.

So did she.

The script was clear; his role set. The next move was hers.

"Don't put this on me," he said. "You've done enough damage."

She gestured to the front door, to the world beyond it. "No choice," she said.

Starke moved a step closer to the gun on the floor, intending to kick it away. His eyes fixed on Kerrigan's, he extended his foot, searching by feel for the elusive metal lump. He was still searching when the house's front door burst open. An explosive rush of air made the flames inside the house roar even higher.

They both turned. A filthy firefighter in a yellow flame-resistant suit stood silhouetted in the doorframe, his sooty face hidden behind a full-face breathing mask. From inside it, the man's eyes swept the scene—the now-billowing flames in the foyer, Shelby's body curled on the floor, a man threatening another woman with a gun.

Kerrigan turned her pleading eyes to the intruder. "He'll kill me, too, for God's sake!" she screamed. "Do something!" Starke aimed the barrel of his gun at the center of the man's chest.

"Stay where you are," he commanded. "Los Colmas PD. This is a crime scene."

Kerrigan unclipped her badge from her belt and waved it at the man. "*I'm* Los Colmas PD."

For a second, maybe two, the three of them stood frozen amid the flames.

"He'll kill us both!" Kerrigan screamed.

The firefighter took one step forward. Starke raised his arm until the gun's barrel was pointing at the man's helmeted head. Slowly, carefully, the firefighter lifted the mask away from a face Starke recognized immediately despite the layers of grime. They'd played soccer together in high school.

"Ron?" the firefighter said. "That you?"

It wasn't much, but it was enough. Kerrigan's shoulders slumped, and she seemed to shrink. She'd done the calculus and come to a fast conclusion.

She was the outsider.

Again.

She turned back to Starke. Now there was no rage or hate in her eyes. Only a plea.

"You know the deal," she said again.

Her move for her gun wasn't a desperate lunge, but rather a deliberate stride and reach. The whole time, she was looking at him.

"Don't," he pleaded.

But then she had the bloody weapon in her hand, and she was lifting it from the floor, and she was pointing it at him. Just that quick, the balance shifted. He was the one without options.

His first shot spun her like a top—he'd aimed for her shoulder—but she was holding tight to the gun as she dropped to the floor. She landed on her hands and knees, then fell forward facing away from him. Kerrigan's back heaved from the pain. The bullet had gone straight through, he could see now, leaving a two-inch exit wound in her left shoulder. She coughed, but made no other move.

A deep voice. "Jesus, Ron. What the fuck?"

From the corner of his eye, Starke could see the firefighter still silhouetted in the doorway. He leveled the gun at the back of Kerrigan's head and braced its butt in the palm of his left hand.

"Leave the weapon," he commanded. "Goddamn it, Chief. Leave it."

Kerrigan was motionless for a long moment. Not even a cough. Finally, Kerrigan pushed herself back up until she was again on her hands and knees. The firefighter watched from the doorway, still as a statue.

"Push the gun out of reach," Starke ordered. "Now."

Kerrigan turned her head, looking back at him over her right shoulder. Her hair was still pulled into an efficient ponytail, and she smiled a smile he knew would haunt him forever. When she shifted her weight to her shaking left arm, it gave way. She sealed her fate as she dropped, raising her right arm and pointing her gun directly at him.

Starke's head shot finished it. Kerrigan died sprawled beside Shelby Dwyer's body. In the stunned-silent moment that followed, just before the ceiling at the back of the house collapsed, Starke thought again of the online phantom's name.

64

Starke didn't know the name of the sedative, but he was feeling no pain as he lay face down on the emergency-room exam table. He was wearing an open-back hospital gown, but it was untied, and he was basically naked. Every few seconds, he'd hear the *tink!* of another shard after the nurse tweezered it from the flesh of his back and butt and dropped it into the metal pan beside his head. After two hours, there was an impressive little mound of bloody glass in the center of the pan.

"Almost done, baby," she said.

"Take your time."

He checked his wristwatch. Five hours since he'd collapsed outside the Dwyer house and ended up here. He'd regained consciousness in an ambulance at the bottom of the hill, face-to-face with the firefighter whose name he instantly remembered. Dry. Ed Dry. Hell of a striker.

"Ron?" he'd asked. "What the hell just happened up there?"

Starke had gulped a few breaths and tried to answer. "Long story. Just say what you saw. The truth, straight out."

The firefighter nodded as the paramedics closed the ambulance doors.

Tink!

"You won't sparkle as much after I'm done, *mijo*."

"Never been a sparkly guy."

Starke turned his head so he could see the nurse's face. She was lovely—Mexican, he assumed—but young. Said her name was—hell, what was it? Was it the drugs, or his middle-aged man's imagination? He could swear she'd been flirting with him.

"Just be glad it was your back," she said. "This was the other side? Hoo-baby. Plus you'd have to watch me do this, know what I mean? It's one thing—"

Starke felt the air shift. The nurse looked up toward the blue curtain that offered them the thinnest pretense of privacy in the emergency room. He followed her eyes to where the curtain now split and saw Ramon Chavez standing there like an undertaker.

The Los Colmas police captain didn't smile often—something that stood him well with Kerrigan as she shuffled and reshuffled the department's power structure in recent months. Now was no exception. He looked like a man trying to pass a cantaloupe.

"'Bout wrapped up in here?" Chavez said.

"Sir?" she said. "Please wait outside."

"How long?"

The nurse set the tweezers on Starke's bare, bloodied ass and crossed her arms across her chest. Her playful voice changed as she shifted into pro mode. "Don't make me call security."

Captain Chavez casually held up his shield.

"I don't care who you are," she snapped. "This man's medicated, he's in no condition to talk, and he's undergoing treatment. So you just turn around and walk out of this exam area now before I—now who's this?"

The curtain parted even wider as Corie Rosen stepped into the cramped space. Starke had known the county deputy DA for years, but her face was all business until her eyes swept across the exam table. She blanched. Starke made no effort to cover himself, and Rosen quickly looked away.

"Corie, does this gown make my butt look big?" Starke asked.

Rosen covered her eyes with her hand. "Chipped Christ on toast, Starke. Your back looks like hamburger. What the hell?"

Starke pushed himself up onto his elbows and turned to face the nurse. "Sorry. What's your name again?"

She didn't take her eyes off the intruders. "Madonna."

"As much as I've enjoyed our time together, Madonna, I really do need to talk to these folks. I know them both, and I'm pretty sure they're in a hurry to get some answers. Can we finish this up after I do that?"

When she finally looked at him, he smiled and said, "It's OK. Really."

Madonna grabbed a bottle of some sort of disinfectant wash, soaked a wad of sterile gauze, and swabbed down the parts of his back where she'd removed his sparkles. He could feel it snag here and there on the remaining bits. "Didn't get it all," she said. "Least let me clean you up a little so it won't get infected."

Chavez and Rosen stared at their shoes as the nurse blotted the blood from Starke's glass-peppered glutes. When she was done, she snapped off her surgical gloves with a bit more violence than necessary, then maneuvered around the visitors and disappeared through the curtain. Still, Starke made no effort to cover himself. Couldn't hurt to let Chavez and Rosen squirm. He could always blame it on the painkillers.

"Do you know why we're here, detective?" Chavez said.

The most loaded of questions. Starke already knew his answer. "I'm prepared to make a full statement."

Chavez and Rosen seemed startled. Rosen stepped forward and looked Starke in the eye.

"About?"

"The Dwyer killings. Also, the death of Chief Donna Kerrigan."

Chavez and Rosen looked at one another. Chavez spoke first.

"She's dead?"

Starke nodded. "Figured you knew by now."

"We got two bodies, both badly burned. No ID yet, but Kerrigan's car was out front. And she's missing. A county fire captain told us you might know something about it."

"It's her."

"And the other?"

"Shelby Dwyer."

Chavez and Rosen look at each other again. This time Rosen spoke.

"Ron, you need an attorney."

He shrugged. "Couldn't hurt. Know any?"

She stepped forward and pressed a card into his hand: San Bernardino County Public Defender. "Call them," she said. "And be down at the cop shop in two hours. If they can't assign anybody that soon, we'll wait. But you need somebody there. Understood?"

He nodded.

"Captain Chavez will stay with you," she added.

Chavez stepped forward. He looked uncomfortable as he reached toward the back of his belt. "Precaution, is all."

Starke knew the drill, so he held out his left wrist. Chavez clamped a cuff around it, probably tighter than was necessary.

"I'll wait for you at reception," Chavez said. "Just have your little girlfriend call me when she's done cleaning you up." Before he and Rosen stepped back out, Chavez clicked the other cuff around the metal leg of the exam table.

65

The computer?

Starke's eyes shot open. The sedatives had overtaken him shortly after Chavez and Rosen left, just as nurse Madonna tweezered the last of the sparkles from his back. How long had he dozed? He was still face down on the table, so he lifted his head and looked around.

His blue curtain was gone, pushed back along its ceiling track all the way to the wall. He could see now how his privacy, such as it had been, was an illusion. He was square in the middle of a vast emergency room. Here and there small treatment areas were partitioned off by those blue curtains, but for the most part he was one of a dozen people receiving treatment. Four stations down, a team worked furiously over someone who'd been unable to outrun the fire. The smell of charred meat drifted through the room.

Starke tried to focus on the thought that woke him— Shelby Dwyer's computer. He'd seen Kerrigan carry it into the house, then again on a table in the front hall as he'd faced her down. He remembered reaching for it as he staggered toward the front door of the burning house, remembered firefighter Ed Dry shoving him outside before he could grab it. Then—nothing. He'd passed out, and those final moments were a blur. Could it have survived as the house went up in flames? Did it matter?

Starke pushed himself up on his elbows, relieved to see his flash drive still dangling from a cord around his neck. At least he had that.

Then, a voice: "Thank you."

He couldn't place it, but it came from the treatment station next to him. He turned his head. A young woman was sitting up on an empty exam table nearby. She was wearing the same clothes she was wearing when he last saw her, climbing down the tree at the corner of her burning house. She'd pushed her own oxygen mask up onto her forehead.

"Chloe." He smiled. "You're OK."

He tried to imagine the kid's state of mind—suddenly alone, both parents dead. Did she know her house was gone, too? Just hours before, she'd heard her mother confront Kerrigan, heard the shots, seen her mother sprawled in the downstairs hall. He'd coaxed her out of shock as she cowered in her upstairs bedroom. That had been the easy part. The complicated stuff was still to come.

Chloe brought the mask down and took a deep hit of oxygen, then lifted it again. "I told," she gasped. "When I got out. Of the house. Fireman guy. Helped me. So I told him. My mom. Was hurt."

Hurt? Could she still not know?

"Where is she?" Chloe asked. "My mom?"

Starke tried to roll onto his side to slide off the treatment table, but the sound of metal on metal reminded him that his wrist was cuffed to one of the table's legs. Chloe noticed the restraints, stared long and hard at them, but said nothing. Just waited.

Starke shook his head. "Couldn't save her. Chloe, I'm sorry. She died before I even came upstairs and found you."

The girl's face registered nothing, at first. It was as if he'd told her the time. Then, suddenly, her features crumpled into grief. She'd been floating on the tiniest bit of hope. Starke felt like he'd just handed her an anchor. Chloe clenched her eyes shut, but not tight enough to stop the tears. They flowed down her face, around the outside of her breathing mask, and hung in a little liquid bulb at the bottom of her chin. She didn't make any sound at all except to gulp more air.

Starke had more to tell her, none of it good. Better that she take the lead. After a minute, Chloe blotted her chin with her sleeve, brushed the tear trails from her cheeks, lifted the mask, and gestured toward Starke's shackled wrist.

"But you didn't shoot her," she said. "The lady—"

Starke looked the girl in the eye. "She's dead, too," he said. "I think she killed your dad, and tried to make it look like your mom—"

The girl waved away his words. "I know."

"You knew?"

Chloe shrugged. "More than I. Wanted to know."

"Tell me."

Starke listened as Chloe, between hard-fought breaths, laid out what her mother had told her, about meeting someone online, someone she'd assumed was a man, but whose name and true identity she never knew. How that someone had lured her mother into watching her father's murder, then terrorized her into silence.

"It was. That lady?" she asked.

Starke nodded.

"But why?"

Starke shook his head. "Did your mom say anything that might explain all this, Chloe? Because that's what I still—I know what happened, I just don't know *why*. I'll find out, but right now, I'm not sure why she went after your Dad, or tried to make it look like your Mom was involved."

An awkward silence. The girl's lower lip quivered. Starke tried to imagine being seventeen and as alone as Chloe suddenly found herself. No parents. No brothers or sisters. There was one more bit of bad news.

"Your house, Chloe. It burned. I'm sorry."

The girl closed her eyes. Starke hated delivering that on top of everything else, but at least now she knew everything. Now she could process it. She seemed strong enough, like her mother.

"There are people who can help you," Starke said. "You have grandparents, right? People who can find you a place to live. Help you sort things out."

She nodded, but Starke could tell by her lost look that she was overwhelmed.

"My mom talked. About you," she said. "A lot."

Starke looked away. "We were close friends. A long time ago."

"I know."

"Did you love her?"

Caught off guard, he still managed a smile. "Once."

Chloe smiled back. "I think maybe she loved you."

Starke didn't believe that. He'd once thought what happened between them that summer when they were both twenty-one was real and honest and perfect. But their passion had consequences, and suddenly he was just the guy standing between Shelby and the life she really wanted. She'd made her choice and moved on before he ever knew, and so he moved on, too. Eventually he met Rosaleen, and life happened.

"Your mom was a good person," he said.

Chloe nodded. Could the kid really understand that essential truth, after all that had happened?

"Mom loved being loved," Chloe said.

Starke sat up, the cuffs rattling against the metal leg of the exam table as he tried to gather the open-backed hospital gown around him with his free hand. The effort and noise brought Chavez out of his chair at the far end of emergency room. The police captain attempted a smile as he approached, but it flickered like a candle in a breeze and disappeared. His face resumed its natural scowl as he tossed a pair of jeans and a T-shirt to Starke's free hand.

"Found you something to wear down to the station," Chavez said. "We may be a while sorting this out."

"Thanks."

Starke rattled the cuffs again, and Chavez stepped forward with a key. He unlocked the cuff from the table leg, but left the other one around Starke's wrist. Starke waited until Chloe looked away, then worked around the swinging cuff as he pulled the loose jeans over his tender ass.

"DA already found a lawyer for you," Chavez said. "They're waiting for us. You sure you're feeling up to this now? We've got a lot of questions."

"I've got answers," Starke said. "Just give me a sec, OK?"

He turned to Chloe, who'd stripped off her oxygen mask and was standing beside her exam table. "Everything will be OK," he said. "I just have to tell the police what happened."

The girl looked alarmed, abandoned. "I'll go. With you."

They both looked at Chavez, who seemed confused. He shook his head. "And you are?" he asked.

Chloe sidestepped closer to Starke, then turned and fixed her eyes on his. For the first time they stood face to face, and Starke had a disconcerting moment of familiarity. The girl looked like a younger version of her mother.

Starke was about to back away when she reached across his waist and took his left hand in hers. The girl shifted her eyes to Chavez, and before the police captain could react, she fixed the open cuff around her own thin wrist.

Her answer to Chavez left no room for debate: "I'm Chloe Dwyer. You need to hear my story, too."

ACKNOWLEDGMENTS

I've been blessed to know many amazing and complicated women, and their influences are everywhere in the characters, themes, and random moments of this book. I owe them all a great debt for enriching my life, and my stories, in ways I may never fully understand:

Helen Vance Smith, my mother, my spiritual and moral compass, and surely the most quietly complicated of them all.

Judith Johnson Smith, my wife, whom I love now more than ever, and who after more than thirty years together remains as fascinating to me as the day we met.

Molly Boulware, my first friend, whose death at age twenty-five shaped me in ways too numerous to count. I miss her still, and dedicate this book to her memory.

Lisa Wren, my only sister, a bottomless well of strength, grace, encouragement, and endless good humor until her death in September 2015, just as I was finishing this book.

And Susan Ginsburg, my literary agent, whose unfailing

support and wise counsel over the years have helped me become the person I always imagined I would be.

Also, the members of my former writing group, the Mavericks, offered much-needed feedback on the manuscript as this novel took shape. Their input, as always, was invaluable. In addition, Robin Abcarian of the *Los Angeles Times* let me borrow her daughter's name.

Four remarkable women ran the Writer's Colony at Dairy Hollow in Eureka Springs, Arkansas, when I wrote an early version of this book there in the autumn of 2006—Jane Tucker, Sharon Spurlin, Cindy Duncan, and Sandy Wright. I thank them for the extraordinary gifts of time and space. Among the many talented writers I met while in residence at Dairy Hollow, Paige Britt of Austin, Texas, helped me better understand the character of Ron Starke. I thank her for sharing her scars.

Not all of my support team is female, though. My friend and fellow writer, Philip Reed, offered some great suggestions as I struggled during the late stages of writing this novel. The team at Diversion Books has been terrific, and I especially appreciate editor Randall Klein's unwavering faith in my abilities as a storyteller. His suggestions on the manuscripts of this novel and its predecessor, *The Disappeared Girl*, were invaluable in helping both books reach their potential. And his digital resurrection of the three novels before that, *Time Release*, *Shadow Image*, and *Straw Men*, have introduced those books and characters to new audiences around the world. I hope to someday repay his faith.

Martin J. Smith
Granby, Colorado

MARTIN J. SMITH is a veteran journalist, author, and magazine editor who has won more than 50 newspaper and magazine awards. He's a former senior editor of the *Los Angeles Times Magazine*, and for nine years was editor-in-chief of *Orange Coast* magazine in Orange County, CA. His first three crime novels were nominated for prestigious crime fiction awards—the Edgar, Barry, and Anthony. He also is the author of three nonfiction books, including *The Wild Duck Chase, Poplorica: A Popular History of the Fads, Mavericks, Inventions, and Lore That Shaped Modern America*, and *Oops: 20 Life Lessons From the Fiascoes That Shaped America*.

THE MEMORY SERIES IS AVAILABLE NOW!

TIME RELEASE

Pittsburgh, 1986: The city is gripped in a panic as a maniac slips poison onto pharmacy shelves. All of the evidence has pointed to Ron Corbett, but shoddy policework let Corbett off the hook, left the crime unsolved.

Ten years later, it's happening again. This time, for the most personal of reasons, Detective Downing has made it his mission to see Corbett behind bars. He enlists the help of Jim Christensen, a psychologist who specializes in memory, to interview Corbett's son, now a young man with a painful past and problems of his own. Does the boy remember his father slipping poison into pill containers? Has he blocked memories of a horrific crime spree enacted in his own house? As Christensen explores the boy's memory and Downing grows more obsessive investigating the case, both men fear that the killings now may not be as random as they once thought, and that unlocking memories may draw them too close to a vicious predator.

SHADOW IMAGE

The Underhill family has loomed over Pennsylvania politics for four generations as the most powerful in the state. Now, with their youngest son locked in a tight gubernatorial race, a simple accident threatens to derail the entire campaign. After Floss Underhill, the family matriarch, has been discovered alive after falling from a gazebo into a ravine, Brenna Kennedy gets brought in as a defense attorney to the family. The police don't seem to believe that her fall was an accident, however, and soon neither does Brenna.

Jim Christensen, a psychologist, memory expert, and Brenna's partner as they raise their children together, has been studying Floss Underhill for months in a group of Alzheimer's patients. Her mind ravaged by the disease, her body broken by the fall, Floss Underhill nevertheless knows something, and is trying to tell Christensen a family secret so explosive it could bring down an empire. To help bring it out of her, though, will make them powerful enemies, and bring both the truth—and the danger—very close to home…

STRAW MEN

Eight years ago, Brenna Kennedy defended Carmen DellaVecchio: a loner, a freak, a man accused of a heinous crime. She lost the case, and DellaVecchio was sent to prison for the brutal rape and near murder of Teresa Harnett, a Pittsburgh cop.

But DNA evidence has cast doubt on DellaVecchio's guilt. While he waits for a new trial, he is free, and Brenna still believes that he is an innocent man. But if DellaVecchio is innocent, then that means there's a guilty sociopath out there, and all that's standing in his way from getting away with a grisly crime is one meddling lawyer...

Jim Christensen has the key to unlock memories. Brilliant and compassionate, he's dedicated his career to studying the effects of memory loss, including on victims of trauma. When Teresa Harnett asks him to help her remember that terrible night, he resists. Ethically, it's unsound, as Christensen and Kennedy have been together for six years. But Christensen is drawn into the case, and soon everyone involved is caught in the web of a man who will kill to stay free...

THE DISAPPEARED GIRL

Nothing stays buried forever, especially not the past.

Two men stand out in a crowd overlooking the Ohio River. A plane is being taken from the water where it crashed decades before. Both men helped put it there.

Jim Christensen's daughter, Melissa, has been troubled of late. She has dreams that feel like memories, unsettling images percolate to the surface. She remembers a terrifying past, possibly her own, from a time before she was adopted by her father. Christensen's work as an expert in memory makes him the ideal person to help unlock his daughter's fragile grasp on her own history. But will he want to learn the truth of where Melissa came from? Who she was before? Who might still be looking for her?

This dizzying novel of suspense takes the reader back into a dirty war and its human costs, into the fevered mind of one of its survivors, and through the crosshairs of a man desperate to keep his own history vanished.